THE ONLY ROSE
AND
OTHER TALES

by

SARAH ORNE JEWETT

With an Introduction by
REBECCA WEST

FIRST ISSUED IN THE TRAVELLERS' LIBRARY 1937

ISBN 978-1-4067-9434-2

CONTENTS

	PAGE
INTRODUCTION	7
THE ONLY ROSE	17
THE GUESTS OF MRS. TIMMS	36
THE PASSING OF SISTER BARSETT	57
DECORATION DAY	72
THE COURTING OF SISTER WISBY	90
A NATIVE OF WINBY	111
AUNT CYNTHY DALLETT	138
MISS TEMPY'S WATCHERS	157
THE DULHAM LADIES	171
MISS PECK'S PROMOTION	189
THE FLIGHT OF BETSEY LANE	217
THE HILTONS' HOLIDAY	245
A WHITE HERON	266

INTRODUCTION

It would be easy for an English reader of *The Only Rose*, and its companion volume of New England Tales, *The Country of the Pointed Firs*, to misconceive the nature of these works and their author. Sarah Orne Jewett was a lady, never married, who was born in 1849 and died in 1909, in the State of Maine. Therefore our imagination might, if not restrained, rush to its easel and paint a lean Yankee spinster, Puritan by inheritance and kept on a low diet by a specially strict local interpretation of the Victorian spirit, who wrote of the village life around her because she knew no other, and who achieved simplicity through artlessness. The truth is not so. The perfection of this work comes out of abundance. Miss Jewett was an extremely happy woman, child of a community that approved a full life; and her native sensitiveness was educated and encouraged and taught to communicate its findings by an ancient and liberal culture. Her stories represent the blossoming of a transplanted tradition that has flourished in its new soil.

Sarah Orne Jewett was one of the many and distinguished descendants of a Yorkshireman who emigrated to America in 1638. The family tradition was, as is more often the case in New England than we recognize over here, Cavalier and not Puritan; and indeed in all the likenesses of Miss Jewett there is a full-lipped, clear-browed, unembarrassed handsomeness which speaks of the Cavalier spirit at its best. Her grandfather had been a wealthy shipbuilder, which is to say that she was brought up in a fine sunset glow. The heyday of the New England mercantile marine, before it had lost both its whaling and its East India trade, was almost as romantic as

INTRODUCTION

the great age of Venetian commerce. She was brought up in the detritus of past grandeur in an eighteenth-century house that was renowned as beautiful, even in a State where beautiful houses are common as blackberries; and as she was too delicate to attend school regularly, her father, who was a doctor, took her with him in his chaise on his rounds whenever the weather allowed it, so that from her childhood she knew by heart the length and breadth of one of the most exquisite countrysides the world can show. She came to learn a good deal about the inhabitants of that countryside, for from her childhood she saw them when they were unveiled by calamity; and as she grew older her father used her as a secretary, and she knew almost as much about his patients as he did.

It was Miss Jewett's first desire to be a doctor, but she was not strong enough; all her life long she suffered from slight but persistent ill-health. When she started to write she was fortunate enough to be directed by her early reading straight to the material that was perfectly suited to her talents. As a child she had read again and again Miss Harriet Beecher Stowe's *The Pearl of Orris Island*, a tale about just that Maine landscape and those Maine country folk which she knew so well. She so definitely followed Mrs. Stowe's lead in dialogue and in sense of background that to open this forgotten book is like coming on the quarry which gave Miss Jewett the stone for her sculptures; the substance is there, though not the form. From the beginning she wrote well, and she gained an impressive reputation while she was still in her twenties. She was by then an honoured contributor to *The Atlantic Monthly*, which was at that time and for long after incom-

INTRODUCTION

parably superior to any similar literary publication in England; and through its editor, Thomas Bailey Aldrich, she came to know William Dean Howells and John Greenleaf Whittier, and on her travels met Tennyson and Matthew Arnold, George du Maurier and Henry James.

But she was sustained in her literary life by more than success. Her traditions had put her into a most comfortable relationship with literature. Perhaps because she was of French blood on her mother's side, she knew the great writers of France as well as those of our own tongue; she made a pilgrimage to Madame de Sévigné's fig-tree at the Chateau de Grignan. The purity of her transplanted and strictly preserved culture gave her a self-confidence, a sense of establishment, which enabled her to do without the defensive motions of prudery when she came to discuss the more modern French masters. *Madame Bovary* is a classic that provoked a great many apologies and even titterings among English critics of that time, which compare ill with the unperturbed and penetrating analysis of that work of art, to be found in a letter from this New English gentlewoman, dated from her home in the little town of South Berwick. It is surprising to see which of these opinions bears the imprint of a citizen of the world.

Flaubert, indeed, she understood so well that he was one of the great influences on her literary life. She kept pinned up on her desk 'for a constant reminder' two sayings of his: 'Ecrire la vie ordinaire comme on écrit l'histoire' and 'Ce n'est pas de faire rire—mais d'agir à la façon de la nature, c'est à dire de faire rêver.' What these sayings reminded her was, simply, that since she was a writer what she wrote must

INTRODUCTION

be the truth, the whole truth and nothing but the truth, and at the same time the symbol of a greater truth. It is an onerous enterprise; and the contemplation of it has been known to make writers, including Flaubert himself, melancholy or frenetic. But Miss Jewett was so inherently hale that she only took it as an assurance of having found an occupation which would keep her busy to the very end. There was no chink in her armour of well-being. She was even, so far as can be made out, entirely contented with her life. Her youth was made happy by her love for her father, and after his death a close and lasting friendship with Mrs. Fields, the wife of her publisher, seems to have given her complete emotional satisfaction.

Out of this unusually rich life came the short stories which have earned her the high place in American literature which few critics of any school would deny her, and which certainly deserve to be ranked among the minor masterpieces of classical art. Miss Jewett was not in the least degree a romantic; she never treated of experiences as yet unanalysed, she never contemplated her fellow-men when they spoke without logic and tried to guess what hidden hungers were speaking through them. It was her preference to use material already digested, to deal with experiences on the significance of which the world had long made up its mind, and with fully recognized motives. Her business was not to discover, but to celebrate what had already been discovered; and she performed her task with exquisite aptitude.

She has a few faults that may obscure the brightness of her talents in the eyes of the hasty reader. It must be owned that she writes of a universe which has been unscrupulously

INTRODUCTION

emasculated, swept unnaturally clean of the male and the baggage of forthrightness and violence he carries about with him; and when she is forced to deal with him, she wholly falsifies his quality. The grey delicacy of 'Decoration Day' is in itself enchanting, but it is inappropriate to a representation of the aftermath to the war which, until 1914, ranked as the bloodiest in history; and that is an extreme example of a general tendency in Miss Jewett's art. Here we have to blame both her temperament and the age in which she lived. She appears never to have been interested by any man whatsoever except her father. Her letters abound in ecstatic responses to the charm of all sorts of women, but her male friends had to earn and maintain their position by some sort of extreme literacy. They had to be library-trained, and even then they were not fully existent for her. This blindness was regarded not as a defect but as a virtue by the literary Boston of that day, which in its quality was not merely expressing a preference, but was reacting against tremendous historical events. The Puritan element in the North had made it force its idealism on the South, and the Civil War had been the result. Since it was not in the nature of Puritanism to admit a flaw in its premises, it defiantly exaggerated its character, and turned a disapproving face on the virility of the rest of America, as if to affirm that there and there alone would be the source of any ill that might befall the United States. That attitude profoundly impressed and deformed the genius of Mark Twain; it would be surprising if it had not affected the more passive gift of Miss Jewett.

It might often be charged against her, also, that she spoils her stories by touches of the didactic and the sentimental; but

INTRODUCTION

this is sometimes true. 'The Flight of Betsey Lane' tells the story of an innocent soul who at the very end of her days enjoyed a golden holiday, and not once embittered her enjoyment by reflecting that never before had anything but dreariness come her way. It is an exquisite study of that exquisite possession, the capacity for pleasure. It is, however, marred by the encounter between Betsey and the surgeon who promises to operate on Peggy Bond's cataract; before our eyes the picture changes from a Peter de Hoogh to Luke Fildes's 'The Doctor.' Betsey had already been saved by grace, there was no need to drag in good works. When such lapses occur it must be remembered that though Miss Jewett was sound on the classics she did not escape the depravation of taste regarding her contemporaries which was the peculiar misfortune of her age. Bad writers have been popular in every century; but there can never have been a time when good writers were as wrong about their own craft and who plied it best, as they were in the last half of the nineteenth century. In a letter to a friend about a novel by Mrs. Humphry Ward, Miss Jewett wrote: 'One says at certain moments with happy certainty that here is the one solitary master of fiction.' To this astonishing degree had even she been persuaded of the supreme value of novels so deficient in any literary quality that their maker had to give them weight by the insertion of moralistic platitude. It is no wonder that this critical weakness sometimes betrayed her into imitation of that trick; but in her case the fault could be only superficial, because her work had every necessary literary quality. The platitude was merely pinned on to an object satisfying in content, form and style.

INTRODUCTION

Most of Miss Jewett's lapses into sentimentality, however, are more apparent than real. We suspect her of it when we need not, simply because she so often uses the same material as the sentimental writer. But this is not because she is tainted with his vice of handling his subject with the aim, not of conveying what his imagination tells him about it, but of causing certain emotional effects in his audience. It is simply that he seeks out, for his own voluptuous purposes, the very scenes she knew from her childhood: the household stricken by sickness or maintaining itself with dignity in an unkindly changing economy. But always when she treats that material she does so honestly, forcing herself to relive the human experience so that the truth about them is set down on her page, in order not that her readers may feel, but that they may know. 'Miss Tempy's Watchers' is not a calculated effect to cozen from our eyes all such tears as can be shed at the death of a saintly spinster; it is what Miss Jewett learned when she used her imagination to project herself into a New Hampshire farmhouse where two women of different temperaments were keeping vigil over their loved friend, the night before her funeral. 'The Dulham Ladies' is not, as it looks at the first glance, a piece of debased Cranfordism that angles for a snigger; it tells with precision how time and altered circumstances can evoke idiocy in worthy human beings, and how such idiocy makes a both sensible and kindly community show exasperation and tolerance at one and the same time. Everywhere, even in the Hawthorne-like ecstasy of 'A White Heron,' is the solemn sense that the writer's first obligation is to give a just account of the universe so far as he knows it.

There is a passage in one of the last letters Miss Jewett

INTRODUCTION

wrote which illustrates how far on the road towards fulfilling that obligation a lifetime of honest writing brought her. Her destiny was not so kind at its end as at the beginning, for in 1905 she had a serious carriage accident which kept her an invalid till her death five years later. In that distressing period she found it hard to write, but nevertheless kept enough power to write these words about a writer's day:

'I chiefly wish to tell you about a drive yesterday down the river; the river frozen; the snow very white and thinly spread like nicest frosting over the fields and the pine-woods black as they could be—no birds, but the tracks of every sort of little beastie. They seem to have been all out on visits and errands and going such distances on their little paws and claws: somehow it looks too much for a mouse to go half a mile along the road or across a field. Think how a hawk would see him! I think we knew every track but one,—it had long claws and a tail that never lifted;—we settled upon a big old rat who had come up from an old wharf by the riverside.'

This simple-seeming writing shows how nearly she had come to satisfying the requirements of Flaubert. 'Ecrire la vie ordinaire comme on écrit l'histoire': she had made the coming and going of beasties as definite an event as Waterloo. 'Ce n'est pas de faire rire—mais d'agir à la façon de la nature, c'est à dire de faire rêver': from the paw-tracks faithfully observed, there stretches out a whole countryside, a whole world.

REBECCA WEST.

THE ONLY ROSE AND OTHER TALES

THE ONLY ROSE

★

I

JUST where the village abruptly ended, and the green mowing fields began, stood Mrs. Bickford's house, looking down the road with all its windows, and topped by two prim chimneys that stood up like ears. It was placed with an end to the road, and fronted southward; you could follow a straight path from the gate past the front door and find Mrs. Bickford sitting by the last window of all in the kitchen, unless she were solemnly stepping about, prolonging the stern duties of her solitary housekeeping.

One day in early summer, when almost everyone else in Fairfield had put her house plants out of doors, there were still three flower pots on a kitchen window-sill. Mrs. Bickford spent but little time over her rose and geranium and Jerusalem cherry-tree, although they had gained a kind of personality born of long association. They rarely undertook to bloom, but had most courageously maintained life in spite of their owner's unsympathetic but conscientious care. Later in the season she would carry them out of doors, and leave them, until the time of frosts, under the shade of a great apple-tree, where they might make the best of what the summer had to give.

The afternoon sun was pouring in, the Jerusalem cherry-tree drooped its leaves in the heat and looked pale, when a neighbour, Miss Pendexter, came in from the next house but one to make a friendly call. As she passed the parlour with its shut blinds, and the sitting-room, also shaded carefully from the light, she wished, as she had done many times before, that somebody beside the owner might have the pleasure of living in and using so good and pleasant a house. Mrs. Bickford always complained of having so much care, even while she valued herself intelligently upon having the right to do as she pleased with one of the best houses in Fairfield. Miss Pendexter was a cheerful, even gay little person, who always brought a pleasant flurry of excitement, and usually had a genuine though small piece of news to tell, or some new aspect of already received information.

Mrs. Bickford smiled as she looked up to see this sprightly neighbour coming. She had no gift at entertaining herself, and was always glad, as one might say, to be taken off her own hands.

Miss Pendexter smiled back, as if she felt herself to be equal to the occasion.

'How be you to-day?' the guest asked kindly, as she entered the kitchen. 'Why, what a sight o' flowers, Mis' Bickford! What be you goin' to do with 'em all?'

Mrs. Bickford wore a grave expression as she glanced over her spectacles. 'My sister's boy fetched 'em over,' she answered. 'You know my sister Parsons's a great hand to raise flowers, an' this boy takes after her. He said his mother thought the gardin never looked handsomer and she picked me these to send over. They was sendin' a team to Westbury for some fertilizer to put on the land, an' he come with the men, an' stopped to eat his dinner 'long o' me. He's been growin' fast, and looks peakëd. I expect sister 'Liza thought the ride, this pleasant day, would do him good. 'Liza sent word for me to come over and pass some days next week, but it ain't so that I can.'

THE ONLY ROSE

'Why, it's a pretty time of year to go off and make a little visit,' suggested the neighbour encouragingly.

'I ain't got my sitting-room chamber carpet taken up yet,' sighed Mrs. Bickford. 'I do feel condemned. I might have done it to-day, but 't was all at end when I saw Tommy coming. There, he's a likely boy, an' so relished his dinner; I happened to be well prepared. I don't know but he's my favourite o' that family. Only I've been sittin' here thinkin', since he went, an' I can't remember that I ever was so belated with my spring cleaning.'

"T was owin' to the weather,' explained Miss Pendexter. 'None of us could be so smart as common this year, not even the lazy ones that always get one room done the first o' March, and brag of it to others' shame, and then never let on when they do the rest.'

The two women laughed together cheerfully. Mrs. Bickford had put up the wide leaf of her large table between the windows and spread out the flowers. She was sorting them slowly into three heaps.

'Why, I do declare if you haven't got a rose in bloom yourself!' exclaimed Miss Pendexter abruptly, as if the bud had not been announced weeks before, and its progress regularly commented upon. 'Ain't it a lovely rose? Why, Mis' Bickford!'

'Yes'm, it's out to-day,' said Mrs. Bickford, with a somewhat plaintive air. 'I'm glad you come in so as to see it.'

The bright flower was like a face. Somehow, the beauty and life of it were surprising in the plain room, like a gay little child who might suddenly appear in a doorway. Miss Pendexter forgot herself and her hostess and the tangled mass of

19

garden flowers in looking at the red rose. She even forgot that it was incumbent upon her to carry forward the conversation. Mrs. Bickford was subject to fits of untimely silence which made her friends anxiously sweep the corners of their minds in search of something to say, but anyone who looked at her now could easily see that it was not poverty of thought that made her speechless, but an overburdening sense of the inexpressible.

'Goin' to make up all your flowers into bo'quets? I think the short-stemmed kinds is often pretty in a dish,' suggested Miss Pendexter compassionately.

'I thought I should make them into three bo'quets. I wish there wa'n't quite so many. Sister Eliza's very lavish with her flowers; she's always been a kind sister, too,' said Mrs. Bickford vaguely. She was not apt to speak with so much sentiment, and as her neighbour looked at her narrowly she detected unusual signs of emotion. It suddenly became evident that the three nosegays were connected in her mind with her bereavement of three husbands, and Miss Pendexter's easily roused curiosity was quieted by the discovery that her friend was bent upon a visit to the burying-ground. It was the time of year when she was pretty sure to spend an afternoon there, and sometimes they had taken the walk in company. Miss Pendexter expected to receive the usual invitation, but there was nothing further said at the moment, and she looked again at the pretty rose.

Mrs. Bickford aimlessly handled the syringas and flowering almond sprays, choosing them out of the fragrant heap only to lay them down again. She glanced out of the window; then gave Miss Pendexter a long expressive look.

THE ONLY ROSE

'I expect you're going to carry 'em over to the burying-ground?' inquired the guest, in a sympathetic tone.

'Yes'm,' said the hostess, now well started in conversation and in quite her every-day manner. 'You see I was goin' over to my brother's folks to-morrow in South Fairfield, to pass the day; they said they were goin' to send over to-morrow to leave a wagon at the blacksmith's, and they'd hitch that to their best chaise, so I could ride back very comfortable. You know I have to avoid bein' out in the mornin' sun?'

Miss Pendexter smiled to herself at this moment; she was obliged to move from her chair at the window, the May sun was so hot on her back, for Mrs. Bickford always kept the curtains rolled high up, out of the way, for fear of fading and dust. The kitchen was a blaze of light. As for the Sunday chaise being sent, it was well known that Mrs. Bickford's married brothers and sisters comprehended the truth that she was a woman of property, and had neither chick nor child.

'So I thought 't was a good opportunity to just stop an' see if the lot was in good order, – last spring Mr. Wallis's stone hove with the frost; an' so I could take these flowers.' She gave a sigh. 'I ain't one that can bear flowers in a close room, – they bring on a headache; but I enjoy 'em as much as anybody to look at, only you never know what to put 'em in. If I could be out in the mornin' sun, as some do, and keep flowers in the house, I should have me a gardin, certain,' and she sighed again.

'A garden's a sight o' care, but I don't begrudge none o' the care I give to mine. I have to scant on flowers so's to make room for pole beans,' said Miss Pendexter gayly. She had only

21

a tiny strip of land behind her house, but she always had something to give away, and made riches out of her narrow poverty. 'A few flowers gives me just as much pleasure as more would,' she added. 'You get acquainted with things when you've only got one or two roots. My sweet-williams is just like folks.'

'Mr. Bickford was partial to sweet-williams,' said Mrs. Bickford. 'I never knew him to take notice of no other sort of flowers. When we'd be over to Eliza's, he'd walk down her gardin, an' he'd never make no comments until he come to them, and then he'd say, "Those is sweet-williams." How many times I've heard him!'

'You ought to have a sprig of 'em for his bo'quet,' suggested Miss Pendexter.

'Yes, I've put a sprig in,' said her companion.

At this moment Miss Pendexter took a good look at the bouquets, and found that they were as nearly alike as careful hands could make them. Mrs. Bickford was evidently trying to reach absolute impartiality.

'I don't know but you think it's foolish to tie 'em up this afternoon,' she said presently, as she wound the first with a stout string. 'I thought I could put 'em in a bucket o' water out in the shed, where there's a draught o' air, and then I should have all my time in the morning. I shall have a good deal to do before I go. I always sweep the setting-room and front entry Wednesdays. I want to leave everything nice, goin' away for all day so. So I meant to get the flowers out o' the way this afternoon. Why, it's most half-past four, ain't it? But I sha'n't pick the rose till mornin'; 't will be blowed out better then.'

THE ONLY ROSE

'The rose?' questioned Miss Pendexter. 'Why, are you goin' to pick that, too?'

'Yes, I be. I never like to let 'em fade on the bush. There, that's just what's a-troublin' me,' and she turned to give a long, imploring look at the friend who sat beside her. Miss Pendexter had moved her chair before the table in order to be out of the way of the sun. 'I don't seem to know which of 'em ought to have it,' said Mrs. Bickford despondently. 'I do so hate to make a choice between 'em; they all had their good points, especially Mr. Bickford, and I respected 'em all. I don't know but what I think of one on 'em 'most as much as I do of the other.'

'Why, 't is difficult for you, ain't it?' responded Miss Pendexter. 'I don't know's I can offer advice.'

'No, I s'pose not,' answered her friend slowly, with a shadow of disappointment coming over her calm face. 'I feel sure you would if you could, Abby.'

Both of the women felt as if they were powerless before a great emergency.

'There's one thing, – they're all in a better world now,' said Miss Pendexter, in a self-conscious and constrained voice; 'they can't feel such little things or take note o' slights same's we can.'

'No; I suppose 't is myself that wants to be just,' answered Mrs. Bickford. 'I feel under obligations to my last husband when I look about and see how comfortable he left me. Poor Mr. Wallis had his great projects, an' perhaps if he'd lived longer he'd have made a record; but when he died he'd failed all up, owing to that patent corn-sheller he'd put everything into, and, as you know, I had to get along 'most any way I could for the next few years. Life was very disappointing with Mr. Wallis, but he meant well, an' used to be an amiable person to dwell with, until his temper got spoilt makin' so many hopes an' havin' 'em turn out failures. He had consider'ble of an air, an' dressed very handsome when I was first acquainted with him, Mr. Wallis did. I don't know's you ever knew Mr. Wallis in his prime?'

'He died the year I moved over here from North Denfield,' said Miss Pendexter, in a tone of sympathy. 'I just knew him by sight. I was to his funeral. You know you lived in what we call the Wells house then, and I felt it wouldn't be an intrusion, we was such near neighbours. The first time I ever was in your house was just before that, when he was sick, an' Mary 'Becca Wade an' I called to see if there was anything we could do.'

'They used to say about town that Mr. Wallis went to an' fro like a mail-coach an' brought nothin' to pass,' announced Mrs. Bickford without bitterness. 'He ought to have had a better chance than he did in this little neighbourhood. You see, he had excellent ideas, but he never'd learned the machinist's trade, and there was somethin' the matter with every model he contrived. I used to be real narrow-minded when he talked about moving 'way up to Lowell, or some o' them places; I hated to think of leaving my folks; and now I see that I never done right by him. His ideas was good. I know once he was on a jury, and there was a man stopping to the tavern where he was, near the court house, a man that travelled for a firm to Lowell; and they engaged in talk, an' Mr. Wallis let out some o' his notions an' contrivances, an' he said that man wouldn't hardly stop to eat, he was so

THE ONLY ROSE

interested, an' said he'd look for a chance for him up to Lowell. It all sounded so well that I kind of begun to think about goin' myself. Mr. Wallis said we'd close the house here, and go an' board through the winter. But he never heard a word from him, and the disappointment was one he never got over. I think of it now different from what I did then. I often used to be kind of disapproving to Mr. Wallis; but there, he used to be always tellin' over his great projects. Somebody told me once that a man by the same name of the one he met while he was to court had got some patents for the very things Mr. Wallis used to be workin' over; but 't was after he died, an' I don't know's 't was in him to ever really set things up so other folks could ha' seen their value. His machines always used to work kind of rickety, but folks used to come from all round to see 'em; they was curiosities if they wa'n't nothin' else, an' gave him a name.'

Mrs. Bickford paused a moment, with some geranium leaves in her hand, and seemed to suppress with difficulty a desire to speak even more freely.

'He was a dreadful notional man,' she said at last, regretfully, and as if this fact were a poor substitute for what had just been in her mind. 'I recollect one time he worked all through the early winter over my churn, an' got it so it would go three quarters of an hour all of itself if you wound it up; an' if you'll believe it, he went an' spent all that time for nothin' when the cow was dry, an' we was with difficulty borrowin' a pint o' milk a day somewheres in the neighbourhood just to get along with.' Mrs. Bickford flushed with displeasure, and turned to look at her visitor. 'Now what do you think of such a man as that, Miss Pendexter?' she asked.

'Why, I don't know but 'twas just as good for an invention,' answered Miss Pendexter timidly; but her friend looked doubtful, and did not appear to understand.

'Then I asked him where it was, one day that spring when I'd got tired to death churnin', an' the butter wouldn't come in a churn I'd had to borrow, and he'd gone an' took ours all to pieces to get the works to make some other useless contrivance with. He had no sort of a business turn, but he was well meanin', Mr. Wallis was, an' full o' divertin' talk; they used to call him very good company. I see now that he never had no proper chance. I've always regretted Mr. Wallis,' said she who was now the widow Bickford.

'I'm sure you always speak well of him,' said Miss Pendexter. ''T was a pity he hadn't got among good business men, who could push his inventions an' do all the business part.'

'I was left very poor an' needy for them next few years,' said Mrs. Bickford mournfully; 'but he never'd give up but what he should die worth his fifty thousand dollars. I don't see now how I ever did get along them next few years without him; but there, I always managed to keep a pig, an' sister Eliza gave me my potatoes, and I made out somehow. I could dig me a few greens, you know, in spring, and then 't would come strawberry-time, and other berries a-followin' on. I was always decent to go to meetin' till within the last six months, an' then I went in bad weather, when folks wouldn't notice; but 't was a rainy summer, an' I managed to get considerable preachin' after all. My clothes looked proper enough when 't was a wet Sabbath. I often think o' them pinched days now, when I'm left so comfortable by Mr. Bickford.'

THE ONLY ROSE

'Yes'm, you've everything to be thankful for,' said Miss Pendexter, who was as poor herself at that moment as her friend had ever been, and who could never dream of venturing upon the support and companionship of a pig. 'Mr. Bickford was a very personable man,' she hastened to say, the confidences were so intimate and interesting.

'Oh, very,' replied Mrs. Bickford; 'there was something about him that was very marked. Strangers would always ask who he was as he come into meetin'. His words counted; he never spoke except he had to. 'T was a relief at first after Mr. Wallis's being so fluent; but Mr. Wallis was splendid company for winter evenings, – 't would be eight o'clock before you knew it. I didn't use to listen to it all, but he had a great deal of information. Mr. Bickford was dreadful dignified; I used to be sort of meechin' with him along at the first, for fear he'd disapprove of me; but I found out 't wa'n't no need; he was always just that way, an' done everything by rule an' measure. He hadn't the mind of my other husbands, but he was a very dignified appearing man; he used 'most always to sleep in the evenin's, Mr. Bickford did.'

'Them is lovely bo'quets, certain!' exclaimed Miss Pendexter. 'Why, I couldn't tell 'em apart; the flowers are comin' out just right, aren't they?'

Mrs. Bickford nodded assent, and then, startled by sudden recollection, she cast a quick glance at the rose in the window.

'I always seem to forget about your first husband, Mr. Fraley,' Miss Pendexter suggested bravely. 'I've often heard you speak of him, too, but he'd passed away long before I ever knew you.'

'He was but a boy,' said Mrs. Bickford. 'I thought

the world was done for me when he died, but I've often thought since 't was a mercy for him. He come of a very melancholy family, and all his brothers an' sisters enjoyed poor health; it might have been his lot. Folks said we was as pretty a couple as ever come into church; we was both dark, with black eyes an' a good deal o' colour, – you wouldn't expect it to see me now. Albert was one that held up his head, and looked as if he meant to own the town, an' he had a good word for everybody. I don't know what the years might have brought.'

There was a long pause. Mrs. Bickford leaned over to pick up a heavy-headed Guelder-rose that had dropped on the floor.

'I expect 't was what they call fallin' in love,' she added, in a different tone; 'he wa'n't nothin' but a boy, an' I wa'n't nothin' but a girl, but we was dreadful happy. He didn't favour his folks, – they all had hay-coloured hair and was faded-looking, except his mother; they was alike, and looked alike, an' set everything by each other. He was just the kind of strong, hearty young man that goes right off if they get a fever. We was just settled on a little farm, an' he'd have done well if he'd had time; as it was, he left debts. He had a hasty temper, that was his great fault, but Albert had a lovely voice to sing; they said there wa'n't no such tenor voice in this part o' the State. I could hear him singin' to himself right out in the field a'ploughin' or hoein', an' he didn't know it half o' the time, no more'n a common bird would. I don't know's I valued his gift as I ought to, but there was nothin' ever sounded so sweet to me. I ain't one that ever had much fancy, but I knowed Albert had a pretty voice.'

Mrs. Bickford's own voice trembled a little, but she held

THE ONLY ROSE

up the last bouquet and examined it critically. 'I must hurry now an' put these in water,' she said, in a matter-of-fact tone. Little Miss Pendexter was so quiet and sympathetic that her hostess felt no more embarrassed than if she had been talking only to herself.

'Yes, they do seem to droop some; 't is a little warm for them here in the sun,' said Miss Pendexter; 'but you'll find they'll all come up if you give them their fill o' water. They'll look very handsome to-morrow; folks'll notice them from the road. You've arranged them very tasty, Mis' Bickford.'

'They do look pretty, don't they?' Mrs. Bickford regarded the three in turn. 'I want to have them all pretty. You may deem it strange, Abby.'

'Why, no, Mis' Bickford,' said the guest sincerely, although a little perplexed by the solemnity of the occasion. 'I know how 't is with friends, – that having one don't keep you from wantin' another; 't is just like havin' somethin' to eat, and then wantin' somethin' to drink just the same. I expect all friends find their places.'

But Mrs. Bickford was not interested in this figure, and still looked vague and anxious as she began to brush the broken stems and wilted leaves into her wide calico apron. 'I done the best I could while they was alive,' she said, 'and mourned 'em when I lost 'em, an' I feel grateful to be left so comfortable now when all is over. It seems foolish, but I'm still at a loss about that rose.'

'Perhaps you'll feel sure when you first wake up in the morning,' answered Miss Pendexter solicitously. 'It's a case where I don't deem myself qualified to offer you any advice. But I'll say one thing, seeing's you've been so friendly spoken and confiding with me. I never was married myself, Mis' Bickford, because it wa'n't so that I could have the one I liked.'

'I suppose he ain't livin', then? Why, I wa'n't never aware you had met with a disappointment, Abby,' said Mrs. Bickford instantly. None of her neighbours had ever suspected little Miss Pendexter of a romance.

'Yes'm, he's livin',' replied Miss Pendexter humbly. 'No'm, I never have heard that he died.'

'I want to know!' exclaimed the woman of experience. 'Well, I'll tell you this, Abby: you may have regretted your lot, and felt lonesome and hardshipped, but they all have their faults, and a single woman's got her liberty, if she ain't got other blessin's.'

"T wouldn't have been my choice to live alone,' said Abby, meeker than before. 'I feel very thankful for my blessin's, all the same. You've always been a kind neighbour, Mis' Bickford.'

'Why can't you stop to tea?' asked the elder woman, with unusual cordiality; but Miss Pendexter remembered that her hostess often expressed a dislike for unexpected company, and promptly took her departure after she had risen to go, glancing up at the bright flower as she passed outside the window. It seemed to belong most to Albert, but she had not liked to say so. The sun was low; the green fields stretched away southward into the misty distance.

II

Mrs. Bickford's house appeared to watch her out of sight down the road, the next morning. She had lost all spirit for her

THE ONLY ROSE

holiday. Perhaps it was the unusual excitement of the afternoon's reminiscences, or it might have been simply the bright moonlight night which had kept her broad awake until dawn, thinking of the past, and more and more concerned about the rose. By this time it had ceased to be merely a flower, and had become a definite symbol and assertion of personal choice. She found it very difficult to decide. So much of her present comfort and well-being was due to Mr. Bickford; still, it was Mr. Wallis who had been most unfortunate, and to whom she had done least justice. If she owed recognition to Mr. Bickford, she certainly owed amends to Mr. Wallis. If she gave him the rose, it would be for the sake of affectionate apology. And then there was Albert, to whom she had no thought of being either indebted or forgiving. But she could not escape from the terrible feeling of indecision.

It was a beautiful morning for a drive, but Mrs. Bickford was kept waiting some time for the chaise. Her nephew, who was to be her escort, had found much social advantage at the blacksmith's shop, so that it was after ten when she finally started with the three large flat-backed bouquets, covered with a newspaper to protect them from the sun. The petals of the almond flowers were beginning to scatter, and now and then little streams of water leaked out of the newspaper and trickled down the steep slope of her best dress to the bottom of the chaise. Even yet she had not made up her mind; she had stopped trying to deal with such an evasive thing as decision, and leaned back and rested as best she could.

'What an old fool I be!' she rebuked herself from time to time, in so loud a whisper that her companion ventured a respectful 'What, ma'am?' and was astonished that she made no reply. John was a handsome young man, but Mrs. Bickford could never cease thinking of him as a boy. He had always been her favourite among the younger members of the family, and now returned this affectionate feeling, being possessed of an instinctive confidence in the sincerities of his prosaic aunt.

As they drove along, there had seemed at first to be something unsympathetic and garish about the beauty of the summer day. After the shade and shelter of the house, Mrs. Bickford suffered even more from a contracted and assailed feeling out of doors. The very trees by the roadside had a curiously fateful, trying way of standing back to watch her, as she passed in the acute agony of indecision, and she was annoyed and startled by a bird that flew too near the chaise in a moment of surprise. She was conscious of a strange reluctance to the movement of the Sunday chaise, as if she were being conveyed against her will; but the companionship of her nephew John grew every moment to be more and more a reliance. It was very comfortable to sit by his side, even though he had nothing to say; he was manly and cheerful, and she began to feel protected.

'Aunt Bickford,' he suddenly announced, 'I may's well out with it! I've got a piece o' news to tell you, if you won't let on to nobody. I expect you'll laugh, but you know I've set everything by Mary Lizzie Gifford ever since I was a boy. Well, sir!'

'Well, sir!' exclaimed aunt Bickford in her turn, quickly roused into most comfortable self-forgetfulness. 'I am really pleased. She'll make you a good, smart wife, John. Ain't all the folks pleased, both sides?'

THE ONLY ROSE

'Yes, they be,' answered John soberly, with a happy, important look that became him well.

'I guess I can make out to do something for you to help along, when the right time comes,' said aunt Bickford impulsively, after a moment's reflection. 'I've known what it is to be starting out in life with plenty o' hope. You ain't calculatin' on gettin' married before fall, – or be ye?'

"Long in the fall,' said John regretfully. 'I wish t' we could set up for ourselves right away this summer. I ain't got much ahead, but I can work well as anybody, an' now I'm out o' my time.'

'She's a nice, modest, pretty girl. I thought she liked you, John,' said the old aunt. 'I saw her over to your mother's, last day I was there. Well, I expect you'll be happy.'

'Certain,' said John, turning to look at her affectionately, surprised by this outspokenness and lack of embarrassment between them. 'Thank you, aunt,' he said simply; 'you're a real good friend to me'; and he looked away again hastily, and blushed a fine scarlet over his sun-browned face. 'She's coming over to spend the day with the girls,' he added. 'Mother thought of it. You don't get over to see us very often.'

Mrs. Bickford smiled approvingly. John's mother looked for her good opinion, no doubt, but it was very proper for John to have told his prospects himself, and in such a pretty way. There was no shilly-shallying about the boy.

'My gracious!' said John suddenly. 'I'd like to have drove right by the burying-ground. I forgot we wanted to stop.'

Strange as it may appear, Mrs. Bickford herself had not noticed the burying-ground, either, in her excitement and pleasure; now she felt distressed and responsible again, and showed it in her face at once. The young man leaped lightly to the ground, and reached for the flowers.

'Here, you just let me run up with 'em,' he said kindly. "T is hot in the sun to-day, an' you'll mind it risin' the hill. We'll stop as I fetch you back to-night, and you can go up comfortable an' walk the yard after sundown when it's cool, an' stay as long as you're a mind to. You seem sort of tired, aunt.'

'I don't know but what I will let you carry 'em,' said Mrs. Bickford slowly.

To leave the matter of the rose in the hands of fate seemed weakness and cowardice, but there was not a moment for consideration. John was a smiling fate, and his proposition was a great relief. She watched him go away with a terrible inward shaking, and sinking of pride. She had held the flowers with so firm a grasp that her hands felt weak and numb, and as she leaned back and shut her eyes she was afraid to open them again at first for fear of knowing the bouquets apart even at that distance, and giving instructions which she might regret. With a sudden impulse she called John once or twice eagerly; but her voice had a thin and piping sound, and the meditative early crickets that chirped in the fresh summer grass probably sounded louder in John's ears. The bright light on the white stones dazzled Mrs. Bickford's eyes; and then all at once she felt light-hearted, and the sky seemed to lift itself higher and wider from the earth, and she gave a sigh of relief as her messenger came back along the path. 'I know who I do hope's got the right one,' she said to herself. 'There, what a touse I be in! I don't see what I had to go and pick the old rose for, anyway.'

THE ONLY ROSE

'I declare, they did look real handsome, aunt,' said John's hearty voice as he approached the chaise. 'I set 'em up just as you told me. This one fell out, an' I kept it. I don't know's you'll care. I can give it to Lizzie.'

He faced her now with a bright, boyish look. There was something gay in his buttonhole, – it was the red rose.

Aunt Bickford blushed like a girl. 'Your choice is easy made,' she faltered mysteriously, and then burst out laughing, there in front of the burying-ground. 'Come, get right in, dear,' she said. 'Well, well! I guess the rose was made for you; it looks very pretty in your coat, John.'

She thought of Albert, and the next moment the tears came into her old eyes. John was a lover, too.

'My first husband was just such a tall, straight young man as you be,' she said as they drove along. 'The flower he first give me was a rose.'

THE GUESTS OF MRS. TIMMS

★

I

MRS. PERSIS FLAGG stood in her front doorway taking leave of Miss Cynthia Pickett, who had been making a long call. They were not intimate friends. Miss Pickett always came formally to the front door and rang when she paid her visits, but, the week before, they had met at the county conference, and happened to be sent to the same house for entertainment, and so had deepened and renewed the pleasures of acquaintance.

It was an afternoon in early June; the syringa-bushes were tall and green on each side of the stone doorsteps, and were covered with their lovely white and golden flowers. Miss Pickett broke off the nearest twig, and held it before her prim face as she talked. She had a pretty childlike smile that came and went suddenly, but her face was not one that bore the marks of many pleasures. Mrs. Flagg was a tall, commanding sort of person, with an air of satisfaction and authority.

'Oh, yes, gather all you want,' she said stiffly, as Miss Pickett took the syringa without having asked beforehand; but she had an amiable expression, and just now her large countenance was lighted up by pleasant anticipation.

'We can tell early what sort of a day it's goin' to be,' she said eagerly. 'There ain't a cloud in the sky now. I'll stop for you as I come along, or if there should be anything unforeseen to detain me, I'll send you word. I don't expect you'd want to go if it wa'n't so that I could?'

'Oh my sakes, no!' answered Miss Pickett discreetly, with

THE GUESTS OF MRS. TIMMS

a timid flush. 'You feel certain that Mis' Timms won't be put out? I shouldn't feel free to go unless I went 'long o' you.'

'Why, nothin' could be plainer than her words,' said Mrs. Flagg in a tone of reproval. 'You saw how she urged me, an' had over all that talk about how we used to see each other often when we both lived to Longport, and told how she'd been thinkin' of writin', and askin' if it wa'n't so I should be able to come over and stop three or four days as soon as settled weather come, because she couldn't make no fire in her best chamber on account of the chimbley smokin' if the wind wa'n't just right. You see how she felt toward me, kissin' of me comin' and goin'? Why, she even asked me who I employed to do over my bonnet, Miss Pickett, just as interested as if she was a sister; an' she remarked she should look for us any pleasant day after we all got home, an' were settled after the conference.'

Miss Pickett smiled, but did not speak, as if she expected more arguments still.

'An' she seemed just about as much gratified to meet with you again. She seemed to desire to meet you again very particular,' continued Mrs. Flagg. 'She really urged us to come together an' have a real good day talkin' over old times – there, don't le' 's go all over it again! I've always heard she'd made that old house of her aunt Bascoms' where she lives look real handsome. I once heard her best parlour carpet described as being an elegant carpet, different from any there was round here. Why, nobody couldn't be more cordial, Miss Pickett; you ain't goin' to give out just at the last?'

'Oh, no!' answered the visitor hastily; 'no, 'm! I want to go full as much as you do, Mis' Flagg, but you see I never was so well acquainted with Mis' Cap'n Timms, an' I always seem to dread putting myself for'ard. She certain was very urgent, an' she said plain enough to come any day next week, an' here 't is Wednesday, though of course she wouldn't look for us either Monday or Tuesday. 'T will be a real pleasant occasion, an' now we've been to the conference it don't seem near so much effort to start.'

'Why, I don't think nothin' of it,' said Mrs. Flagg proudly. 'We shall have a grand good time, goin' together an' all, I feel sure.'

Miss Pickett still played with her syringa flower, tapping her thin cheek, and twirling the stem with her fingers. She looked as if she were going to say something more, but after a moment's hesitation she turned away.

'Good afternoon, Mis' Flagg,' she said formally, looking up with a quick little smile; 'I enjoyed my call; I hope I ain't kep' you too late; I don't know but what it's 'most tea-time. Well, I shall look for you in the mornin'.'

'Good afternoon, Miss Pickett; I'm glad I was in when you came. Call again, won't you?' said Mrs. Flagg. 'Yes; you may expect me in good season,' and so they parted. Miss Pickett went out at the neat clicking gate in the white fence, and Mrs. Flagg a moment later looked out of her sitting-room window to see if the gate were latched, and felt the least bit disappointed to find that it was. She sometimes went out after the departure of a guest, and fastened the gate herself with a loud, rebuking sound. Both of these Woodville women lived alone, and were very precise in their way of doing things.

THE GUESTS OF MRS. TIMMS

II

The next morning dawned clear and bright, and Miss Pickett rose even earlier than usual. She found it most difficult to decide which of her dresses would be best to wear. Summer was still so young that the day had all the freshness of spring, but when the two friends walked away together along the shady street, with a chorus of golden robins singing high overhead in the elms, Miss Pickett decided that she had made a wise choice of her second-best black silk gown, which she had just turned again and freshened. It was neither too warm for the season nor too cool, nor did it look overdressed. She wore her large cameo pin, and this, with a long watch-chain, gave an air of proper mural decoration. She was a straight, flat little person, as if, when not in use, she kept herself, silk dress and all, between the leaves of a book. She carried a noticeable parasol with a fringe, and a small shawl, with a pretty border, neatly folded over her left arm. Mrs. Flagg always dressed in black cashmere, and looked, to hasty observers, much the same one day as another; but her companion recognized the fact that this was the best black cashmere of all, and for a moment quailed at the thought that Mrs. Flagg was paying such extreme deference to their prospective hostess. The visit turned for a moment into an unexpectedly solemn formality, and pleasure seemed to wane before Cynthia Pickett's eyes, yet with great courage she never slackened a single step. Mrs. Flagg carried a somewhat worn black leather handbag, which Miss Pickett regretted; it did not give the visit that casual and unpremeditated air which she felt to be more elegant.

'Sha'n't I carry your bag for you?' she asked timidly. Mrs. Flagg was the older and more important person.

'Oh, dear me, no,' answered Mrs. Flagg. 'My pocket's so remote, in case I should desire to sneeze or anything, that I thought 't would be convenient for carrying my handkerchief and pocket-book; an' then I just tucked in a couple o' glasses o' my crab-apple jelly for Mis' Timms. She used to be a great hand for preserves of every sort, an' I thought 't would be a kind of an attention, an' give rise to conversation. I know she used to make excellent drop-cakes when we was both residin' to Longport; folks used to say she never would give the right receipt, but if I get a real good chance, I mean to ask her. Or why can't you, if I start talkin' about receipts – why can't you say, sort of innocent, that I have always spoken frequently of her drop-cakes, an' ask for the rule? She would be very sensible to the compliment, and could pass it off if she didn't feel to indulge us. There, I do so wish you would!'

'Yes, 'm,' said Miss Pickett doubtfully; 'I'll try to make the opportunity. I'm very partial to drop-cakes. Was they flour or rye, Mis' Flagg?'

'They was flour, dear,' replied Mrs. Flagg approvingly; 'crisp an' light as any you ever see.'

'I wish I had thought to carry somethin' to make it pleasant,' said Miss Pickett, after they had walked a little farther; 'but there, I don't know's 't would look just right, this first visit, to offer anything to such a person as Mis' Timms. In case I ever go over to Baxter again I won't forget to make her some little present, as nice as I've got. 'T was certain very polite of her to urge me to come with you. I did feel very doubtful at first. I didn't know but she thought it behooved

THE GUESTS OF MRS. TIMMS

her, because I was in your company at the conference, and she wanted to save my feelin's, and yet expected I would decline. I never was well acquainted with her; our folks wasn't well off when I first knew her; 't was before uncle Cap'n Dyer passed away an' remembered mother an' me in his will. We couldn't make no han'some companies in them days, so we didn't go to none, an' kep' to ourselves; but in my grandmother's time, mother always said, the families was very friendly. I shouldn't feel like goin' over to pass the day with Mis' Timms if I didn't mean to ask her to return the visit. Some don't think o' these things, but mother was very set about not bein' done for when she couldn't make no return.'

' "When it rains porridge hold up your dish," ' said Mrs. Flagg; but Miss Pickett made no response beyond a feeble 'Yes, 'm,' which somehow got caught in her pale-green bonnet-strings.

'There, 't ain't no use to fuss too much over all them things,' proclaimed Mrs. Flagg, walking along at a good pace with a fine sway of her skirts, and carrying her head high. 'Folks walks right by an' forgits all about you; folks can't always be going through with just so much. You'd had a good deal better time, you an' your ma, if you'd been freer in your ways; now don't you s'pose you would? 'T ain't what you give folks to eat so much as 't is makin' 'em feel welcome. Now, there's Mis' Timms; when we was to Longport she was dreadful methodical. She wouldn't let Cap'n Timms fetch nobody home to dinner without lettin' of her know, same's other cap'ns' wives had to submit to. I was thinkin', when she was so cordial over to Danby, how she'd softened with time. Years do learn folks somethin'! She did seem very pleasant an' desirous. There, I am so glad we got started; if she'd gone an' got up a real good dinner to-day, an' then not had us come till to-morrow, 't would have been real too bad. Where anybody lives alone such a thing is very tryin'.'

'Oh, so 't is!' said Miss Pickett. 'There, I'd like to tell you what I went through with year before last. They come an' asked me one Saturday night to entertain the minister, that time we was having candidates' —

'I guess we'd better step along faster,' said Mrs. Flagg suddenly. 'Why, Miss Pickett, there's the stage comin' now! It's dreadful prompt, seems to me. Quick! there's folks awaitin', an' I sha'n't get to Baxter in no state to visit Mis' Cap'n Timms if I have to ride all the way there backward!'

III

The stage was not full inside. The group before the store proved to be made up of spectators, except one man, who climbed at once to a vacant seat by the driver. Inside there was only one person, after two passengers got out, and she preferred to sit with her back to the horses, so that Mrs. Flagg and Miss Pickett settled themselves comfortably in the coveted corners of the back seat. At first they took no notice of their companion, and spoke to each other in low tones, but presently something attracted the attention of all three and engaged them in conversation.

'I never was over this road before,' said the stranger. 'I s'pose you ladies are well acquainted all along.'

'We have often travelled it in past years. We was over this part of it last week goin' and comin' from the county conference,' said Mrs. Flagg in a dignified manner.

THE GUESTS OF MRS. TIMMS

'What persuasion?' inquired the fellow-traveller, with interest.

'Orthodox,' said Miss Pickett quickly, before Mrs. Flagg could speak. 'It was a very interestin' occasion; this other lady an' me stayed through all the meetin's.'

'I ain't Orthodox,' announced the stranger, waiving any interest in personalities. 'I was brought up amongst the Freewill Baptists.'

'We're well acquainted with several of that denomination in our place,' said Mrs. Flagg, not without an air of patronage. 'They've never built 'em no church; there ain't but a scattered few.'

'They prevail where I come from,' said the traveller. 'I'm goin' now to visit with a Freewill lady. We was to a conference together once, same's you an' your friend, but 't was a state conference. She asked me to come some time an' make her a good visit, and I'm on my way now. I didn't seem to have nothin' to keep me to home.'

'We're all goin' visitin' to-day, ain't we?' said Mrs. Flagg sociably; but no one carried on the conversation.

The day was growing very warm; there was dust in the sandy road, but the fields of grass and young growing crops looked fresh and fair. There was a light haze over the hills, and birds were thick in the air. When the stage-horses stopped to walk, you could hear the crows caw, and the bobolinks singing, in the meadows. All the farmers were busy in their fields.

'It don't seem but little ways to Baxter, does it?' said Miss Pickett, after a while. 'I felt we should pass a good deal o' time on the road, but we must be pretty near half-way there a'ready.'

'Why, more'n half!' exclaimed Mrs. Flagg. 'Yes; there's Beckett's Corner right ahead, an' the old Beckett house. I haven't been on this part of the road for so long that I feel kind of strange. I used to visit over here when I was a girl. There's a nephew's widow owns the place now. Old Miss Susan Beckett willed it to him, an' he died; but she resides there an' carries on the farm, an unusual smart woman, everybody says. Ain't it pleasant here, right out among the farms!'

'Mis' Beckett's place, did you observe?' said the stranger, leaning forward to listen to what her companions said. 'I expect that's where I'm goin' – Mis' Ezra Beckett's?'

'That's the one,' said Miss Pickett and Mrs. Flagg together, and they both looked out eagerly as the coach drew up to the front door of a large old yellow house that stood close upon the green turf of the roadside.

The passenger looked pleased and eager, and made haste to leave the stage with her many bundles and bags. While she stood impatiently tapping at the brass knocker, the stage-driver landed a large trunk, and dragged it toward the door across the grass. Just then a busy-looking middle-aged woman made her appearance, with floury hands and a look as if she were prepared to be somewhat on the defensive.

'Why, how do you do, Mis' Beckett?' exclaimed the guest. 'Well, here I be at last. I didn't know's you thought I was ever comin'. Why, I do declare, I believe you don't recognize me, Mis' Beckett.'

'I believe I don't,' said the self-possessed hostess. 'Ain't you made some mistake, ma'am?'

'Why, don't you recollect we was together that time to the state conference, an' you said you should be pleased to

THE GUESTS OF MRS. TIMMS

have me come an' make you a visit some time, an' I said I would certain. There, I expect I look more natural to you now.'

Mrs. Beckett appeared to be making the best possible effort, and gave a bewildered glance, first at her unexpected visitor, and then at the trunk. The stage-driver, who watched this encounter with evident delight, turned away with reluctance. 'I can't wait all day to see how they settle it,' he said, and mounted briskly to the box, and the stage rolled on.

'He might have waited just a minute to see,' said Miss Pickett indignantly, but Mrs. Flagg's head and shoulders were already far out of the stage window — the house was on her side. 'She ain't got in yet,' she told Miss Pickett triumphantly. 'I could see 'em quite a spell. With that trunk, too! I do declare, how inconsiderate some folks is!'

"'T was pushin' an acquaintance most too far, wa'n't it?" agreed Miss Pickett. 'There, 't will be somethin' laughable to tell Mis' Timms. I never see anything more divertin'. I shall kind of pity that woman if we have to stop an' git her as we go back this afternoon.'

'Oh, don't let's forgit to watch for her,' exclaimed Mrs. Flagg, beginning to brush off the dust of travel. 'There, I feel an excellent appetite, don't you? And we ain't got more'n three or four miles to go, if we have that. I wonder what Mis' Timms is likely to give us for dinner; she spoke of makin' a good many chicken-pies, an' I happened to remark how partial I was to 'em. She felt above most of the things we had provided for us over to the conference. I know she was always counted the best o' cooks when I knew her so well to Longport. Now, don't you forget, if there's a suitable opportunity, to inquire about the drop-cakes;' and Miss Pickett, a little less doubtful than before, renewed her promise.

IV

'My gracious, won't Mis' Timms be pleased to see us! It's just exactly the day to have company. And ain't Baxter a sweet pretty place?' said Mrs. Flagg, as they walked up the main street. 'Cynthy Pickett, now ain't you proper glad you come? I felt sort o' calm about it part o' the time yesterday, but I ain't felt so like a girl for a good while. I do believe I'm goin' to have a splendid time.'

Miss Pickett glowed with equal pleasure as she paced along. She was less expansive and enthusiastic than her companion, but now that they were fairly in Baxter, she lent herself generously to the occasion. The social distinction of going away to spend a day in company with Mrs. Flagg was by no means small. She arranged the folds of her shawl more carefully over her arm so as to show the pretty palm-leaf border, and then looked up with great approval to the row of great maples that shaded the broad sidewalk. 'I wonder if we can't contrive to make time to go an' see old Miss Nancy Fell?' she ventured to ask Mrs. Flagg. 'There ain't a great deal o' time before the stage goes at four o'clock; 't will pass quickly, but I should hate to have her feel hurt. If she was one we had visited often at home, I shouldn't care so much, but such folks feel any little slight. She was a member of our church; I think a good deal of that.'

'Well, I hardly know what to say,' faltered Mrs. Flagg coldly. 'We might just look in a minute; I shouldn't want her to feel hurt.'

THE GUESTS OF MRS. TIMMS

'She was one that always did her part, too,' said Miss Pickett, more boldly. 'Mr. Cronin used to say that she was more generous with her little than many was with their much. If she hadn't lived in a poor part of the town, and so been occupied with a different kind of people from us, 't would have made a difference. They say she's got a comfortable little home over here, an' keeps house for a nephew. You know she was to our meeting one Sunday last winter, and 'peared dreadful glad to get back; folks seemed glad to see her, too. I don't know as you were out.'

'She always wore a friendly look,' said Mrs. Flagg indulgently. 'There, now, there's Mis' Timms's residence; it's handsome, ain't it, with them big spruce-trees? I expect she may be at the window now, an' see us as we come along. Is my bonnet on straight, an' everything? The blinds looks open in the room this way; I guess she's to home fast enough.'

The friends quickened their steps, and with shining eyes and beating hearts hastened forward. The slightest mists of uncertainty were now cleared away; they gazed at the house with deepest pleasure; the visit was about to begin.

They opened the front gate and went up the short walk, noticing the pretty herring-bone pattern of the bricks, and as they stood on the high steps Cynthia Pickett wondered whether she ought not to have worn her best dress, even though there was lace at the neck and sleeves, and she usually kept it for the most formal of tea-parties and exceptional parish festivals. In her heart she commended Mrs. Flagg for that familiarity with the ways of a wider social world which had led her to wear the very best among her black cashmeres.

'She's a good while coming to the door,' whispered Mrs.

Flagg presently. 'Either she didn't see us, or else she's slipped upstairs to make some change, an' is just goin' to let us ring again. I've done it myself sometimes. I'm glad we come right over after her urgin' us so; it seems more cordial than to keep her expectin' us. I expect she'll urge us terribly to remain with her over-night.'

'Oh, I ain't prepared,' began Miss Pickett, but she looked pleased. At that moment there was a slow withdrawal of the bolt inside, and a key was turned, the front door opened, and Mrs. Timms stood before them with a smile. Nobody stopped to think at that moment what kind of smile it was.

'Why, if it ain't Mis' Flagg,' she exclaimed politely, 'an' Miss Pickett too! I am surprised!'

The front entry behind her looked well furnished, but not exactly hospitable; the stairs with their brass rods looked so clean and bright that it did not seem as if anybody had ever gone up or come down. A cat came purring out, but Mrs. Timms pushed her back with a determined foot, and hastily closed the sitting-room door. Then Miss Pickett let Mrs. Flagg precede her, as was becoming, and they went into a darkened parlour, and found their way to some chairs, and seated themselves solemnly.

"'T is a beautiful day, ain't it?' said Mrs. Flagg, speaking first. 'I don't know's I ever enjoyed the ride more. We've been having a good deal of rain since we saw you at the conference, and the country looks beautiful.'

'Did you leave Woodville this morning? I thought I hadn't heard you was in town,' replied Mrs. Timms formally. She was seated just a little too far away to make things seem exactly pleasant. The darkness of the best room seemed to

THE GUESTS OF MRS. TIMMS

retreat somewhat, and Miss Pickett looked over by the door, where there was a pale gleam from the side-lights in the hall, to try to see the pattern of the carpet; but her effort failed.

'Yes, 'm,' replied Mrs. Flagg to the question. 'We left Woodville about half-past eight, but it is quite a ways from where we live to where you take the stage. The stage does come slow, but you don't seem to mind it such a beautiful day.'

'Why, you must have come right to see me first!' said Mrs. Timms, warming a little as the visit went on. 'I hope you're going to make some stop in town. I'm sure it was very polite of you to come right an' see me; well, it's very pleasant, I declare. I wish you'd been in Baxter last Sabbath; our minister did give us an elegant sermon on faith an' works. He spoke of the conference, and gave his views on some o' the questions that came up, at Friday evenin' meetin'; but I felt tired after getting home, an' so I wasn't out. We feel very much favoured to have such a man amon'st us. He's building up the parish very considerable. I understand the pew-rents come to thirty-six dollars more this quarter than they did last.'

'We also feel grateful in Woodville for our pastor's efforts,' said Miss Pickett; but Mrs. Timms turned her head away sharply, as if the speech had been untimely, and trembling Miss Pickett had interrupted.

'They're thinking here of raisin' Mr. Barlow's salary another year,' the hostess added; 'a good many of the old parishioners have died off, but every one feels to do what they can. Is there much interest among the young people in Woodville, Mis' Flagg?'

'Considerable at this time, ma'am,' answered Mrs. Flagg,

without enthusiasm, and she listened with unusual silence to the subsequent fluent remarks of Mrs. Timms.

The parlour seemed to be undergoing the slow processes of a winter dawn. After a while the three women could begin to see one another's faces, which aided them somewhat in carrying on a serious and impersonal conversation. There were a good many subjects to be touched upon, and Mrs. Timms said everything that she should have said, except to invite her visitors to walk upstairs and take off their bonnets. Mrs. Flagg sat her parlour-chair as if it were a throne, and carried her banner of self-possession as high as she knew how, but toward the end of the call even she began to feel hurried.

'Won't you ladies take a glass of wine an' a piece of cake after your ride?' inquired Mrs. Timms, with an air of hospitality that almost concealed the fact that neither cake nor wine was anywhere to be seen; but the ladies bowed and declined with particular elegance. Altogether it was a visit of extreme propriety on both sides, and Mrs. Timms was very pressing in her invitation that her guests should stay longer.

'Thank you, but we ought to be going,' answered Mrs. Flagg, with a little show of ostentation, and looking over her shoulder to be sure that Miss Pickett had risen too. 'We've got some little ways to go,' she added with dignity. 'We should be pleased to have you call an' see us in case you have occasion to come to Woodville,' and Miss Pickett faintly seconded the invitation. It was in her heart to add, 'Come any day next week,' but her courage did not rise so high as to make the words audible. She looked as if she were ready to cry; her usual smile had burnt itself out into grey ashes; there was a white, appealing look about her mouth. As they emerged

THE GUESTS OF MRS. TIMMS

from the dim parlour and stood at the open front door, the bright June day, the golden-green trees, almost blinded their eyes. Mrs. Timms was more smiling and cordial than ever.

'There, I ought to have thought to offer you fans; I am afraid you was warm after walking,' she exclaimed, as if to leave no stone of courtesy unturned. 'I have so enjoyed meeting you again, I wish it was so you could stop longer. Why, Mis' Flagg, we haven't said one word about old times when we lived to Longport. I've had news from there, too, since I saw you; my brother's daughter-in-law was here to pass the Sabbath after I returned.'

Mrs. Flagg did not turn back to ask any questions as she stepped stiffly away down the brick walk. Miss Pickett followed her, raising the fringed parasol; they both made ceremonious little bows as they shut the high white gate behind them. 'Good-bye,' said Mrs. Timms finally, as she stood in the door with her set smile; and as they departed she came out and began to fasten up a rose-bush that climbed a narrow white ladder by the steps.

'Oh, my goodness alive!' exclaimed Mrs. Flagg, after they had gone some distance in aggrieved silence, 'if I haven't gone and forgotten my bag! I ain't goin' back, whatever happens. I expect she'll trip over it in that dark room and break her neck!'

'I brought it; I noticed you'd forgotten it,' said Miss Pickett timidly, as if she hated to deprive her companion of even that slight consolation.

'There, I'll tell you what we'd better do,' said Mrs. Flagg gallantly; 'we'll go right over an' see poor old Miss Nancy Fell; 't will please her about to death. We can say we felt like goin' somewhere to-day, an' 't was a good many years since either one of us had seen Baxter, so we come just for the ride, an' to make a few calls. She'll like to hear all about the conference; Miss Fell was always one that took a real interest in religious matters.'

Miss Pickett brightened, and they quickened their step. It was nearly twelve o'clock, they had breakfasted early, and now felt as if they had eaten nothing since they were grown up. An awful feeling of tiredness and uncertainty settled down upon their once buoyant spirits.

'I can forgive a person,' said Mrs. Flagg, once, as if she were speaking to herself; 'I can forgive a person, but when I'm done with 'em, I'm done.'

V

'I do declare, 't was like a scene in Scriptur' to see that poor good-hearted Nancy Fell run down her walk to open the gate for us!' said Mrs. Persis Flagg later that afternoon, when she and Miss Pickett were going home in the stage. Miss Pickett nodded her head approvingly.

'I had a good sight better time with her than I should have had at the other place,' she said with fearless honesty. 'If I'd been Mis' Cap'n Timms, I'd made some apology or just passed us the compliment. If it wa'n't convenient, why couldn't she just tell us so after all her urgin' and sayin' how she should expect us?'

'I thought then she'd altered from what she used to be,' said Mrs. Flagg. 'She seemed real sincere an' open away from home. If she wa'n't prepared to-day, 't was easy enough to say so; we was reasonable folks, an' should have gone away

THE GUESTS OF MRS. TIMMS

with none but friendly feelin's. We did have a grand good time with Nancy. She was as happy to see us as if we'd been queens.'

"T was a real nice little dinner,' said Miss Pickett gratefully. 'I thought I was goin' to faint away just before we got to the house, and I didn't know how I should hold out if she undertook to do anything extra, and keep us a-waitin'; but there, she just made us welcome, simple-hearted, to what she had. I never tasted such dandelion greens; an' that nice little piece o' pork and new biscuit, why, they was just splendid. She must have an excellent good cellar, if 't is such a small house. Her potatoes was truly remarkable for this time o' year. I myself don't deem it necessary to cook potatoes when I'm goin' to have dandelion greens. Now, didn't it put you in mind of that verse in the Bible that says, "Better is a dinner of herbs where love is"? An' how desirous she'd been to see somebody that could tell her some particulars about the conference!'

'She'll enjoy tellin' folks about our comin' over to see her. Yes, I'm glad we went; 't will be of advantage every way, an' our bein' of the same church an' all, to Woodville. If Mis' Timms hears of our bein' there, she'll see we had reason, an' knew of a place to go. Well, I needn't have brought this old bag!'

Miss Pickett gave her companion a quick resentful glance, which was followed by one of triumph directed at the dust that was collecting on the shoulders of the best black cashmere; then she looked at the bag on the front seat, and suddenly felt illuminated with the suspicion that Mrs. Flagg had secretly made preparations to pass the night in Baxter. The bag looked plump, as if it held much more than the pocket-book and the jelly.

Mrs. Flagg looked up with unusual humility. 'I did think about that jelly,' she said, as if Miss Pickett had openly reproached her. 'I was afraid it might look as if I was tryin' to pay Nancy for her kindness.'

'Well, I don't know,' said Cynthia; 'I guess she'd been pleased. She'd thought you just brought her over a little present: but I do' know as 't would been any good to her after all; she'd thought so much of it, comin' from you, that she'd kep' it till 't was all candied.' But Mrs. Flagg didn't look exactly pleased by this unexpected compliment, and her fellow-traveller coloured with confusion and a sudden feeling that she had shown undue forwardness.

Presently they remembered the Beckett house, to their great relief, and, as they approached, Mrs. Flagg reached over and moved her hand-bag from the front seat to make room for another passenger. But nobody came out to stop the stage, and they saw the unexpected guest sitting by one of the front windows comfortably swaying a palm-leaf fan, and rocking to and fro in calm content. They shrank back into their corners, and tried not to be seen. Mrs. Flagg's face grew very red.

'She got in, didn't she?' said Miss Pickett, snipping her words angrily, as if her lips were scissors. Then she heard a call, and bent forward to see Mrs. Beckett herself appear in the front doorway, very smiling and eager to stop the stage.

The driver was only too ready to stop his horses. 'Got a passenger for me to carry back, ain't ye?' said he facetiously. 'Them's the kind I like; carry both ways, make somethin' on a double trip,' and he gave Mrs. Flagg and Miss Pickett a

THE GUESTS OF MRS. TIMMS

friendly wink as he stepped down over the wheel. Then he hurried toward the house, evidently in a hurry to put the baggage on; but the expected passenger still sat rocking and fanning at the window.

'No, sir; I ain't got any passengers,' exclaimed Mrs. Beckett, advancing a step or two to meet him, and speaking very loud in her pleasant excitement. 'This lady that come this morning wants her large trunk with her summer things that she left to the depot in Woodville. She's very desirous to git into it, so don't you go an' forget; ain't you got a book or somethin', Mr. Ma'sh? Don't you forget to make a note of it; here's her cheque, an' we've kep' the number in case you should mislay it or anything. There's things in the trunk she needs; you know how you overlooked stoppin' to the milliner's for my bunnit last week.'

'Other folks disremembers things as well's me,' grumbled Mr. Marsh. He turned to give the passengers another wink more familiar than the first, but they wore an offended air, and were looking the other way. The horses had backed a few steps, and the guest at the front window had ceased the steady motion of her fan to make them a handsome bow, and been puzzled at the lofty manner of their acknowledgment.

'Go 'long with your foolish jokes, John Ma'sh!' Mrs. Beckett said cheerfully, as she turned away. She was a comfortable, hearty person, whose appearance adjusted the beauties of hospitality. The driver climbed to his seat, chuckling, and drove away with the dust flying after the wheels.

'Now, she's a friendly sort of a woman, that Mis' Beckett,' said Mrs. Flagg unexpectedly, after a few moments of silence, when she and her friend had been unable to look at each other.

'I really ought to call over an' see her some o' these days, knowing her husband's folks as well as I used to, an' visitin' of 'em when I was a girl.' But Miss Pickett made no answer.

'I expect it was all for the best, that woman's comin',' suggested Mrs. Flagg again hopefully. 'She looked like a willing person who would take right hold. I guess Mis' Beckett knows what she's about, and must have had her reasons. Perhaps she thought she'd chance it for a couple o' weeks anyway, after the lady'd come so fur, an' bein' one o' her own denomination. Hayin'-time'll be here before we know it. I think myself, gen'rally speakin', 't is just as well to let anybody know you're comin'.'

'Them seemed to be Mis' Cap'n Timms's views,' said Miss Pickett in a low tone; but the stage rattled a good deal, and Mrs. Flagg looked up inquiringly, as if she had not heard.

THE PASSING OF SISTER BARSETT

★

MRS. MERCY CRANE was of such firm persuasion that a house is meant to be lived in, that during many years she was never known to leave her own neat two-storied dwelling-place on the Ridge road. Yet being very fond of company, in pleasant weather she often sat in the side doorway looking out on her green yard, where the grass grew short and thick and was undisfigured even by a path toward the steps. All her faded green blinds were securely tied together and knotted on the inside by pieces of white tape; but now and then, when the sun was not too hot for her carpets, she opened one window at a time for a few hours, having pronounced views upon the necessity of light and air. Although Mrs. Crane was acknowledged by her best friends to be a peculiar person and very set in her ways, she was much respected, and one acquaintance vied with another in making up for her melancholy seclusion by bringing her all the news they could gather. She had been left alone many years before by the sudden death of her husband from sunstroke, and though she was by no means poor, she had, as someone said, 'such a pretty way of taking a little present that you couldn't help being pleased when you gave her anything.'

For a lover of society, such a life must have had its difficulties at times, except that the Ridge road was more travelled than any other in the township, and Mrs. Crane had invented a system of signals, to which she always resorted in case of wishing to speak to some one of her neighbours.

The afternoon was wearing late, one day toward the end

57

of summer, and Mercy Crane sat in her doorway dressed in a favourite old-fashioned light calico and a small shoulder shawl figured with large palm leaves. She was making some tatting of a somewhat intricate pattern; she believed it to be the prettiest and most durable of trimmings, and having decorated her own wardrobe in the course of unlimited leisure, she was now making a few yards apiece for each of her more intimate friends, so that they might have something to remember her by. She kept glancing up the road as if she expected someone, but the time went slowly by, until at last a woman appeared to view, walking fast, and carrying a large bundle in a checked handkerchief.

Then Mercy Crane worked steadily for a short time without looking up, until the desired friend was crossing the grass between the dusty road and the steps. The visitor was out of breath, and did not respond to the polite greeting of her hostess until she had recovered herself to her satisfaction. Mrs. Crane made her the kind offer of a glass of water or a few peppermints, but was answered only by a shake of the head, so she resumed her work for a time until the silence should be broken.

'I have come from the house of mourning,' said Sarah Ellen Dow at last, unexpectedly.

'You don't tell me that Sister Barsett' –

'She's left us this time, she's really gone,' and the excited news-bringer burst into tears. The poor soul was completely overwrought; she looked tired and wan, as if she had spent her forces in sympathy as well as hard work. She felt in her great bundle for a pocket handkerchief, but was not successful in the search, and finally produced a faded gingham apron with

THE PASSING OF SISTER BARSETT

long, narrow strings, with which she hastily dried her tears. The sad news appealed also to Mercy Crane, who looked across to the apple-trees, and could not see them for a dazzle of tears in her own eyes. The spectacle of Sarah Ellen Dow going home with her humble workaday possessions, from the house where she had gone in haste only a few days before to care for a sick person well known to them both, was a very sad sight.

'You sent word yesterday that you should be returnin' early this afternoon, and would stop. I presume I received the message as you gave it?' asked Mrs. Crane, who was tenacious in such matters; 'but I do declare I never looked to hear she was gone.'

'She's been failin' right along sence yesterday about this time,' said the nurse. 'She's taken no notice to speak of, an' been eatin' the vally o' nothin', I may say, since I went there a-Tuesday. Her sisters both come back yisterday, an' of course I was expected to give up charge to them. They're used to sickness, an' both havin' such a name for bein' great housekeepers!'

Sarah Ellen spoke with bitterness, but Mrs. Crane was reminded instantly of her own affairs. 'I feel condemned that I ain't begun my own fall cleanin' yet,' she said, with an ostentatious sigh.

'Plenty o' time to worry about that,' her friend hastened to console her.

'I do desire to have everything decent about my house,' resumed Mrs. Crane. 'There's nobody to do anything but me. If I was to be taken away sudden myself, I shouldn't want to have it said afterwards that there was wisps under my sofy or

— There! I can't dwell on my own troubles with Sister Barsett's loss right before me. I can't seem to believe she's really passed away; she always was saying she should go in some o' these spells, but I deemed her to be troubled with narves.'

Sarah Ellen Dow shook her head. 'I'm all nerved up myself,' she said brokenly. 'I made light of her sickness when I went there first, I'd seen her what she called dreadful low so many times; but I saw her looks this morning, an' I begun to believe her at last. Them sisters o' hers is the master for unfeelin' hearts. Sister Barsett was a-layin' there yisterday, an' one of 'em was a-settin' right by her tellin' how difficult 't was for her to leave home, her niece was goin' to graduate to the high school, an' they was goin' to have a time in the evening, an' all the exercises promised to be extry interesting. Poor Sister Barsett knew what she said an' looked at her with contempt, an' then she give a glance at me an' closed up her eyes as if 't was for the last time. I know she felt it.'

Sarah Ellen Dow was more and more excited by a sense of bitter grievance. Her rule of the afflicted household had evidently been interfered with; she was not accustomed to be ignored and set aside at such times. Her simple nature and uncommon ability found satisfaction in the exercise of authority, but she had now left her post feeling hurt and wronged, besides knowing something of the pain of honest affliction.

'If it hadn't been for esteemin' Sister Barsett as I always have done, I should have told 'em no, an' held to it, when they asked me to come back an' watch to-night. 'T ain't for none o' their sakes, but Sister Barsett was a good friend to me in her way.' Sarah Ellen broke down once more, and

THE PASSING OF SISTER BARSETT

felt in her bundle again hastily, but the handkerchief was again elusive, while a small object fell out upon the doorstep with a bounce.

"'T ain't nothin' but a little taste-cake I spared out o' the loaf I baked this mornin',' she explained, with a blush. 'I was so shoved out that I seemed to want to turn my hand to somethin' useful an' feel I was still doin' for Sister Barsett. Try a little piece, won't you, Mis' Crane? I thought it seemed light an' good.'

They shared the taste-cake with serious enjoyment, and pronounced it very good indeed when they had finished and shaken the crumbs out of their laps. 'There's nobody but you shall come an' do for me at the last, if I can have my way about things,' said Mercy Crane impulsively. She meant it for a tribute to Miss Dow's character and general ability, and as such it was meekly accepted.

'You're a younger person than I be, an' less wore,' said Sarah Ellen, but she felt better now that she had rested, and her conversational powers seemed to be refreshed by her share of the little cake. 'Doctor Bangs has behaved real pretty, I can say that,' she continued presently in a mournful tone.

'Heretofore, in the sickness of Sister Barsett, I have always felt to hope certain that she would survive; she's recovered from a sight o' things in her day. She has been the first to have all the new diseases that's visited this region. I know she had the spinal mergeetis months before there was any other case about,' observed Mrs. Crane with satisfaction.

'An' the new throat troubles, all of 'em,' agreed Sarah Ellen; 'an' has made trial of all the best patent medicines, an' could tell you their merits as no one else could in this vicinity. She never was one that depended on herbs alone, though she considered 'em extremely useful in some cases. Everybody has their herb, as we know, but I'm free to say that Sister Barsett sometimes done everything she could to kill herself with such rovin' ways o' dosin'. She must see it now she's gone an' can't stuff down no more invigorators.' Sarah Ellen Dow burst out suddenly with this, as if she could no longer contain her honest opinion.

'There, there! you're all worked up,' answered placid Mercy Crane, looking more interested than ever.

'An' she was dreadful handy to talk religion to other folks, but I've come to a realizin' sense that religion is somethin' besides opinions. She an' Elder French has been mostly of one mind, but I don't know's they've got hold of all the religion there is.'

'Why, why, Sarah Ellen!' exclaimed Mrs. Crane, but there was still something in her tone that urged the speaker to further expression of her feelings. The good creature was much excited, her face was clouded with disapproval.

'I ain't forgettin' nothin' about their good points either,' she went on in a more subdued tone, and suddenly stopped.

'Preachin' 'll be done away with soon or late, – preachin' o' Elder French's kind,' announced Mercy Crane, after waiting to see if her guest did not mean to say anything more. 'I should like to read 'em out that verse another fashion: "Be ye doers o' the word, not preachers only," would hit it about right; but there, it's easy for all of us to talk. In my early days I used to like to get out to meetin' regular, because sure as I didn't I had bad luck all the week. I didn't feel pacified 'less

THE PASSING OF SISTER BARSETT

I'd been half a day, but I was out all day the Sabbath before Mr. Barlow died as he did. So you mean to say that Sister Barsett's really gone?'

Mrs. Crane's tone changed to one of real concern, and her manner indicated that she had put the preceding conversation behind her with decision.

'She was herself to the last,' instantly responded Miss Dow. 'I see her put out a thumb an' finger from under the spread an' pinch up a fold of her sister Deckett's dress, to try an' see if 't was all wool. I thought 't wa'n't all wool, myself, an' I know it now by the way she looked. She was a very knowin' person about materials; we shall miss poor Mis' Barsett in many ways, she was always the one to consult with about matters o' dress.'

'She passed away easy at the last, I hope?' asked Mrs. Crane with interest.

'Why, I wa'n't there, if you'll believe it!' exclaimed Sarah Ellen, flushing, and looking at her friend for sympathy. 'Sister Barsett revived up the first o' the afternoon, an' they sent for Elder French. She took notice of him, and he exhorted quite a spell, an' then he spoke o' there being need of air in the room, Mis' Deckett havin' closed every window, an' she asked me of all folks if I hadn't better step out; but Elder French come too, an' he was very reasonable, an' had a word with me about Mis' Deckett an' Mis' Peak, an' the way they was workin' things. I told him right out how they never come near when the rest of us was havin' it so hard with her along in the spring, but now they thought she was re'lly goin' to die, they come settlin' down like a pair o' old crows in a field to pick for what they could get. I just made up my mind they should have all the care if they wanted it. It didn't seem as if there was anything more I could do for Sister Barsett, an' I set there in the kitchen within call an' waited, an' when I heard 'em sayin', "There, she's gone, she's gone!" and Mis' Deckett a-weepin', I put on my bunnit and stepped myself out into the road. I felt to repent after I had gone but a rod, but I was so worked up, an' I thought they'd call me back, an' then I was put out because they didn't, an' so here I be. I can't help it now.' Sarah Ellen was crying again; she and Mrs. Crane could not look at each other.

'Well, you set an' rest,' said Mrs. Crane kindly, and with the merest shadow of disapproval. 'You set an' rest, an' by an' by, if you'd feel better, you could go back an' just make a little stop an' inquire about the arrangements. I wouldn't harbour no feelin's, if they be inconsiderate folks. Sister Barsett has often deplored their actions in my hearin' an' wished she had sisters like other folks. With all her faults she was a useful person an' a good neighbour,' mourned Mercy Crane sincerely. 'She was one that always had somethin' interestin' to tell, an' if it wa'n't for her dyin' spells an' all that sort o' nonsense, she'd make a figger in the world, she would so. She walked with an air always, Mis' Barsett did; you'd ask who she was if you hadn't known, as she passed you by. How quick we forget the outs about anybody that's gone! but I always feel grateful to anybody that's friendly, situated as I be. I shall miss her runnin' over. I can seem to see her now, comin' over the rise in the road. But don't you get in a way of takin' things too hard, Sarah Ellen! You've worked yourself all to pieces since I saw you last; you're gettin' to be as lean as a meetin'-house fly. Now, you're comin' in to have a cup o' tea with me, an' then you'll feel better. I've got some new molasses gingerbread that I baked this mornin'.'

'I do feel beat out, Mis' Crane,' acknowledged the poor little soul, glad of a chance to speak, but touched by this unexpected mark of consideration. 'If I could ha' done as I wanted to I should be feelin' well enough, but to be set aside an' ordered about, where I'd taken the lead in sickness so much, an' knew how to deal with Sister Barsett so well! She might be livin' now, perhaps' –

'Come; we'd better go in, 't is gettin' damp,' and the mistress of the house rose so hurriedly as to seem bustling. 'Don't dwell on Sister Barsett an' her foolish folks no more; I wouldn't, if I was you.'

They went into the front room, which was dim with the twilight of the half-closed blinds and two great syringa bushes that grew against them. Sarah Ellen put down her bundle and bestowed herself in the large, cane-seated rocking-chair. Mrs. Crane directed her to stay there awhile and rest, and then come out into the kitchen when she got ready.

A cheerful clatter of dishes was heard at once upon Mrs. Crane's disappearance. 'I hope she's goin' to make one o' her nice short-cakes, but I don't know's she'll think it quite worth while,' thought the guest humbly. She desired to go out into the kitchen, but it was proper behaviour to wait until she should be called. Mercy Crane was not a person with whom one could venture to take liberties. Presently Sarah Ellen began to feel better. She did not often find such a quiet place, or the quarter of an hour of idleness in which to enjoy it, and was glad to make the most of this opportunity. Just now she felt tired and lonely. She was a busy, unselfish, eager-minded creature by nature, but now, while grief was sometimes uppermost in her mind and sometimes a sense of wrong, every moment found her more peaceful, and the great excitement little by little faded away.

'What a person poor Sister Barsett was to dread growing old so she couldn't get about. I'm sure I shall miss her as much as anybody,' said Mrs. Crane, suddenly opening the kitchen door, and letting in an unmistakable and delicious odour of short-cake that revived still more the drooping spirits of her guest. 'An' a good deal of knowledge has died with her,' she added, coming into the room and seeming to make it lighter.

'There, she knew a good deal, but she didn't know all, especially o' doctorin',' insisted Sarah Ellen from the rocking-chair, with an unexpected little laugh. 'She used to lay down the law to me as if I had neither sense nor experience, but when it came to her bad spells she'd always send for me. It takes everybody to know everything, but Sister Barsett was of an opinion that her information was sufficient for the town. She was tellin' me the day I went there how she disliked to have old Mis' Doubleday come an' visit with her, an' remarked that she called Mis' Doubleday very officious. "Went right down on her knees an' prayed," says she. "Anybody would have thought I was a heathen!" But I kind of pacified her feelin's, an' told her I supposed the old lady meant well.'

'Did she give away any of her things? – Mis' Barsett, I mean,' inquired Mrs. Crane.

'Not in my hearin',' replied Sarah Ellen Dow. 'Except one day, the first of the week, she told her oldest sister, Mis' Deckett, – 't was that first day she rode over, – that she might

THE PASSING OF SISTER BARSETT

have her green quilted petticoat; you see it was a rainy day, an' Mis' Deckett had complained o' feelin' thin. She went right up an' got it, and put it on an' wore it off, an' I'm sure I thought no more about it, until I heard Sister Barsett groanin' dreadful in the night. I got right up to see what the matter was, an' what do you think but she was wantin' that petticoat back, and not thinking any too well o' Nancy Deckett for takin' it when 't was offered. "Nancy never showed no sense o' propriety," says Sister Barsett; I just wish you'd heard her go on!'

'If she had felt to remember me,' continued Sarah Ellen, after they had laughed a little, 'I'd full as soon have some of her nice crockery-ware. She told me once, years ago, when I was stoppin' to tea with her an' we were havin' it real friendly, that she should leave me her Britannia tea-set, but I ain't got it in writin', and I can't say she's ever referred to the matter since. It ain't as if I had a home o' my own to keep it in, but I should have thought a great deal of it for her sake,' and the speaker's voice faltered. 'I must say that with all her virtues she never was a first-class housekeeper, but I wouldn't say it to any but a friend. You never eat no preserves o' hers that wa'n't commencin' to work, an' you know as well as I how little forethought she had about putting away her woollens. I sat behind her once in meetin' when I was stoppin' with the Tremletts and so occupied a seat in their pew, an' I see between ten an' a dozen moth millers come workin' out o' her fitch-fur tippet. They was flutterin' round her bonnet same's 't was a lamp. I should be mortified to death to have such a thing happen to me.'

'Every housekeeper has her weak point; I've got mine as

much as anybody else,' acknowledged Mercy Crane with spirit, 'but you never see no moth millers come workin' out o' me in a public place.'

'Ain't your oven beginning to get over-het?' anxiously inquired Sarah Ellen Dow, who was sitting more in the draught, and could not bear to have any accident happen to the supper. Mrs. Crane flew to a short-cake's rescue, and presently called her guest to the table.

The two women sat down to deep and brimming cups of tea. Sarah Ellen noticed with great gratification that her hostess had put on two of the best tea-cups and some citron-melon preserves. It was not an every-day supper. She was used to hard fare, poor, hard-working Sarah Ellen, and this handsome social attention did her good. Sister Crane rarely entertained a friend, and it would be a pleasure to speak of the tea-drinking for weeks to come.

'You've put yourself out quite a consid'able for me,' she acknowledged. 'How pretty these cups is! You oughtn't to use 'em so common as for me. I wish I had a home I could really call my own to ask you to, but 't ain't never been so I could. Sometimes I wonder what's goin' to become o' me when I get so I'm past work. Takin' care o' sick folks an' bein' in houses where there's a sight goin' on an' everybody in a hurry kind of wears on me now I'm most a-gittin' in years. I was wishin' the other day that I could get with some comfortable kind of a sick person, where I could live right along quiet as other folks do, but folks never sends for me 'less they're drove to it. I ain't laid up anything to really depend upon.'

The situation appealed to Mercy Crane, well-to-do as she

THE PASSING OF SISTER BARSETT

was and not burdened with responsibilities. She stirred uneasily in her chair, but could not bring herself to the point of offering Sarah Ellen the home she coveted.

'Have some hot tea,' she insisted, in a matter-of-fact tone, and Sarah Ellen's face, which had been lighted by a sudden eager hopefulness, grew dull and narrow again.

'Plenty, plenty, Mis' Crane,' she said sadly, "t is beautiful tea, – you always have good tea;' but she could not turn her thoughts from her own uncertain future. 'None of our folks has ever lived to be a burden,' she said presently, in a pathetic tone, putting down her cup. 'My mother was thought to be doing well until four o'clock an' was dead at ten. My Aunt Nancy came to our house well at twelve o'clock an' died that afternoon; my father was sick but ten days. There was dear sister Betsy, she did go in consumption, but 't wa'n't an expensive sickness.'

'I've thought sometimes about you, how you'd get past rovin' from house to house one o' these days. I guess your friends will stand by you.' Mrs. Crane spoke with unwonted sympathy, and Sarah Ellen's heart leaped with joy.

'You're real kind,' she said simply. 'There's nobody I set so much by. But I shall miss Sister Barsett, when all's said an' done. She's asked me many a time to stop with her when I wasn't doin' nothin'. We all have our failin's, but she was a friendly creatur'. I shan't want to see her laid away.'

'Yes, I was thinkin' a few minutes ago that I shouldn't want to look out an' see the funeral go by. She's one o' the old neighbours. I s'pose I shall have to look, or I shouldn't feel right afterward,' said Mrs. Crane mournfully. 'If I hadn't got so kind of housebound,' she added with touching frankness, ' I'd just as soon go over with you an' offer to watch this night.'

''T would astonish Sister Barsett so I don't know but she'd return.' Sarah Ellen's eyes danced with amusement; she could not resist her own joke, and Mercy Crane herself had to smile.

'Now I must be goin', or 't will be dark,' said the guest, rising and sighing after she had eaten her last crumb of gingerbread. 'Yes, thank ye, you're real good, I will come back if I find I ain't wanted. Look what a pretty sky there is!' and the two friends went to the side door and stood together in a moment of affectionate silence, looking out towards the sunset across the wide fields. The country was still with that deep rural stillness which seems to mean the absence of humanity. Only the thrushes were singing far away in the walnut woods beyond the orchard, and some crows were flying over and cawed once loudly, as if they were speaking to the women at the door.

Just as the friends were parting, after most grateful acknowledgments from Sarah Ellen Dow, someone came driving along the road in a hurry and stopped.

'Who's that with you, Mis' Crane?' called one of their near neighbours.

'It's Sarah Ellen Dow,' answered Mrs. Crane. 'What's the matter?'

'I thought so, but I couldn't rightly see. Come, they are in a peck o' trouble up to Sister Barsett's, wonderin' where you be,' grumbled the man. 'They can't do nothin' with her; she's drove off everybody an' keeps a-screechin' for you. Come, step along, Sarah Ellen, do!'

THE PASSING OF SISTER BARSETT

'Sister Barsett!' exclaimed both the women. Mercy Crane sank down upon the doorstep, but Sarah Ellen stepped out upon the grass all of a tremble, and went toward the wagon. 'They said this afternoon that Sister Barsett was gone,' she managed to say. 'What did they mean?'

'Gone where?' asked the impatient neighbour. 'I expect 't was one of her spells. She's come to; they say she wants somethin' hearty for her tea. Nobody can't take one step till you get there, neither.'

Sarah Ellen was still dazed; she returned to the doorway, where Mercy Crane sat shaking with laughter. 'I don't know but we might as well laugh as cry,' she said in an aimless sort of way. 'I know you too well to think you're going to repeat a single word. Well, I'll get my bonnet an' start; I expect I've got considerable to cope with, but I'm well rested. Good night, Mis' Crane, I certain did have a beautiful tea, whatever the future may have in store.'

She wore a solemn expression as she mounted into the wagon in haste and departed, but she was far out of sight when Mercy Crane stopped laughing and went into the house.

DECORATION DAY

★

I

A WEEK before the thirtieth of May, three friends – John Stover and Henry Merrill and Asa Brown – happened to meet on Saturday evening at Barton's store at the Plains. They were ready to enjoy this idle hour after a busy week. After long easterly rains, the sun had at last come out bright and clear, and all the Barlow farmers had been planting. There was even a good deal of ploughing left to be done, the season was so backward.

The three middle-aged men were old friends. They had been school-fellows, and when they were hardly out of their boyhood the war came on, and they enlisted in the same company, on the same day, and happened to march away elbow to elbow. Then came the great experience of a great war, and the years that followed their return from the South had come to each almost alike. These men might have been members of the same rustic household, they knew each other's history so well.

They were sitting on a low wooden bench at the left of the store door as you went in. People were coming and going on their Saturday night errands, – the post-office was in Barton's store, – but the friends talked on eagerly, without being interrupted, except by an occasional nod of recognition. They appeared to take no notice at all of the neighbours whom they saw oftenest. It was a most beautiful evening; the two great elms were almost half in leaf over the blacksmith's shop which stood across the wide road. Farther along were two small

DECORATION DAY

old-fashioned houses and the old white church, with its pretty belfry of four arched sides and a tiny dome at the top. The large cockerel on the vane was pointing a little south of west, and there was still light enough to make it shine bravely against the deep blue eastern sky. On the western side of the road, near the store, were the parsonage and the storekeeper's modern house, which had a French roof and some attempt at decoration, which the long-established Barlow people called gingerbread-work, and regarded with mingled pride and disdain. These buildings made the tiny village called Barlow Plains. They stood in the middle of a long narrow strip of level ground. They were islanded by green fields and pastures. There were hills beyond; the mountains themselves seemed very near. Scattered about on the hill slopes were farmhouses, which stood so far apart, with their clusters of out-buildings, that each looked lonely, and the pine woods above seemed to besiege them all. It was lighter on the uplands than it was in the valley, where the three men sat on their bench, with their backs to the store and the western sky.

'Well, here we be 'most into June, an' I 'ain't got a bush-bean above ground,' lamented Henry Merrill.

'Your land's always late, ain't it? But you always catch up with the rest on us,' Asa Brown consoled him. 'I've often observed that your land, though early planted, was late to sprout. I view it there's a good week's difference betwixt me an' Stover an' your folks, but come first o' July we all even up.'

"'T is just so,' said John Stover, taking his pipe out of his mouth, as if he had a good deal more to say, and then replacing it, as if he had changed his mind.

'Made it extry hard having that long wet spell. Can't none on us take no day off this season,' said Asa Brown; but nobody thought it worth his while to respond to such evident truth.

'Next Saturday 'll be the thirtieth o' May – that's Decoration Day, ain't it? – come round again. Lord! how the years slip by after you git to be forty-five an' along there!' said Asa again. 'I s'pose some o' our folks 'll go over to Alton to see the procession, same's usual. I've got to git one o' them small flags to stick on our Joel's grave, an' Mis' Dexter always counts on havin' some for Harrison's lot. I calculate to get 'em somehow. I must make time to ride over, but I don't know where the time 's comin' from out o' next week. I wish the women folks would tend to them things. There's the spot where Eb Munson an' John Tighe lays in the poor-farm lot, an' I did mean certain to buy flags for 'em last year an' year before, but I went an' forgot it. I'd like to have folks that rode by notice 'em for once, if they was town paupers. Eb Munson was as darin' a man as ever stepped out to tuck o' drum.'

'So he was,' said John Stover, taking his pipe with decision and knocking out the ashes. 'Drink was his ruin; but I wan't one that could be harsh with Eb, no matter what he done. He worked hard long's he could, too; but he wa'n't like a sound man, an' I think he took somethin' first not so much 'cause he loved it, but to kind of keep his strength up so's he could work, an' then, all of a sudden, rum clinched with him an' threw him. Eb was talkin' 'long o' me one day when he was about half full, an' says he, right out, "I wouldn't have fell to this state," says he, "if I'd had me a home an' a little

DECORATION DAY

fam'ly; but it don't make no difference to nobody, and it's the best comfort I seem to have, an' I ain't goin' to do without it. I'm ailin' all the time," says he, "an' if I keep middlin' full, I make out to hold my own an' to keep along o' my work." I pitied Eb. I says to him, "You ain't goin' to bring no disgrace on us old army boys, be you, Eb?" an' he says no, he wa'n't. I think if he'd lived to get one o' them big fat pensions, he'd had it easier. Eight dollars a month paid his board, while he'd pick up what cheap work he could, an' then he got so that decent folks didn't seem to want the bother of him, an' so he come on the town.'

'There was somethin' else to it,' said Henry Merrill soberly. 'Drink come natural to him, 't was born in him, I expect, an' there wa'n't nobody that could turn the divil out same's they did in Scriptur'. His father an' his gran'father was drinkin' men; but they was kind-hearted an' good neighbours, an' never set out to wrong nobody. 'T was the custom to drink in their day; folks was colder an' lived poorer in early times, an' that's how most of 'em kept a-goin'. But what stove Eb all up was his disapp'intment with Marthy Peck – her forsakin' of him an' marryin' old John Down whilst Eb was off to war. I've always laid it up ag'inst her.'

'So've I,' said Asa Brown. 'She didn't use the poor fellow right. I guess she was full as well off, but it's one thing to show judgment, an' another thing to have heart.'

There was a long pause; the subject was too familiar to need further comment.

'There ain't no public sperit here in Barlow,' announced Asa Brown, with decision. 'I don't s'pose we could ever get up anything for Decoration Day. I've felt kind of 'shamed, but it always comes in a busy time; 't wa'n't no time to have it, anyway, right in late plantin'.'

"'T ain't no use to look for public sperit 'less you've got some yourself,' observed John Stover soberly; but something had pleased him in the discouraged suggestion. 'Perhaps we could mark the day this year. It comes on a Saturday; that ain't nigh so bad as bein' in the middle of the week.'

Nobody made any answer, and presently he went on:

'There was a time along back when folks was too nigh the war-time to give much thought to the bigness of it. The best fellows was them that had stayed to home an' worked their trades an' laid up money; but I don't know's it's so now.'

'Yes, the fellows that stayed at home got all the fat places, an' when we come back we felt dreadful behind the times,' grumbled Asa Brown. 'I remember how 't was.'

'They begun to call us heroes an' old stick-in-the-mud just about the same time,' resumed Stover, with a chuckle. 'We wa'n't no hand for strippin' woodland nor even tradin' hosses them first few years. I don' know why 't was we were so beat out. The best most on us could do was to sag right on to the old folks. Father he never wanted me to go to the war, – 't was partly his Quaker breed, – an' he used to be dreadful mortified with the way I hung round down here to the store an' loafed round a-talkin' about when I was out South, an' arguin' with folks that didn't know nothin', about what the generals done. There! I see me now just as he see me then; but after I had my boy-strut out, I took holt o' the old farm 'long o' father, an' I've made it bounce. Look at them old meadows an' see the herd's grass that come off of 'em last year! I ain't ashamed o' my place now, if I did go to the war.'

DECORATION DAY

'It all looks a sight bigger to me now than it did then,' said Henry Merrill. 'Our goin' to the war, I refer to. We didn't sense it no more than other folks did. I used to be sick o' hearin' their stuff about patriotism and lovin' your country, an' them pieces o' poetry women folks wrote for the papers on the old flag, an' our fallen heroes, an' them things; they didn't seem to strike me in the right place; but I tell ye it kind o' starts me now every time I come on the flag sudden, – it does so. A spell ago – 'long in the fall, I guess it was – I was over to Alton, an' there was a fire company paradin'. They'd got the prize at a fair, an' had just come home on the cars, an' I heard the band; so I stepped to the front o' the store where me an' my woman was tradin', an' the company felt well, an' was comin' along the street 'most as good as troops. I see the old flag a-comin', kind of blowin' back, an' it went all over me. Somethin' worked round in my throat; I vow I come near cryin'. I was glad nobody see me.'

'I'd go to war again in a minute,' declared Stover, after an expressive pause; 'but I expect we should know better what we was about. I don't know but we've got too many rooted opinions now to make us the best o' soldiers.'

'Martin Tighe an' John Tighe was considerable older than the rest, and they done well,' answered Henry Merrill quickly. 'We three was the youngest of any, but we did think at the time we knew the most.'

'Well, whatever you may say, that war give the country a great start,' said Asa Brown. 'I tell ye we just begin to see the scope on 't. There was my cousin, you know, Dan'l Evins, that stopped with us last winter; he was tellin' me that one o'

THE ONLY ROSE AND OTHER TALES

his coastin' trips he was into the port o' Beaufort lo'din' with yaller-pine lumber, an' he roved into an old buryin'-ground there is there, an' he see a stone that had on it some young Southern fellow's name that was killed in the war, an' under it was, "He died for his country." Dan'l knowed how I used to feel about them South Car'lina goings on, an' I did feel kind o' red an' ugly for a minute, an' then somethin' come over me, an' I says, "Well, I don' know but what the poor chap did, Dan Evins, when you come to view it all round."'

The other men made no answer.

'Le's see what we can do this year. I don't care if we be a poor han'ful,' urged Henry Merrill. 'The young folks ought to have the good of it; I'd like to have my boys see somethin' different. Le's get together what men there is. How many's left, anyhow? I know there was thirty-seven went from old Barlow, three-months' men an' all.'

'There can't be over eight now, countin' out Martin Tighe; he can't march,' said Stover. 'No, 't ain't worth while.' But the others did not notice his disapproval.

'There's nine in all,' announced Asa Brown, after pondering and counting two or three times on his fingers. 'I can't make us no more. I never could carry figur's in my head.'

'I make nine,' said Merrill. ' We'll have Martin ride, an' Jesse Dean too, if he will. He's awful lively on them canes o' his. An' there's Jo Wade with his crutch; he's amazin' spry for a short distance. But we can't let 'em go far afoot; they're decripped men. We'll make 'em all put on what they've got left o' their uniforms, an' we'll scratch round an' have us a fife an' drum, an' make the best show we can.'

'Why, Martin Tighe's boy, the next to the oldest, is an

DECORATION DAY

excellent hand to play the fife!' said John Stover, suddenly growing enthusiastic. ' If you two are set on it, let's have a word with the minister to-morrow, an' see what he says. Perhaps he'll give out some kind of a notice. You have to have a good many bunches o' flowers. I guess we'd better call a meetin', some few on us, an' talk it over first o' the week. 'T wouldn't be no great of a range for us to take to march from the old buryin'-ground at the meetin'-house here up to the poor-farm an' round by Deacon Elwell's lane, so's to notice them two stones he set up for his boys that was sunk on the man-o'-war. I expect they notice stones same's if the folks laid there, don't they?'

He spoke wistfully. The others knew that Stover was thinking of the stone he had set up to the memory of his only brother, whose nameless grave had been made somewhere in the Wilderness.

'I don't know but what they'll be mad if we don't go by every house in town,' he added anxiously, as they rose to go home. ''Tis a terrible scattered population in Barlow to favour with a procession.'

It was a mild starlit night. The three friends took their separate ways presently, leaving the Plains road and crossing the fields by foot-paths toward their farms.

II

The week went by, and the next Saturday morning brought fair weather. It was a busy morning on the farms – like any other; but long before noon the teams of horses and oxen were seen going home from work in the fields, and everybody got ready in haste for the great event of the afternoon. It was so seldom that any occasion roused public interest in Barlow that there was an unexpected response, and the green before the old white meeting-house was covered with country wagons and groups of people, whole families together, who had come on foot. The old soldiers were to meet in the church; at half-past one the procession was to start, and on its return the minister was to make an address in the old burying-ground. John Stover had been first lieutenant in the war, so he was made captain of the day. A man from the next town had offered to drum for them, and Martin Tighe's proud boy was present with his fife. He had a great longing – strange enough in that peaceful, sheep-raising neighbourhood – to go into the army; but he and his elder brother were the mainstay of their crippled father, and he could not be spared from the large household until a younger brother could take his place; so that all his fire and military zeal went for the present into martial tunes, and the fife was a safety-valve for his enthusiasm.

The army men were used to seeing each other; everybody knew everybody in the little country town of Barlow; but when one comrade after another appeared in what remained of his accoutrements, they felt the day to be greater than they had planned, and the simple ceremony proved more solemn than anyone expected. They could make no use of their every-day jokes and friendly greetings. Their old blue coats and tarnished army caps looked faded and antiquated enough. One of the men had nothing left but his rusty canteen and rifle; but these he carried like sacred emblems. He had worn out all his army clothes long ago, because he was too poor when he was discharged to buy any others.

DECORATION DAY

When the door of the church opened, the veterans were not abashed by the size and silence of the crowd. They came walking two by two down the steps, and took their places in line as if there were nobody looking on. Their brief evolutions were like a mystic rite. The two lame men refused to do anything but march as best they could; but poor Martin Tighe, more disabled than they, was brought out and lifted into Henry Merrill's best wagon, where he sat up, straight and soldierly, with his boy for driver. There was a little flag in the whip-socket before him, which flapped gayly in the breeze. It was such a long time since he had been seen out-of-doors that everybody found him a great object of interest, and paid him much attention. Even those who were tired of being asked to contribute to his support, who resented the fact of his having a helpless wife and great family; who always insisted that with his little pension and hopeless lameness, his fingerless left hand and failing sight, he could support himself and his household if he chose, — even those persons came forward now to greet him handsomely and with large approval. To be sure, he enjoyed the conversation of idlers, and his wife had a complaining way that was the same as begging, especially since her boys began to grow up and be of some use; and there were one or two near neighbours who never let them really want; so other people, who had cares enough of their own, could excuse themselves for forgetting him the year round, and even call him shiftless. But there were none to look askance at Martin Tighe on Decoration Day, as he sat in the wagon, with his bleached face like a captive's, and his thin, afflicted body. He stretched out his whole hand impartially to those who had remembered and those who had forgotten both his courage at Fredericksburg and his sorry need in Barlow.

Henry Merrill had secured the engine company's large flag in Alton, and now carried it proudly. There were eight men in line, two by two, and marching a good bit apart, to make their line the longer. The fife and drum struck up gallantly together, and the little procession moved away slowly along the country road. It gave an unwonted touch of colour to the landscape, — the scarlet, the blue, between the new-ploughed fields and budding roadside thickets, between the wide dim ranges of the mountains, under the great white clouds of the spring sky. Such processions grow more pathetic year by year; it will not be so long now before wondering children will have seen the last. The ageing faces of the men, the renewed comradeship, the quick beat of the hearts that remember, the tenderness of those who think upon old sorrows, — all these make the day a lovelier and a sadder festival. So men's hearts were stirred, they knew not why, when they heard the shrill fife and the incessant drum along the quiet Barlow road, and saw the handful of old soldiers marching by. Nobody thought of them as familiar men and neighbours alone, — they were a part of that army which had saved its country. They had taken their lives in their hands and gone out to fight for their country, plain John Stover and Jesse Dean and the rest. No matter if every other day in the year they counted for little or much, whether they were lame-footed and lagging, whether their farms were of poor soil or rich.

The little troop went in slender line along the road; the crowded country wagons and all the people who went afoot

DECORATION DAY

followed Martin Tighe's wagon as if it were a great gathering at a country funeral. The route was short, and the long, straggling line marched slowly; it could go no faster than the lame men could walk.

In one of the houses by the roadside an old woman sat by a window, in an old-fashioned black gown, and clean white cap with a prim border which bound her thin, sharp features closely. She had been for a long time looking out eagerly over the snowberry and cinnamon-rose bushes; her face was pressed close to the pane, and presently she caught sight of the great flag as it came down the road.

'Let me see 'em! I've got to see 'em go by!' she pleaded, trying to rise from her chair alone when she heard the fife, and the women helped her to the door, and held her so that she could stand and wait. She had been an old woman when the war began; she had sent sons and grandsons to the field; they were all gone now. As the men came by, she straightened her bent figure with all the vigour of youth. The fife and drum stopped suddenly; the colours lowered. She did not heed that, but her old eyes flashed and then filled with tears to see the flag going to salute the soldiers' graves. 'Thank ye, boys; thank ye!' she cried, in her quavering voice, and they all cheered her. The cheer went back along the straggling line for old Grandmother Dexter, standing there in her front door between the lilacs. It was one of the great moments of the day.

The few old people at the poor-house, too, were waiting to see the show. The keeper's young son, knowing that it was a day of festivity, and not understanding exactly why, had put his toy flag out of the gable window, and there it showed against the grey clap-boards like a gay flower. It was the only bit of decoration along the veterans' way, and they stopped and saluted it before they broke ranks and went out to the field corner beyond the poor-farm barn to the bit of ground that held the paupers' unmarked graves. There was a solemn silence while Asa Brown went to the back of Tighe's wagon, where such light freight was carried, and brought two flags, and he and John Stover planted them straight in the green sod. They knew well enough where the right graves were, for these had been made in a corner by themselves, with unwonted sentiment. And so Eben Munsen and John Tighe were honoured like the rest, both by their flags and by great and unexpected nosegays of spring flowers, daffies and flowering currant and red tulips, which lay on the graves already. John Stover and his comrade glanced at each other curiously while they stood singing, and then laid their own bunches of lilacs down and came away.

Then something happened that almost none of the people in the wagons understood. Martin Tighe's boy, who played the fife, had studied well his part, and on his poor short-winded instrument now sounded taps as well as he could. He had heard it done once in Alton at a soldier's funeral. The plaintive notes called sadly over the fields, and echoed back from the hills. The few veterans could not look at each other; their eyes brimmed up with tears; they could not have spoken. Nothing called back old army days like that. They had a sudden vision of the Virginian camp, the hillside dotted white with tents, the twinkling lights in other camps, and far away the glow of smouldering fires. They heard the bugle call from post to post; they remembered the chilly winter night,

DECORATION DAY

the wind in the pines, the laughter of the men. Lights out! Martin Tighe's boy sounded it again sharply. It seemed as if poor Eb Munson and John Tighe must hear it too in their narrow graves.

The procession went on, and stopped here and there at the little graveyards on the farms, leaving their bright flags to flutter through summer and winter rains and snows, and to bleach in the wind and sunshine. When they returned to the church, the minister made an address about the war, and everyone listened with new ears. Most of what he said was familiar enough to his listeners; they were used to reading those phrases about the results of the war, the glorious future of the South, in their weekly newspapers; but there never had been such a spirit of patriotism and loyalty waked in Barlow as was waked that day by the poor parade of the remnant of the Barlow soldiers. They sent flags to all the distant graves, and proud were those households who claimed kinship with valour, and could drive or walk away with their flags held up so that others could see that they, too, were of the elect.

III

It is well that the days are long in the last of May, but John Stover had to hurry more than usual with his evening work, and then, having the longest distance to walk, he was much the latest comer to the Plains store, where his two triumphant friends were waiting for him impatiently on the bench. They also had made excuse of going to the post-office and doing an unnecessary errand for their wives, and were talking together so busily that they had gathered a group about them before the store. When they saw Stover coming, they rose hastily and crossed the road to meet him, as if they were a committee in special session. They leaned against the post-and-board fence, after they had shaken hands with each other solemnly.

'Well, we've had a great day, ain't we, John?' asked Henry Merrill. 'You did lead off splendid. We've done a grand thing, now, I tell you. All the folks say we've got to keep it up every year. Everybody had to have a talk about it as I went home. They say they had no idea we should make such a show. Lord! I wish we'd begun while there was more of us!'

'That han'some flag was the great feature,' said Asa Brown generously. 'I want to pay my part for hirin' it. An' then folks was glad to see poor old Martin made o' some consequence.'

'There was half a dozen said to me that another year they was goin' to have flags out, and trim up their places somehow or 'nother. Folks has feelin' enough, but you've got to rouse it,' said Merrill.

'I have thought o' joinin' the Grand Army over to Alton time an' again, but it's a good ways to go, an' then the expense has been o' some consideration,' Asa continued. 'I don't know but two or three over there. You know, most o' the Alton men nat'rally went out in the rigiments t' other side o' the State line, an' they was in other battles, an' never camped nowheres nigh us. Seems to me we ought to have home feelin' enough to do what we can right here.'

'The minister says to me this afternoon that he was goin' to arrange an' have some talks in the meetin'-house next winter, an' have some of us tell where we was in the South; an' one

DECORATION DAY

night 't will be about camp life, an' one about the long marches, an' then about the battles, – that would take some time, – an' tell all we could about the boys that was killed, an' their record, so they wouldn't be forgot. He said some of the folks must have the letters we wrote home from the front, an' we could make out quite a history of us. I call Elder Dallas a very smart man; he'd planned it all out a'ready, for the benefit o' the young folks, he said,' announced Henry Merrill, in a tone of approval.

'I s'pose there ain't none of us but could add a little somethin',' answered John Stover modestly. "'T would re'lly learn the young folks a good deal. I should be scared numb to try an' speak from the pulpit. That ain't what the Elder means, is it? Now I was one that had a good chance to see somethin' o' Washin'ton. I shook hands with President Lincoln, an' I always think I'm worth lookin' at for that, if I ain't for nothin' else. 'T was that time I was just out o' hospit'l, an' able to crawl about some. I've often told you how 't was I met him, an' he stopped an' shook hands an' asked where I'd been at the front an' how I was gettin' along with my hurts. Well, we'll see how 't is when winter comes. I never thought I had no gift for public speakin', 'less 't was for drivin' cattle or pollin' the house town-meetin' days. Here! I've got somethin' in mind. You needn't speak about it if I tell it to ye,' he added suddenly. 'You know all them han'some flowers that was laid on to Eb Munson's grave an' Tighe's? I mistrusted you thought the same thing I did by the way you looked. They come from Marthy Down's front yard. My woman told me when we got home that she knew 'em in a minute; there wa'n't nobody in town had that kind o' red flowers but her. She must ha' kind o' harked back to the days when she was Marthy Peck. She must have come over with 'em after dark, or else dreadful early in the mornin'.'

Henry Merrill cleared his throat. 'There ain't nothin' half-way 'bout Mis' Down,' he said. 'I wouldn't ha' spoken 'bout this 'less you had led right on to it; but I overtook her when I was gittin' towards home this afternoon, an' I see by her looks she was worked up a good deal; but we talked about how well things had gone off, an' she wanted to know what expenses we'd been put to, an' I told her; and she said she'd give five dollars any day I'd stop in for it. An' then she spoke right out. "I'm alone in the world," says she, "and I've got somethin' to do with, an' I'd like to have a plain stone put up to Eb Munson's grave, with the number of his rigiment on it, an' I'll pay the bill. 'T ain't out o' Mr. Down's money," she says; "'t is mine, an' I want you to see to it." I said I would, but we'd made a plot to git some o' them soldiers' headstones that's provided by the government. 'T was a shame it had been overlooked so long. "No," says she; "I'm goin' to pay for Eb's myself." An' I told her there wouldn't be no objection. Don't ary one o' you speak about it. 'T wouldn't be fair. She was real well-appearin'. I never felt to respect Marthy so before.'

'We was kind o' hard on her sometimes, but folks couldn't help it. I've seen her pass Eb right by in the road an' never look at him when he first come home,' said John Stover.

'If she hadn't felt bad, she wouldn't have cared one way or t' other,' insisted Henry Merrill. "Tain't for us to judge. Sometimes folks has to get along in years before they see

DECORATION DAY

things fair. Come; I must be goin' home. I'm tired as an old dog.'

'It seemed kind o' natural to be steppin' out together again. Strange we three got through with so little damage, an' so many dropped round us,' said Asa Brown. 'I've never been one mite sorry I went out in old A Company. I was thinkin' when I was marchin' to-day, though, that we should all have to take to the wagons before long an' do our marchin' on wheels, so many of us felt kind o' stiff. There's one thing, – folks won't never say again that we can't show no public sperit here in old Barlow.'

THE COURTING OF SISTER WISBY

★

ALL the morning there had been an increasing temptation to take an outdoor holiday, and early in the afternoon the temptation outgrew my power of resistance. A far-away pasture on the long south-western slope of a high hill was persistently present to my mind, yet there seemed to be no particular reason. I was not sure that I wanted anything from the pasture, and there was no sign, except the temptation, that the pasture wanted anything of me. But I was on the farther side of as many as three fences before I stopped to think again where I was going, and why.

There is no use in trying to tell another person about that afternoon unless he distinctly remembers weather exactly like it. This was one of those perfect New England days in late summer, when the spirit of autumn takes a first stealthy flight, like a spy, through the ripening country-side, and, with feigned sympathy for those who droop with August heat, puts her cool cloak of bracing air about leaf and flower and human shoulders. Every living thing grows suddenly cheerful and strong; it is only when you catch sight of a horror-stricken little maple in swampy soil – a little maple that has second sight and foreknowledge of coming disaster to her race – only then does a distrust of autumn's friendliness dim your joyful satisfaction.

In midwinter there is always a day when one has the first foretaste of spring; in late August there is a morning when the air is for the first time autumn-like. Perhaps it is a hint to the squirrels to get in their first supplies for the winter

THE COURTING OF SISTER WISBY

hoards, or a reminder that summer will soon end, and everybody had better make the most of it. We are always looking forward to the passing and ending of winter, but when summer is here it seems as if summer must always last. As I went across the fields that day, I found myself half lamenting that the world must fade again, even that the best of her budding and bloom was only a preparation for another spring-time, for an awakening beyond the coming winter's sleep.

The sun was slightly veiled; there was a chattering group of birds, which had gathered for a conference about their early migration. Yet, oddly enough, I heard the voice of a belated bobolink, and presently saw him rise from the grass, and hover leisurely, while he sang a brief tune. He was much behind time if he were still a housekeeper; but as for the other birds, who listened, they cared only for their own notes. An old crow went sagging by, and gave a croak at his despised neighbour, just as a black reviewer croaked at Keats: so hard it is to be just to one's contemporaries. The bobolink was indeed singing out of season, and it was impossible to say whether he really belonged most to this summer or to the next. He might have been delayed on his northward journey; at any rate, he had a light heart now, to judge from his song, and I wished that I could ask him a few questions — how he liked being the last man among the bobolinks, and where he had taken singing lessons in the South.

Presently I left the lower fields, and took a path that led higher, where I could look beyond the village to the northern country mountain-ward. Here the sweet fern grew, thick and fragrant, and I also found myself heedlessly treading on pennyroyal. Near by, in a field corner, I long ago made a most comfortable seat by putting a stray piece of board and bit of rail across the angle of the fences. I have spent many a delightful hour there, in the shade and shelter of a young pitch-pine and a wild cherry-tree, with a lovely outlook towards the village, just far enough away beyond the green slopes and tall elms of the lower meadows. But that day I still had the feeling of being outward bound, and did not turn aside nor linger. The high pasture land grew more and more enticing.

I stopped to pick some blackberries that twinkled at me like beads among their dry vines, and two or three yellow birds fluttered up from the leaves of a thistle, and then came back again, as if they had complacently discovered that I was only an overgrown yellow-bird, in strange disguise but perfectly harmless. They made me feel as if I were an intruder, though they did not offer to peck at me, and we parted company very soon. It was good to stand at last on the great shoulder of the hill. The wind was coming in from the sea, there was a fine fragrance from the pines, and the air grew sweeter every moment. I took new pleasure in the thought that in a piece of wild pasture land like this one may get closest to Nature, and subsist upon what she gives of her own free will. There have been no drudging, heavy-shod ploughmen to overturn the soil, and vex it into yielding artificial crops. Here one has to take just what Nature is pleased to give, whether one is a yellow-bird or a human being. It is very good entertainment for a summer wayfarer, and I am asking my reader now to share the winter provision which I harvested that day. Let us hope that the small birds are also faring well after their fashion, but I give them an anxious

THE COURTING OF SISTER WISBY

thought while the snow goes hurrying in long waves across the buried fields, this windy winter night.

Farther down the hill, I got a drink of fresh cool water from the brook, and pulled a tender sheaf of sweet flag beside it. The mossy old fence just beyond was the last barrier between me and the pasture which had sent an invisible messenger earlier in the day, but I saw that somebody else had come first to the rendezvous: there was a brown gingham cape-bonnet and a sprigged shoulder shawl bobbing up and down, a little way off among the junipers. I had taken such uncommon pleasure in being alone that I instantly felt a sense of disappointment; then a warm glow of pleasant satisfaction rebuked my selfishness. This could be no one but dear old Mrs. Goodsoe, the friend of my childhood and fond dependence of my maturer years. I had not seen her for many weeks, but here she was, out on one of her famous campaigns for herbs, or perhaps just returning from a blueberrying expedition. I approached with care, so as not to startle the gingham bonnet; but she heard the rustle of the bushes against my dress, and looked up quickly, as she knelt bending over the turf. In that position she was hardly taller than the luxuriant junipers themselves.

'I'm a-gettin' in my mulleins,' she said, briskly, 'an' I've been thinking o' you these twenty times since I come out o' the house. I begun to believe you must ha' forgot me at last.'

'I have been away from home,' I explained. 'Why don't you get in your pennyroyal too? There's a great plantation of it beyond the next fence but one.'

'Pennyr'yal!' repeated the dear little old woman, with an

air of compassion for inferior knowledge; "taint the right time, darlin'. Pennyr'yal's too rank now. But for mulleins this day is prime. I've got a dreadful graspin' fit for 'em this year; seems as if I must be goin' to need 'em extry. I feel as the squirrels must when they know a hard winter's comin'.' And Mrs. Goodsoe bent over her work again, while I stood by and watched her carefully cut the best, fullgrown leaves with a clumsy pair of scissors, which might have served through at least half a century of herb gathering. They were fastened to her apron-strings by a long piece of list.

'I'm going to take my jack-knife and help you,' I suggested, with some fear of refusal. 'I just passed a flourishing family of six or seven heads that must have been growing on purpose for you.'

'Now, be keerful, dear heart,' was the anxious response; 'choose 'em well. There's odds in mulleins same's there is in angels. Take a plant that's all run up to stalk, and there ain't but little goodness in the leaves. This one I'm at now must ha' been stepped on by some creatur' and blighted of its bloom, and the leaves is han'some! When I was small I used to have a notion that Adam an' Eve must a took mulleins for their winter wear. Ain't they just like flannel, for all the world? I've had experience, and I know there's plenty of sickness might be saved to folks if they'd quit horseradish and such fiery, exasperating things, and use mullein drarves in proper season. Now I shall spread these an' dry 'em nice on my spare floor in the garrit, an', come to steam 'em for use along in the winter, there'll be the vally of the whole summer's goodness in 'em, sartin.' And she snipped away with the dull scissors,

THE COURTING OF SISTER WISBY

while I listened respectfully, and took great pains to have my part of the harvest present a good appearance.

'That is most too dry a head,' she added presently, a little out of breath. 'There! I can tell you there's win'rows o' young doctors, bilin' over with book-larnin', that is truly ignorant of what to do for the sick, or how to p'int out those paths that well people foller towards sickness. Book-fools I call 'em, them young men, an' some on 'em never'll live to know much better, if they git to be Methuselahs. In my time every middle-aged woman who had brought up a family had some proper ideas o' dealin' with complaints. I won't say but there was some fools amongst *them*, but I'd rather take my chances, unless they'd forsook herbs and gone to dealin' with patent stuff. Now my mother really did sense the use of herbs and roots. I never see anybody that come up to her. She was a meek-looking woman, but very understandin', mother was.'

'Then that's where you learned so much yourself, Mrs. Goodsoe?' I ventured to say.

'Bless your heart, I don't hold a candle to her; 'tis but little I can recall of what she used to say. No, her l'arnin' died with her,' said my friend, in a self-depreciating tone. 'Why, there was as many as twenty kinds of roots alone that she used to keep by her, that I forget the use of; an' I'm sure I shouldn't know where to find the most of 'em, any. There was an herb' – *airb* she called it – 'an herb called masterwort, that she used to get away from Pennsylvany; and she used to think everything of noble-liverwort, but I never could seem to get the right effects from it as she could. Though I don't know as she ever really did use masterwort where somethin' else

THE ONLY ROSE AND OTHER TALES

wouldn't a served. She had a cousin married out in Pennsylvany that used to take pains to get it to her every year or two, and so she felt 't was important to have it. Some set more by such things as come from a distance, but I rec'lect mother always used to maintain that folks was meant to be doctored with the stuff that grew right about 'em; 't was sufficient, an' so ordered. That was before the whole population took to livin' on wheels, the way they do now. 'T was never my idee that we was meant to know what's goin' on all over the world to once. There's going to be some sort of a set-back one o' these days, with these telegraphs an' things, an' letters comin' every hand's turn, and folks leavin' their proper work to answer 'em. I may not live to see it. 'T was allowed to be difficult for folks to git about in olden times, or to git word across the country, an' they stood in their lot an' place, and weren't all just alike, either, same as pine-spills.'

We were kneeling side by side now, as if in penitence for the march of progress, but we laughed as we turned to look at each other.

'Do you think it did much good when everybody brewed a cracked quart mug of herb-tea?' I asked, walking away on my knees to a new mullein.

'I've always lifted my voice against the practice, far's I could,' declared Mrs. Goodsoe; 'an' I won't deal out none o' the herbs I save for no such nonsense. There was three houses along our road – I call no names – where you couldn't go into the livin' room without findin' a mess o' herb-tea drorin' on the stove or side o' the fireplace, winter or summer, sick or well. One was thoroughwut, one would be camomile, and the other, like as not, yellow dock; but they all used to put in

THE COURTING OF SISTER WISBY

a little new rum to git out the goodness, or keep it from spilin'.' (Mrs. Goodsoe favoured me with a knowing smile.) 'Land, how mother used to laugh! But, poor creatur's, they had to work hard, and I guess it never done 'em a mite o' harm; they was all good herbs. I wish you could hear the quawkin' there used to be when they was indulged with a real case o' sickness. Everybody would collect from far and near; you'd see 'em coming along the road and across the pastures then; everybody clamourin' that nothin' wouldn't do no kind o' good but her choice o' teas or drarves to the feet. I wonder there was a babe lived to grow up in the whole lower part o' the town; an' if nothin' else 'peared to ail 'em, word was passed about that 'twas likely Mis' So-and-So's last young one was goin' to be foolish. Land, how they'd gather! I know one day the doctor come to Widder Peck's and the house was crammed so't he could scercely get inside the door; and he says, just as polite, "Do send for some of the neighbours!" as if there wa'n't a soul to turn to, right or left. You'd ought to seen 'em begin to scatter.'

'But don't you think the cars and telegraphs have given people more to interest them, Mrs. Goodsoe? Don't you believe people's lives were narrower then, and more taken up with little things?' I asked, unwisely, being a product of modern times.

'Not one mite, dear,' said my companion, stoutly. 'There was as big thoughts then as there is now; these times was born o' them. The difference is in folks themselves; but now, instead o' doin' their own housekeepin' and watchin' their own neighbours – though that was carried to excess – they get word that a niece's child is ailin' the other side o' Massachusetts, and they drop everything and git on their best clothes, and off they jiggit in the cars. 'T is a bad sign when folks wears out their best clothes faster'n they do their everyday ones. The other side o' Massachusetts has got to look after itself by rights. An' besides that, Sunday-keepin's all gone out o' fashion. Some lays it to one thing and some another, but some o' them old ministers, that folks are all a-sighin' for, did preach a lot o' stuff that wa'n't nothin' but chaff; 'twa'n't the word o' God out o' either Old Testament or New. But everybody went to meetin' and heard it, and come home, and was set to fighting with their next door neighbour over it. Now, I'm a believer, and I try to live a Christian life, but I'd as soon hear a surveyor's book read out, figgers an' all, as try to get any simple truth out o' most sermons. It's them as is most to blame.'

'What was the matter that day at Widow Peck's?' I hastened to ask, for I knew by experience that the good, clear-minded soul beside me was apt to grow unduly vexed and distressed when she contemplated the state of religious teaching.

'Why, there wa'n't nothing the matter, only a gal of Miss Peck's had met with a dis'pintment, and had gone into screechin' fits. 'T was a roving creatur' that had come along hayin' time, and he'd gone off an' forsook her betwixt two days; nobody ever knew what become of him. Them Pecks was "Good Lord, anybody!" kind o' gals, and took up with whoever they could get. One of 'em married Heron, the Irishman; they lived in that little house that was burnt this summer, over on the edge o' the plains. He was a good-hearted creatur', with a laughin' eye and a clever word for

THE COURTING OF SISTER WISBY

everybody. He was the first Irishman that ever came this way, and we was all for gettin' a look at him, when he first used to go by. Mother's folks was what they call Scotch-Irish, though; there was an old race of 'em settled about here. They could foretell events, some on 'em, and had the second sight. I know folks used to say mother's grandmother had them gifts, but mother was never free to speak about it to us. She remembered her well, too.'

'I suppose that you mean old Jim Heron, who was such a famous fiddler?' I asked, with great interest, for I am always delighted to know more about that rustic hero, parochial Orpheus that he must have been!

'Now, dear heart, I suppose you don't remember him, do you?' replied Mrs. Goodsoe, earnestly. 'Fiddle! He'd about break your heart with them tunes of his, or else set your heels flying up the floor in a jig, though you was minister o' the First Parish and all wound up for a funeral prayer. I tell ye there ain't no tunes sounds like them used to. It used to seem to me summer nights when I was comin' along the plains road, and he set by the window playin', as if there was a bewitched human creatur' in that old red fiddle o' his. He could make it sound just like a woman's voice tellin' somethin' over and over, as if folks could help her out o' her sorrows if she could only make 'em understand. I've set by the stone-wall and cried as if my heart was broke, and dear knows it wa'n't in them days. How he would twirl off them jigs and dance tunes! He used to make somethin' han'some out of 'em in fall an' winter, playin' at huskin's and dancin' parties; but he was unstiddy by spells as he got along in years, and never knew what it was to be forehanded. Everybody felt bad when he died; you couldn't help likin' the creatur'. He'd got the gift – that's all you could say about it.

'There was a Mis' Jerry Foss, that lived over by the brook bridge, on the plains road, that had lost her husband early, and was left with three child'n. She set the world by 'em, and was a real pleasant, ambitious little woman, and was workin' on as best she could with that little farm, when there come a rage o' scarlet fever, and her boy and two girls was swept off and laid dead within the same week. Everyone o' the neighbours did what they could, but she'd had no sleep since they was taken sick, and after the funeral she sat there just like a piece o' marble, and would only shake her head when you spoke to her. They all thought her reason would go; and 't would certain, if she couldn't have shed tears. An' one o' the neighbours – 't was like mother's sense, but it might have been somebody else – spoke o' Jim Heron. Mother an' one or two o' the women that knew her best was in the house with her. 'T was right in the edge o' the woods and some of us younger ones was over by the wall on the other side of the road where there was a couple of old willows – I remember just how the brook damp felt – and we kept quiet's we could, and some other folks come along down the road, and stood waitin' on the little bridge, hopin' somebody'd come out, I suppose, and they'd git news. Everybody was wrought up, and felt a good deal for her, you know. By-an'-by Jim Heron come stealin' right out o' the shadows an' set down on the doorstep, an' 't was a good while before we heard a sound; then, oh, dear me! 't was what the whole neighbourhood felt for that mother all spoke in the notes, an' they told me afterwards that Mis' Foss's face changed in a minute, and she come right over

THE COURTING OF SISTER WISBY

an' got into my mother's lap – she was a little woman – an' laid her head down, and there she cried herself into a blessed sleep. After awhile one o' the other women stole out an' told the folks, and we all went home. He only played that one tune.

'But there!' resumed Mrs. Goodsoe, after a silence, during which my eyes were filled with tears, 'his wife always complained that the fiddle made her nervous. She never 'peared to think nothin' o' poor Heron after she'd once got him.'

'That's often the way,' said I, with harsh cynicism, though I had no guilty person in my mind at the moment; and we went straying off, not very far apart, up through the pasture. Mrs. Goodsoe cautioned me that we must not get so far off that we could not get back the same day. The sunshine began to feel very hot on our backs, and we both turned toward the shade. We had already collected a large bundle of mullein leaves, which were carefully laid into a clean calico apron, held together by the four corners, and proudly carried by me, though my companion regarded them with anxious eyes. We sat down together at the edge of the pine woods, and Mrs. Goodsoe proceeded to fan herself with her limp cape-bonnet.

'I declare, how hot it is! The east wind's all gone again,' she said. 'It felt so cool this forenoon that I overburdened myself with as thick a petticoat as any I've got. I'm despri't afeared of having a chill, now that I ain't so young as once. I hate to be housed up.'

'It's only August, after all,' I assured her, unnecessarily, confirming my statement by taking two peaches out of my pocket, and laying them side by side on the brown pine needles between us.

'Dear sakes alive!' exclaimed the old lady, with evident pleasure. 'Where did you get them, now? Doesn't anything taste twice better out-o'-doors? I ain't had such a peach for years. Do le's keep the stones, an' I'll plant 'em; it only takes four years for a peach pit to come to bearing, an' I guess I'm good for four year, 'thout I meet with some accident.'

I could not help agreeing, or taking a fond look at the thin little figure, and her wrinkled brown face and kind, twinkling eyes. She looked as if she had properly dried herself, by mistake, with some of her mullein leaves, and was likely to keep her goodness, and to last the longer in consequence. There never was a truer, simple-hearted soul made out of the old-fashioned country dust than Mrs. Goodsoe. I thought, as I looked away from her across the wide country, that nobody was left in any of the farm houses, so original, so full of rural wisdom and reminiscence, so really able and dependable as she. And nobody had made better use of her time in a world foolish enough to sometimes undervalue medicinal herbs.

When we had eaten our peaches we still sat under the pines, and I was not without pride when I had poked about in the ground with a little twig, and displayed to my crony a long fine root, bright yellow to the eye, and a wholesome bitter to the taste.

'Yis, dear, goldthread,' she assented, indulgently. 'Seems to me there's more of it than anything except grass an' hardhack. Good for canker, but no better than two or three other things I can call to mind; but I always lay in a good wisp of it, for old times' sake. Now, I want to know why you should a bit it, and took away all the taste o' your nice peach? I was just thinkin' what a han'some entertainment we've had. I've got

THE COURTING OF SISTER WISBY

so I 'sociate certain things with certain folks, and goldthread was somethin' Lizy Wisby couldn't keep house without, no ways whatever. I believe she took so much it kind o' puckered her disposition.'

'Lizy Wisby?' I repeated, inquiringly.

'You knew her, if ever, by the name of Mis' Deacon Brimblecom,' answered my friend, as if this were only a brief preface to further information, so I waited with respectful expectation. Mrs. Goodsoe had grown tired, out in the sun, and a good story would be an excuse for sufficient rest. It was a most lovely place where we sat, half-way up the long hillside; for my part, I was perfectly contented and happy. 'You've often heard of Deacon Brimblecom?' she asked, as if a great deal depended upon his being properly introduced.

'I remember him,' said I. 'They called him Deacon Brimfull, you know, and he used to go about with a witch-hazel branch to show people where to dig wells.'

'That's the one,' said Mrs. Goodsoe, laughing. 'I didn't know's you could go so far back. I'm always divided between whether you can remember everything I can, or are only a babe in arms.'

'I have a dim recollection of there being something strange about their marriage,' I suggested, after a pause, which began to appear dangerous. I was so much afraid the subject would be changed.

'I can tell you all about it,' I was quickly answered. 'Deacon Brimblecom was very pious accordin' to his lights in his early years. He lived way back in the country then, and there come a rovin' preacher along, and set everybody up that way all by the ears. I've heard the old folks talk it over, but I forget most of his doctrine, except some of his followers was persuaded they could dwell among the angels while yet on airth, and this Deacon Brimfull, as you call him, felt sure he was called by the voice of a spirit bride. So he left a good, deservin' wife he had, an' four children, and built him a new house over to the other side of the land he'd had from his father. They didn't take much pains with the buildin', because they expected to be translated before long, and then the spirit brides and them folks was goin' to appear and divide up the airth amongst 'em, and the world's folks and onbelievers was goin' to serve 'em or be sent to torments. They had meetin's about in the school-houses, an' all sorts o' goin's on; some on 'em went crazy, but the deacon held on to what wits he had, an' by-an'-by the spirit bride didn't turn out to be much of a housekeeper, an' he had always been used to good livin', so he sneaked home ag'in. One o' mother's sisters married up to Ash Hill, where it all took place; that's how I come to have the particulars.'

'Then how did he come to find his Eliza Wisby?' I inquired. 'Do tell me the whole story; you've got mullein leaves enough.'

'There's all yesterday's at home, if I haven't,' replied Mrs. Goodsoe. 'The way he come a-courtin' o' Sister Wisby was this: she went a-courtin' o' him.

'There was a spell he lived to home, and then his poor wife died, and he had a spirit bride in good earnest, an' the child'n was placed about with his folks and hers, for they was both out o' good families; and I don't know what come over him, but he had another pious fit that looked for all the world like the real thing. He hadn't no family cares, and he lived with

THE COURTING OF SISTER WISBY

his brother's folks, and turned his land in with theirs. He used to travel to every meetin' an' conference that was within reach of his old sorrel hoss's feeble legs; he j'ined the Christian Baptists that was just in their early prime, and he was a great exhorter, and got to be called deacon, though I guess he wa'n't deacon, 'less it was for a spare hand when deacon timber was scercer'n usual. An' one time there was a four days' protracted meetin' to the church in the lower part of the town. 'T was a real solemn time: something more'n usual was goin' forward, an' they collected from the whole country round. Women folks liked it, an' the men too; it give 'em a change, an' they was quartered round free, same as conference folks now. Some on 'em, for a joke, sent Silas Brimblecom up to Lizy Wisby's, though she'd give out she couldn't accommodate nobody, because of expectin' her cousin's folks. Everybody knew 't was a lie; she was amazin' close considerin' she had plenty to do with. There was a streak that wa'n't just right somewheres in Lizy's wits, I always thought. She was very kind in case o' sickness, I'll say that for her.

'You know where the house is, over there on what they call Windy Hill? There the deacon went, all unsuspectin', and 'stead o' Lizy's resentin' of him she put in her own hoss, and they come back together to evenin' meetin'. She was prominent among the sect herself, an' he bawled and talked, and she bawled and talked, an' took up more'n the time allotted in the exercises, just as if they was showin' off to each other what they was able to do at expoundin'. Everybody was laughin' at 'em after the meetin' broke up, and that next day an' the next, an' all through, they was constant, and seemed to be havin' a beautiful occasion. Lizy had always give out she scorned the men, but when she got a chance at a particular one 't was altogether different, and the deacon seemed to please her somehow or 'nother, and – There! you don't want to listen to this old stuff that's past an' gone?'

'Oh, yes, I do,' said I.

'I run on like a clock that's onset her striking hand,' said Mrs. Goodsoe, mildly. 'Sometimes my kitchen timepiece goes on half the forenoon, and I says to myself, the day before yisterday, I would let it be a warnin', and keep it in mind for a check on my own speech. The next news that was heard was that the deacon an' Lizy – well, opinions differed which of 'em had spoke first, but them fools settled it before the protracted meetin' was over, and give away their hearts before he started for home. They considered 't would be wise, though, considerin' their short acquaintance, to take one another on trial a spell; 'twas Lizy's notion, and she asked him why he wouldn't come over and stop with her till spring, and then, if they both continued to like, they could get married any time 't was convenient. Lizy, she come and talked it over with mother, and mother disliked to offend her, but she spoke pretty plain; and Lizy felt hurt, an' thought they was showin' excellent judgment, so much harm come from hasty unions, and folks comin' to a realizin' sense of each other's failin's when 't was too late.

'So one day our folks saw Deacon Brimfull a-ridin' by with a gre't coopful of hens in the back o' his wagon, and bundles o' stuff tied on top and hitched to the exes underneath; and he riz a hymn just as he passed the house, and was speedin' the old sorrel with a willer-switch. 'T was most Thanksgivin' time, an' sooner'n she expected him. New Year's was

THE COURTING OF SISTER WISBY

the time she set; but he thought he'd better come while the roads was fit for wheels. They was out to meetin' together Thanksgivin' Day, an' that used to be a gre't season for marryin'; so the young folks nudged each other, and some on' 'em ventured to speak to the couple as they come down the aisle. Lizy carried it off real well; she wa'n't afraid o' what nobody said or thought, and so home they went. They'd got out her yellow sleigh and her hoss; she never would ride after the deacon's poor old creatur', and I believe it died long o' the winter from stiffenin' up.

'Yes,' said Mrs. Goodsoe, emphatically, after we had silently considered the situation for a short space of time — 'yes, there was considerable talk, now I tell you! The raskil boys pestered 'em just about to death for a while. They used to collect up there an' rap on the winders, and they'd turn out all the deacon's hens 'long at nine o'clock o' night, and chase 'em all over the dingle; an' one night they even lugged the pig right out o' the sty, and shoved it into the back entry, an' run for their lives. They'd stuffed its mouth full o' somethin', so it couldn't squeal till it got there. There wa'n't a sign o' nobody to be seen when Lizy hasted out with the light, and she an' the deacon had to persuade the creatur' back as best they could; 't was a cold night, and they said it took 'em till towards mornin'. You see, the deacon was just the kind of a man that a hog wouldn't budge for; it takes a masterful man to deal with a hog. Well, there was no end to the works nor the talk, but Lizy left 'em pretty much alone. She did 'pear kind o' dignified about it, I must say!'

'And then, were they married in the spring?'

'I was tryin' to remember whether it was just before Fast

Day or just after,' responded my friend, with a careful look at the sun, which was nearer the west than either of us had noticed. 'I think likely 'twas along in the last o' April. Anyway, some of us looked out o' the window one Monday mornin' early, and says, "For goodness' sake! Lizy's sent the deacon home again!" His old sorrel havin' passed away, he was ridin' in Ezry Welsh's hoss-cart, with his hen-coop and not so many bundles as he had when he come, and he looked as meechin' as ever you see. Ezry was drivin', and he let a glance fly swiftly round to see if any of us was lookin' out; and then I declare if he didn't have the malice to turn right in towards the barn, where he see my oldest brother, Joshuay, an' says he, real natural, "Joshuay, just step out with your wrench. I believe I hear my kingbolt rattlin' kind o' loose." Brother, he went out an' took in the sitooation, an' the deacon bowed kind o' stiff. Joshuay was so full o' laugh, and Ezry Welsh, that they couldn't look one another in the face. There wa'n't nothing ailed the kingbolt, you know, an' when Josh riz up he says, "Goin' up country for a spell, Mr. Brimblecom?"

' "I be," says the deacon, lookin' dreadful mortified and cast down.

' "Ain't things turned out well with you an' Sister Wisby?" says Joshuay. "You had ought to remember that the woman is the weaker vessel."

' "Hang her, let her carry less sail, then!" the deacon bu'st out, and he stood right up an' shook his fist there by the hen-coop, he was so mad; an' Ezry's hoss was a young creatur', an' started up an' set the deacon right over backwards into the chips. We didn't know but he'd broke his neck; but when he

THE COURTING OF SISTER WISBY

see the women folks runnin' out, he jumped up quick as a cat, an' clim' into the cart, an' off they went. Ezry said he told him that he couldn't git along with Lizy, she was so fractious in thundery weather; if there was a rumble in the daytime she must go right to bed an' screech, and if 't was night she must git right up an' call him out of a sound sleep. But everybody knew he'd never a gone home unless she'd sent him.

'Somehow they made it up agin right away, him an' Lizy, and she had him back. She'd been countin' all along on not havin' to hire nobody to work about the gardin an' so on, an' she said she wa'n't goin' to let him have a whole winter's board for nothin'. So the old hens was moved back, and they was married right off fair an' square, an' I don't know but they got along well as most folks. He brought his youngest girl down to live with 'em after a while, an' she was a real treasure to Lizy; everybody spoke well o' Phebe Brimblecom. The deacon got over his pious fit, and there was consider'ble work in him if you kept right after him. He was an amazin' cider drinker, and he airnt the name you know him by in his latter days. Lizy never trusted him with nothin', but she kep' him well. She left everything she owned to Phebe, when she died, 'cept somethin' to satisfy the law. There, they're all gone now: seems to me sometimes, when I get thinkin', as if I'd lived a thousand years!'

I laughed, but I found that Mrs. Goodsoe's thoughts had taken a serious turn.

'There, I come by some old graves down here in the lower edge of the pasture,' she said, as we rose to go. 'I couldn't help thinking how I should like to be laid right out in the pasture ground, when my time comes; it looked sort o' comfortable, and I have ranged these slopes so many summers. Seems as if I could see right up through the turf and tell when the weather was pleasant, and get the goodness o' the sweet fern. Now, dear, just hand me my apernful o' mulleins out o' the shade. I hope you won't come to need none this winter, but I'll dry some special for you.'

'I'm going home by the road,' said I, 'or else by the path across the meadows, so I will walk as far as the house with you. Aren't you pleased with my company?' for she demurred at my going the least bit out of the way.

So we strolled toward the little grey house, with our plunder of mullein leaves slung on a stick which we carried between us. Of course I went in to make a call, as if I had not seen my hostess before; she is the last maker of muster-gingerbread, and, before I came away, I was kindly measured for a pair of mittens.

'You'll be sure to come an' see them two peach-trees after I get 'em well growin'?' Mrs. Goodsoe called after me when I had said good-bye, and was almost out of hearing down the road.

A NATIVE OF WINBY

★

I

ON the teacher's desk, in the little roadside school-house, there was a bunch of Mayflowers, beside a dented and bent brass bell, a small Worcester's Dictionary without any cover, and a worn morocco-covered Bible. These were placed in an orderly row, and behind them was a small wooden box which held some broken pieces of blackboard crayon. The teacher, whom no timid new scholar could look at boldly, wore her accustomed air of authority and importance. She might have been nineteen years old, – not more – but for the time being she scorned the frivolities of youth.

The hot May sun was shining in at the smoky small-paned windows; sometimes an outside shutter swung to with a creak, and eclipsed the glare. The narrow door stood wide open, to the left as you faced the desk, and an old spotted dog lay asleep on the step, and looked wise and old enough to have gone to school with several generations of children. It was half-past three o'clock in the afternoon, and the primer class, settled into the apathy of after-recess fatigue, presented a straggling front, as they stood listlessly on the floor. As for the big boys and girls, they also were longing to be at liberty, but the pretty teacher, Miss Marilla Hender, seemed quite as energetic as when school was begun in the morning.

The spring breeze blew in at the open door, and even fluttered the primer leaves, but the back of the room felt hot and close, as if it were midsummer. The children in the class read their lessons in those high-keyed, droning voices which older teachers learn to associate with faint powers of perception. Only one or two of them had an awakened human look in their eyes, such as Matthew Arnold delighted himself in finding so often in the schoolchildren of France. Most of these poor little students were as inadequate, at that weary moment, to the pursuit of letters as if they had been woolly spring lambs on a sunny hillside. The teacher corrected and admonished with great patience, glancing now and then toward points of danger and insurrection, whence came a suspicious buzz of whispering from behind a desk-lid or a pair of widespread large geographies. Now and then a toiling child would rise and come down the aisle, with his forefinger firm upon a puzzling word as if it were an unclassified insect. It was a lovely beckoning day out-of-doors. The children felt like captives; there was something that provoked rebellion in the droning voices, the buzzing of an early wild bee against the sunlit pane, and even in the stuffy familiar odour of the place – the odour of apples and crumbs of doughnuts and gingerbread in the dinner-pails on the high entry nails, and of all the little gowns and trousers that had brushed through junipers and young pines on their way to school.

The bee left his prisoning pane at last, and came over to the mayflowers, which were in full bloom, although the season was very late, and deep in the woods there were still some greybacked snowdrifts, speckled with bits of bark and moss from the trees above.

'Come, come, Ezra!' urged the young teacher, rapping her

A NATIVE OF WINBY

desk sharply. 'Stop watchin' that common bee! You know well enough what those letters spell. You won't learn to read at this rate until you are a grown man. Mind your book, now; you ought to remember who went to this school when he was a little boy. You've heard folks tell about the Honourable Joseph K. Laneway? He used to be in primer just as you are now, and 't wasn't long before he was out of it, either, and was called the smartest boy in school. He's got to be a general and a Senator, and one of the richest men out West. You don't seem to have the least mite of ambition to-day, any of you!'

The exhortation, entirely personal in the beginning, had swiftly passed to a general rebuke. Ezra looked relieved, and the other children brightened up as they recognized a tale familiar to their ears. Anything was better than trying to study in that dull last hour of afternoon school.

'Yes,' continued Miss Hender, pleased that she had at last roused something like proper attention, 'you all ought to be proud that you are schoolmates of District Number Four, and can remember that the celebrated General Laneway had the same early advantages as you, and think what he has made of himself by perseverance and ambition.'

The pupils were familiar enough with the illustrious history of their noble predecessor. They were sure to be told, in lawless moments, that if Mr. Laneway were to come in and see them he would be mortified to death; and the members of the school committee always referred to him, and said that he had been a poor boy, and was now a self-made man, — as if every man were not self-made as to his character and reputation!

At this point, young Johnny Spencer showed his next neighbour, in the back of his Colburn's Arithmetic, an imaginary portrait of their district hero, which caused them both to chuckle derisively. The Honourable Mr. Laneway figured on the flyleaf as an extremely cross-eyed person, with strangely crooked legs and arms and a terrific expression. He was outlined with red and blue pencils as to coat and trousers, and held a reddened scalp in one hand and a blue tomahawk in the other; being closely associated in the artist's mind with the early settlements of the far West.

There was a noise of wheels in the road near by, and, though Miss Hender had much more to say, everybody ceased to listen to her, and turned toward the windows, leaning far forward over their desks to see who might be passing. They caught a glimpse of a shiny carriage; the old dog bounded out, barking, but nothing passed the open door. The carriage had stopped; someone was coming to the school; somebody was going to be called out! It could not be the committee, whose pompous and uninspiring spring visit had taken place only the week before.

Presently a well-dressed elderly man, with an expectant, masterful look, stood on the doorstep, glanced in with a smile, and knocked. Miss Marilla Hender blushed, smoothed her pretty hair anxiously with both hands, and stepped down from her little platform to answer the summons. There was hardly a shut mouth in the primer class.

'Would it be convenient for you to receive a visitor to the school?' the stranger asked politely, with a fine bow of deference to Miss Hender. He looked much pleased and a little excited, and the teacher said:

A NATIVE OF WINBY

'Certainly; step right in, won't you, sir?' in quite another tone from that in which she had just addressed the school.

The boys and girls were sitting straight and silent in their places, in something like a fit of apprehension and unpreparedness at such a great emergency. The guest represented a type of person previously unknown in District Number Four. Everything about him spoke of wealth and authority. The old dog returned to the doorstep, and after a careful look at the invader approached him, with a funny doggish grin and a desperate wag of the tail, to beg for recognition.

The teacher gave her chair on the platform to the guest, and stood beside him with very red cheeks, smoothing her hair again once or twice, and keeping the hard-wood ruler fast in hand, like a badge of office. 'Primer class may now retire!' she said firmly, although the lesson was not more than half through; and the class promptly escaped to their seats, waddling, and stumbling, until they all came up behind their desks, face foremost, and added themselves to the number of staring young countenances. After this there was a silence, which grew more and more embarrassing.

'Perhaps you would be pleased to hear our first class in geography, sir?' asked the fair Marilla, recovering her presence of mind; and the guest kindly assented.

The young teacher was by no means willing to give up a certainty for an uncertainty. Yesterday's lesson had been well learned; she turned back to the questions about the State of Kansota, and at the first sentence the mysterious visitor's dignity melted into an unconscious smile. He listened intently for a minute, and then seemed to reoccupy himself with his own thoughts and purposes, looking eagerly about the old school-house, and sometimes gazing steadily at the children. The lesson went on finely, and when it was finished Miss Hender asked the girl at the head of the class to name the States and Territories, which she instantly did, mispronouncing nearly all the names of the latter; then others stated boundaries and capitals, and the resources of the New England States, passing on finally to the names of the Presidents. Miss Hender glowed with pride; she had worked hard over the geography class in the winter term, and it did not fail her on this great occasion. When she turned bravely to see if the gentleman would like to ask any questions, she found that he was apparently lost in a deep reverie, so she repeated her own question more distinctly.

'They have done very well, – very well indeed,' he answered kindly; and then, to everyone's surprise, he rose, went up the aisle, pushed Johnny Spencer gently along his bench, and sat down beside him. The space was cramped, and the stranger looked huge and uncomfortable, so that everybody laughed, except one of the big girls, who turned pale with fright, and thought he must be crazy. When this girl gave a faint squeak Miss Hender recovered herself, rapped twice with the ruler to restore order, and then became entirely tranquil. There had been talk of replacing the hacked and worn old school-desks with patent desks and chairs; this was probably an agent connected with that business. At once she was resolute and self-reliant, and said, 'No whispering!' in a firm tone that showed she did not mean to be trifled with. The geography class was dismissed, but the elderly gentleman, in his handsome overcoat, still sat there wedged in at Johnny Spencer's side.

A NATIVE OF WINBY

'I presume, sir, that you are canvassing for new desks,' said Miss Hender, with dignity. 'You will have to see the supervisor and the selectmen.' There did not seem to be any need of his lingering, but she had an ardent desire to be pleasing to a person of such evident distinction. 'We always tell strangers — I thought, sir, you might be gratified to know — that this is the schoolhouse where the Honourable Joseph K. Laneway first attended school. All do not know that he was born in this town, and went West very young; it is only about a mile from here where his folks used to live.'

At this moment the visitor's eyes fell. He did not look at pretty Marilla any more, but opened Johnny Spencer's arithmetic, and, seeing the imaginary portrait of the great General Laneway, laughed a little, — a very deep-down comfortable laugh it was, — while Johnny himself turned cold with alarm, he could not have told why.

It was very still in the school-room; the bee was buzzing and bumping at the pane again; the moment was one of intense expectation.

The stranger looked at the children right and left. 'The fact is this, young people,' said he, in a tone that was half pride and half apology, 'I am Joseph K. Laneway myself.'

He tried to extricate himself from the narrow quarters of the desk, but for an embarrassing moment found that he was stuck fast. Johnny Spencer instinctively gave him an assisting push, and once free the great soldier, statesman, and millionaire took a few steps forward to the open floor; then, after hesitating a moment, he mounted the little platform and stood in the teacher's place. Marilla Hender was as pale as ashes.

'I have thought many times,' the great guest began, 'that some day I should come back to visit this place, which is so closely interwoven with the memories of my childhood. In my counting-room, on the fields of war, in the halls of Congress, and most of all in my Western home, my thoughts have flown back to the hills and brooks of Winby and to this little old school-house. I could shut my eyes and call back the buzz of voices, and fear my teacher's frown, and feel my boyish ambitions waking and stirring in my breast. On that bench where I just sat I saw some notches that I cut with my first jack-knife fifty-eight years ago this very spring. I remember the faces of the boys and girls who went to school with me, and I see their grandchildren before me. I know that one is a Goodsoe and another a Winn by the old family look. One generation goes, and another comes.

'There are many things that I might say to you. I meant, even in those early restricted days, to make my name known, and I dare say that you too have ambition. Be careful what you wish for in this world, for if you wish hard enough you are sure to get it. I once heard a very wise man say this, and the longer I live the more firmly I believe it to be true. But wishing hard means working hard for what you want, and the world's prizes wait for the men and women who are ready to take pains to win them. Be careful and set your minds on the best things. I meant to be a rich man when I was a boy here, and I stand before you a rich man, knowing the care and anxiety and responsibility of wealth. I meant to go to Congress, and I am one of the Senators from Kansota. I say this as humbly as I say it proudly. I used to read of the valour and patriotism of the old Greeks and Romans with my youthful blood leaping

A NATIVE OF WINBY

along my veins, and it came to pass that my own country was in danger, and that I could help to fight her battles. Perhaps some one of these little lads has before him a more eventful life than I have lived, and is looking forward to activity and honour and the pride of fame. I wish him all the joy that I have had, all the toil that I have had, and all the bitter disappointments even; for adversity leads a man to depend upon that which is above him, and the path of glory is a lonely path, beset by temptations and a bitter sense of the weakness and imperfection of man. I see my life spread out like a great picture, as I stand here in my boyhood's place. I regret my failures. I thank God for what in His kind providence has been honest and right. I am glad to come back, but I feel, as I look in your young faces, that I am an old man, while your lives are just beginning. When you remember, in years to come, that I came here to see the old school-house, remember that I said: Wish for the best things, and work hard to win them; try to be good men and women, for the honour of the school and the town, and the noble young country that gave you birth; be kind at home and generous abroad. Remember that I, an old man who had seen much of life, begged you to be brave and good.'

The Honourable Mr. Laneway had rarely felt himself so moved in any of his public speeches, but he was obliged to notice that for once he could not hold his audience. The primer class especially had begun to flag in attention, but one or two faces among the elder scholars fairly shone with vital sympathy and a lovely prescience of their future. Their eyes met his as if they struck a flash of light. There was a sturdy boy who half rose in his place unconsciously, the colour coming and going in his cheeks; something in Mr. Laneway's words lit the altar flame in his reverent heart.

Marilla Hender was pleased and a little dazed; she could not have repeated what her illustrious visitor had said, but she longed to tell everybody the news that he was in town, and had come to school to make an address. She had never seen a great man before, and really needed time to reflect upon him and to consider what she ought to say. She was just quivering with the attempt to make a proper reply and thank Mr. Laneway for the honour of his visit to the school, when he asked her which of the boys could be trusted to drive back his hired horse to the Four Corners. Eight boys, large and small, nearly every boy in the school, rose at once and snapped insistent fingers; but Johnny Spencer alone was desirous not to attract attention to himself. The Colburn's Intellectual Arithmetic with the portrait had been well secreted between his tight jacket and his shirt. Miss Hender selected a trustworthy freckled person in long trousers, who was half way to the door in an instant, and was heard almost immediately to shout loudly at the quiet horse.

Then the hero of District Number Four made his acknowledgments to the teacher. 'I fear that I have interrupted you too long,' he said, with pleasing deference.

Marilla replied that it was of no consequence; she hoped he would call again. She may have spoken primly, but her pretty eyes said everything that her lips forgot. 'My grandmother will want to see you, sir,' she ventured to say. 'I guess you will remember her, – Mis' Hender, she that was Abby Harran. She has often told me how you used to get your lessons out o' the same book.'

A NATIVE OF WINBY

'Abby Harran's granddaughter?' Mr. Laneway looked at her again with fresh interest. 'Yes, I wish to see her more than anyone else. Tell her that I am coming to see her before I go away, and give her my love. Thank you, my dear, as Marilla offered his missing hat. 'Good-bye, boys and girls.' He stopped and looked at them once more from the boys' entry, and turned again to look back from the very doorstep.

'Good-bye, sir, – good-bye,' piped two or three of the young voices; but most of the children only stared, and neither spoke nor moved.

'We will omit the class in Fourth Reader this afternoon. The class in grammar may recite,' said Miss Hender in her most contained and official manner.

The grammar class sighed like a single pupil, and obeyed. She was very stern with the grammar class, but every one in school had an inner sense that it was a great day in the history of District Number Four.

II

The Honourable Mr. Laneway found the outdoor air very fresh and sweet after the closeness of the school-house. It had just that same odour in his boyhood, and as he escaped he had a delightful sense of playing truant or of having an unexpected holiday. It was easier to think of himself as a boy, and to slip back into boyish thoughts, than to bear the familiar burden of his manhood. He climbed the tumble-down stone wall across the road, and went along a narrow path to the spring that bubbled up clear and cold under a great red oak. How many times he had longed for a drink of that water, and now here it was, and the thirst of that warm spring day was hard to quench! Again and again he stopped to fill the birch-bark dipper which the school-children had made, just as his own comrades made theirs years before. The oak-tree was dying at the top. The pine woods beyond had been cut and had grown again since his boyhood, and looked much as he remembered them. Beyond the spring and away from the woods the path led across overgrown pastures to another road, perhaps three-quarters of a mile away, and near this road was the small farm which had been his former home. As he walked slowly along, he was met again and again by some reminder of his youthful days. He had always liked to refer to his early life in New England in his political addresses, and had spoken more than once of going to find the cows at nightfall in the autumn evenings, and being glad to warm his bare feet in the places where the sleepy beasts had lain, before he followed their slow steps homeward through bush and brier. The Honourable Mr. Laneway had a touch of true sentiment which added much to his really stirring and effective campaign speeches. He had often been called the 'king of the platform' in his adopted State. He had long ago grown used to saying 'Go' to one man, and 'Come' to another, like the ruler of old; but all his natural power of leadership and habit of authority disappeared at once as he trod the pasture slopes, calling back the remembrance of his childhood. Here was the place where two lads, older than himself, had killed a terrible woodchuck at bay in the angle of a great rock; and just beyond was the sunny spot where he had picked a bunch of pink and white anemones under a prickly barberry thicket, to give to Abby Harran in morning school. She had put them

A NATIVE OF WINBY

into her desk, and let them wilt there, but she was pleased when she took them. Abby Harran, the little teacher's grandmother, was a year older than he, and had wakened the earliest thought of love in his youthful breast.

It was almost time to catch the first sight of his birthplace. From the knoll just ahead he had often seen the light of his mother's lamp, as he came home from school on winter afternoons; but when he reached the knoll the old house was gone, and so was the great walnut-tree that grew beside it, and a pang of disappointment shot through this devout pilgrim's heart. He never had doubted that the old farm was somebody's home still, and had counted upon the pleasure of spending a night there, and sleeping again in that room under the roof, where the rain sounded loud, and the walnut branches brushed to and fro when the wind blew, as if they were the claws of tigers. He hurried across the worn-out fields, long ago turned into sheep pastures, where the last year's tall grass and golden-rod stood grey and winter-killed; tracing the old walls and fences, and astonished to see how small the fields had been. The prosperous owner of Western farming lands could not help remembering those widespread luxuriant acres, and the broad outlooks of his Western home.

It was difficult at first to find exactly where the house had stood; even the foundations had disappeared. At last, in the long, faded grass he discovered the doorstep, and near by was a little mound where the great walnut-tree stump had been. The cellar was a mere dent in the sloping ground; it had been filled in by the growing grass and slow processes of summer and winter weather. But just at the pilgrim's right were some thorny twigs of an old rosebush. A sudden brightening of memory brought to mind the love that his mother – dead since his fifteenth year – had kept for this sweetbrier. How often she had wished that she had brought it to her new home! So much had changed in the world, so many had gone into the world of light, and here the faithful blooming thing was yet alive! There was one slender branch where green buds were starting, and getting ready to flower in the new year.

The afternoon wore late, and still the grey-haired man lingered. He might have laughed at someone else who gave himself up to sad thoughts, and found fault with himself, with no defendant to plead his cause at the bar of conscience. It was an altogether lonely hour. He had dreamed all his life, in a sentimental, self-satisfied fashion, of this return to Winby. It had always appeared to be a grand affair, but so far he was himself the only interested spectator at his poor occasion. There was even a dismal consciousness that he had been undignified, perhaps even a little consequential and silly, in the old school-house. The picture of himself on the war-path, in Johnny Spencer's arithmetic, was the only tribute that this longed-for day had held, but he laughed aloud delightedly at the remembrance and really liked that solemn little boy who sat at his own old desk. There was another older lad, who sat at the back of the room, who reminded Mr. Laneway of himself in his eager youth. There was a spark of light in that fellow's eyes. Once or twice in the earlier afternoon, as he drove along, he had asked people in the road if there were a Laneway family in that neighbour-hood, but everybody had said no in indifferent fashion. Somehow he had been expecting that everyone would know him and greet him, and give him credit for what he had tried to do, but old Winby had her own affairs to look after, and did very well without any of his help.

Mr. Laneway acknowledged to himself at this point that he was weak and unmanly. There must be some old friends who would remember him, and give him as hearty a welcome as the greeting he had brought for them. So he rose and went his way westward toward the sunset. The air was growing damp and cold, and it was time to make sure of shelter. This was hardly like the visit he had meant to pay to his birthplace. He wished with all his heart that he had never come back. But he walked briskly away, intent upon wider thoughts as the fresh evening breeze quickened his steps. He did not consider where he was going, but was for a time the busy man of affairs, stimulated by the unconscious influence of his surroundings. The slender grey birches and pitch pines of that neglected pasture had never before seen a hat and coat exactly in the fashion. They may have been abashed by the presence of a United States Senator and Western millionaire, though a piece of New England ground that had often felt the tread of his bare feet was not likely to quake because a pair of smart shoes stepped hastily along the school-house path.

III

There was an imperative knock at the side door of the Hender farmhouse, just after dark. The young school-mistress had come home late, because she had stopped all the way along to give people the news of her afternoon's experience. Marilla was not coy and speechless any longer, but sat by the kitchen stove telling her eager grandmother everything she could remember or could imagine.

'Who's that knocking at the door?' interrupted Mrs. Hender. 'No, I'll go myself; I'm nearest.'

The man outside was cold and foot-weary. He was not used to spending a whole day unrecognized, and, after being first amused, and even enjoying a sense of freedom at escaping his just dues of consideration and respect, he had begun to feel as if he were old and forgotten, and was hardly sure of a friend in the world.

Old Mrs. Hender came to the door, with her eyes shining with delight, in great haste to dismiss whoever had knocked, so that she might hear the rest of Marilla's story. She opened the door wide to whoever might have come on some country errand, and looked the tired and faint-hearted Mr. Laneway full in the face.

'Dear heart, come in!' she exclaimed, reaching out and taking him by the shoulder, as he stood humbly on a lower step. 'Come right in, Joe. Why, I should know you anywhere! Why, Joe Laneway, *you same boy!*'

In they went to the warm, bright country kitchen. The delight and kindness of an old friend's welcome and her instant sympathy seemed the loveliest thing in the world. They sat down in two old straight-backed kitchen chairs. They still held each other by the hand, and looked in each other's face. The plain old room was aglow with heat and cheerfulness; the tea-kettle was singing; a drowsy cat sat on the woodbox with her paws tucked in; and the house dog came forward in a friendly way, wagging his tail, and laid his head on their clasped hands.

A NATIVE OF WINBY

'And to think I haven't seen you since your folks moved out West, the next spring after you were thirteen in the winter,' said the good woman. 'But I s'pose there ain't been anybody that has followed your career closer than I have, accordin' to their opportunities. You've done a great work for your country, Joe. I'm proud of you clean through. Sometimes folks has said, "There, there, Mis' Hender, what be you goin' to say now?" but I've always told 'em to wait. I knew you saw your reasons. You was always an honest boy.' The tears started and shone in her kind eyes. Her face showed that she had waged a bitter war with poverty and sorrow, but the look of affection that it wore, and the warm touch of her hard hand, misshapen and worn with toil, touched her old friend in his inmost heart, and for a minute neither could speak.

'They do say that women folks have got no natural head for politics, but I always could seem to sense what was goin' on in Washington, if there was any sense to it,' said grandmother Hender at last.

'Nobody could puzzle you at school, I remember,' answered Mr. Laneway, and they both laughed heartily. 'But surely this granddaughter does not make your household? You have sons?'

'Two besides her father. He died; but they're both away, up toward Canada, buying cattle. We are getting along considerable well these last few years, since they got a mite o' capital together; but the old farm wasn't really able to maintain us, with the heavy expenses that fell on us unexpected year by year. I've seen a great sight of trouble, Joe. My boy John, Marilla's father, and his nice wife, — I lost 'em both early, when Marilla was but a child. John was the flower o' my family. He would have made a name for himself. You would have taken to John.'

'I was sorry to hear of your loss,' said Mr. Laneway. 'He was a brave man. I know what he did at Fredericksburg. You remember that I lost my wife and my only son?'

There was a silence between the friends, who had no need for words now; they understood each other's heart only too well. Marilla, who sat near them, rose and went out of the room.

'Yes, yes, daughter,' said Mrs. Hender, calling her back, 'we ought to be thinkin' about supper.'

'I was going to light a little fire in the parlour,' explained Marilla, with a slight tone of rebuke in her clear girlish voice.

'Oh, no, you ain't, – not now, at least,' protested the elder woman decidedly. 'Now, Joseph, what should you like to have for supper? I wish to my heart I had some fried turnovers, like those you used to come after when you was a boy. I can make 'em just about the same as mother did. I'll be bound you've thought of some old-fashioned dish that you'd relish for your supper.'

'Rye drop-cakes, then, if they wouldn't give you too much trouble,' answered the Honourable Joseph, with prompt seriousness, 'and don't forget some cheese.' He looked up at his old playfellow as she stood beside him, eager with affectionate hospitality.

'You've no idea what a comfort Marilla's been,' she stooped to whisper. 'Always took right hold and helped me when she was a baby. She's as good as made up already to me for my

A NATIVE OF WINBY

having no daughter. I want you to get acquainted with Marilla.'

The granddaughter was still awed and anxious about the entertainment of so distinguished a guest when her grandmother appeared at last in the pantry.

'I ain't goin' to let you do no such a thing, darlin',' said Abby Hender, when Marilla spoke of making something that she called 'fairy gems' for tea, after a new and essentially feminine recipe. 'You just let me get supper to-night. The Gen'ral has enough kickshaws to eat; he wants a good, hearty, old-fashioned supper, – the same country cooking he remembers when he was a boy. He went so far himself as to speak of rye drop-cakes, an' there ain't one in a hundred, nowadays, knows how to make the kind he means. You go an' lay the table just as we always have it, except you can get out them old big sprigged cups o' my mother's. Don't put on none o' the parlour cluset things.'

Marilla went off crestfallen and demurring. She had a noble desire to show Mr. Laneway that they knew how to have things as well as anybody, and was sure that he would consider it more polite to be asked into the best room, and to sit there alone until tea was ready; but the illustrious Mr. Laneway was allowed to stay in the kitchen, in apparent happiness, and to watch the proceedings from beginning to end. The two old friends talked industriously, but he saw his rye dropcakes go into the oven and come out, and his tea made, and his piece of salt fish broiled and buttered, a broad piece of honeycomb set on to match some delightful thick slices of brown-crusted loaf bread, and all the simple feast prepared. There was a sufficient piece of Abby Hender's best cheese;

it must be confessed that there were also some baked beans, and, as one thing after another appeared, the Honourable Joseph K. Laneway grew hungrier and hungrier, until he fairly looked pale with anticipation and delay, and was bidden at that very moment to draw up his chair and make himself a supper if he could. What cups of tea, what uncounted rye drop-cakes, went to the making of that successful supper! How gay the two old friends became, and of what old stories they reminded each other, and how late the dark spring evening grew before the feast was over and the straight-backed chairs were set against the kitchen wall!

Marilla listened for a time with more or less interest, but at last she took one of her school-books, with slight ostentation, and went over to study by the lamp. Mrs. Hender had brought her knitting-work, a blue woollen stocking, out of a drawer, and sat down serene and unruffled, prepared to keep awake as late as possible. She was a woman who had kept her youthful looks through the difficulties of farm life as few women can, and this added to her guest's sense of homelikeness and pleasure. There was something that he felt to be sisterly and comfortable in her strong figure; he even noticed the little plaid woollen shawl that she wore about her shoulders. Dear, uncomplaining heart of Abby Hender! The appealing friendliness of the good woman made no demands except to be allowed to help and to serve everybody who came in her way.

Now began in good earnest the talk of old times, and what had become of this and that old schoolmate; how one family had come to want and another to wealth. The changes and losses and windfalls of good fortune in that rural neighbour-

A NATIVE OF WINBY

hood were made tragedy and comedy by turns in Abby Hender's dramatic speech. She grew younger and more entertaining hour by hour, and beguiled the grave Senator into confidential talk of national affairs. He had much to say, to which she listened with rare sympathy and intelligence. She astonished him by her comprehension of difficult questions of the day, and by her simple good sense. Marilla grew hopelessly sleepy, and departed, but neither of them turned to notice her as she lingered a moment at the door to say good-night. When the immediate subjects of conversation were fully discussed, however, there was an unexpected interval of silence, and, after making sure that her knitting stitches counted exactly right, Abby Hender cast a questioning glance at the Senator to see if he had it in mind to go to bed. She was reluctant to end her evening so soon, but determined to act the part of considerate hostess. The guest was as wide awake as ever: eleven o'clock was the best part of his evening.

'Cider?' he suggested, with an expectant smile, and Abby Hender was on her feet in a moment. When she had brought a pitcher from the pantry, he took a candle from the high shelf and led the way.

'To think of your remembering our old cellar candlestick all these years!' laughed the pleased woman, as she followed him down the steep stairway, and then laughed still more at his delight in the familiar look of the place.

'Unchanged as the pyramids!' he said. 'I suppose those pound sweetings that used to be in that farthest bin were eaten up months ago?'

It was plain to see that the household stores were waning

low, as befitted the time of year, but there was still enough in the old cellar. Care and thrift and gratitude made the poor farmhouse a rich place. This woman of real ability had spent her strength from youth to age, and had lavished as much industry and power of organization in her narrow sphere as would have made her famous in a wider one. Joseph Laneway could not help sighing as he thought of it. How many things this good friend had missed, and yet how much she had been able to win that makes everywhere the very best of life! Poor and early widowed, there must have been a constant battle with poverty on that stony Harran farm, whose owners had been pitied even in his early boyhood, when the best of farming life was none too easy. But Abby Hender had always been one of the leaders of the town.

'Now, before we sit down again, I want you to step into my best room. Perhaps you won't have time in the morning, and I've got something to show you,' she said persuasively.

It was a plain, old-fashioned best room, with a look of pleasantness in spite of the spring chill and the stiffness of the best chairs. They lingered before the picture of Mrs. Hender's soldier son, a poor work of a poorer artist in crayons, but the spirit of the young face shone out appealingly. Then they crossed the room and stood before some bookshelves, and Abby Hender's face brightened into a beaming smile of triumph.

'You didn't expect we should have all those books, now, did you, Joe Laneway?' she asked.

He shook his head soberly, and leaned forward to read the titles. There were no very new ones, as if times had been hard of late; almost every volume was either history, or bio-

A NATIVE OF WINBY

graphy, or travel. Their owner had reached out of her own narrow boundaries into other lives and into far countries. He recognized with gratitude two or three congressional books that he had sent her when he first went to Washington, and there was a life of himself, written from a partisan point of view, and issued in one of his most exciting campaigns; the sight of it touched him to the heart, and then she opened it, and showed him the three or four letters that he had written her, – one, in boyish handwriting, describing his adventures on his first Western journey.

'There are a hundred and six volumes now,' announced the proud owner of such a library. 'I lend 'em all I can, or most of them would look better. I have had to wait a good while for some, and some weren't what I expected 'em to be, but most of 'em 's as good books as there is in the world. I've never been so situated that it seemed best for me to indulge in a daily paper, and I don't know but it's just as well; but stories were never any great of a temptation. I know pretty well what's goin' on about me, and I can make that do. Real life 's interestin' enough for me.'

Mr. Laneway was still looking over the books. His heart smote him for not being thoughtful; he knew well enough that the overflow of his own library would have been delightful to this self-denying, eager-minded soul. 'I've been a very busy man all my life, Abby,' he said impulsively, as if she waited for some apology for his forgetfulness, 'but I'll see to it now that you have what you want to read. I don't mean to lose hold of your advice on state matters.' They both laughed, and he added, 'I've always thought of you, if I haven't shown it.'

'There's more time to read than there used to be; I've had what was best for me,' answered the woman gently, with a grateful look on her face, as she turned to glance at her old friend. 'Marilla takes hold wonderfully and helps me with the work. In the long winter evenings you can't think what a treat a new book is. I wouldn't change places with the Queen.'

They had come back to the kitchen, and she stood before the cupboard, reaching high for two old gayly striped crockery mugs. There were some doughnuts and cheese at hand; their early supper seemed quite forgotten. The kitchen was warm, and they had talked themselves thirsty and hungry; but with what an unexpected tang the cider freshened their throats! Mrs. Hender had picked the apples herself that went to the press; they were all chosen from the old russet tree and the gnarly, red-cheeked, ungrafted fruit that grew along the lane. The flavour made one think of frosty autumn mornings on high hillsides, of north winds and sunny skies. 'It 'livens one to the heart,' as Mrs. Hender remarked proudly, when the Senator tried to praise it as much as it deserved, and finally gave a cheerful laugh, such as he had not laughed for many a day.

'Why, it seems like drinking the month of October,' he told her; and at this the hostess reached over, protesting that the striped mug was too narrow to hold what it ought, and filled it up again.

'Oh, Joe Laneway, to think that I see you at last, after all these years!' she said. 'How rich I shall feel with this evening to live over! I've always wanted to see somebody that I'd read about, and now I've got that to remember; but I've

A NATIVE OF WINBY

always known I should see you again, and I believe 't was the Lord's will.'

Early the next morning they said good-bye. The early breakfast had to be hurried, and Marilla was to drive Mr. Laneway to the station, three miles away. It was Saturday morning, and she was free from school.

Mr. Laneway strolled down the lane before breakfast was ready, and came back with a little bunch of pink anemones in his hand. Marilla thought that he meant to give them to her, but he laid them beside her grandmother's plate. 'You mustn't put those in your desk,' he said with a smile, and Abby Hender blushed like a girl.

'I've got those others now, dried and put away somewhere in one of my books,' she said quietly, and Marilla wondered what they meant.

The two old friends shook hands warmly at parting. 'I wish you could have stayed another day, so I could have had the minister come and see you,' urged Mrs. Hender regretfully.

'You couldn't have done any more for me. I have had the best visit in the world,' he answered, a little shaken, and holding her hand a moment longer, while Marilla sat, young and impatient, in the high wagon. 'You're a dear good woman, Abby. Sometimes when things have gone wrong I've been sorry that I ever had to leave Winby.'

The woman's clear eyes looked straight into his; then fell. 'You wouldn't have done everything you have for the country,' she said.

'Give me a kiss; we're getting to be old folks now,' said the General; and they kissed each other gravely.

A moment later Abby Hender stood alone in her dooryard, watching and waving her hand again and again, while the wagon rattled away down the lane and turned into the highroad.

Two hours afterwards Marilla returned from the station, and rushed into the kitchen.

'Grandma!' she exclaimed, 'you never did see such a crowd in Winby as there was at the depot! Everybody in town had got word about General Laneway, and they were pushing up to shake hands, and cheering same as at election, and the cars waited much as ten minutes, and all the folks was lookin' out of the windows, and came out on the platforms when they heard who it was. Folks say that he'd been to see the selectmen yesterday before he came to school, and he's goin' to build an elegant town hall, and have the names put up in it of all the Winby men that went to the war.' Marilla sank into a chair, flushed with excitement. 'Everybody was asking me about his being here last night and what he said to the school. I wished that you'd gone down to the depot instead of me.'

'I had the best part of anybody,' said Mrs. Hender, smiling and going on with her Saturday morning work. 'I'm real glad they showed him proper respect,' she added a moment afterwards, but her voice faltered.

'Why, you ain't been cryin', grandma?' asked the girl. 'I guess you're tired. You had a real good time, now, didn't you?'

A NATIVE OF WINBY

'Yes, dear heart!' said Abby Hender. "'T ain't pleasant to be growin' old, that's all. I couldn't help noticin' his age as he rode away. I've always been lookin' forward to seein' him again, an' now it's all over.'

AUNT CYNTHY DALLETT

★

I

'No,' said Mrs. Hand, speaking wistfully, – 'no, we never were in the habit of keeping Christmas at our house. Mother died when we were all young; she would have been the one to keep up with all new ideas, but father and grandmother were old-fashioned folks, and – well, you know how 't was then, Miss Pendexter: nobody took much notice of the day except to wish you a Merry Christmas.'

'They didn't do much to make it merry, certain,' answered Miss Pendexter. 'Sometimes nowadays I hear folks complainin' o' bein' overtaxed with all the Christmas work they have to do.'

'Well, others think that it makes a lovely chance for all that really enjoys givin'; you get an opportunity to speak your kind feelin' right out,' answered Mrs. Hand, with a bright smile. 'But there! I shall always keep New Year's Day, too; it won't do no hurt to have an extra day kept an' made pleasant. And there's many of the real old folks have got pretty things to remember about New Year's Day.'

'Aunt Cynthy Dallett's just one of 'em,' said Miss Pendexter. 'She's always very reproachful if I don't get up to see her. Last year I missed it, on account of a light fall o' snow that seemed to make the walkin' too bad, an' she sent a neighbour's boy 'way down from the mount'in to see if I was sick. Her lameness confines her to the house altogether now, an' I have her on my mind a good deal. How anybody does get thinkin' of those that lives alone, as they get older! I waked

AUNT CYNTHY DALLETT

up only last night with a start, thinkin' if Aunt Cynthy's house should get afire or anything, what she would do, 'way up there all alone. I was half dreamin', I s'pose, but I couldn't seem to settle down until I got up an' went upstairs to the north garret window to see if I could see any light; but the mountains was all dark an' safe, same 's usual. I remember noticin' last time I was there that her chimney needed pointin', and I spoke to her about it, – the bricks looked poor in some places.'

'Can you see the house from your north gable window?' asked Mrs. Hand, a little absently.

'Yes'm; it's a great comfort that I can,' answered her companion. 'I have often wished we were near enough to have her make me some sort o' signal in case she needed help. I used to plead with her to come down and spend the winters with me, but she told me one day I might as well try to fetch down one o' the old hemlocks, an' I believe 't was true.'

'Your aunt Dallett is a very self-contained person,' observed Mrs. Hand.

'Oh, very!' exclaimed the elderly niece, with a pleased look. 'Aunt Cynthy laughs, an' says she expects the time will come when age 'll compel her to have me move up an' take care of her; and last time I was there she looked up real funny, an' says, "I do' know, Abby; I'm most afeard sometimes that I feel myself beginnin' to look for'ard to it!" 'T was a good deal, comin' from Aunt Cynthy, an' I so esteemed it.'

'She ought to have you there now,' said Mrs. Hand. 'You'd both make a savin' by doin' it; but I don't expect she needs to save as much as some. There! I know just how you both feel. I like to have my own home an' do everything just my way too.' And the friends laughed, and looked at each other affectionately.

'There was old Mr. Nathan Dunn, – left no debts an' no money when he died,' said Mrs. Hand. "'T was over to his niece's last summer. He had a little money in his wallet, an' when the bill for funeral expenses come in there was just exactly enough; some item or other made it come to so many dollars an' eighty-four cents, and, lo an' behold! there was eighty-four cents in a little separate pocket beside the neat fold o' bills, as if the old gentleman had known beforehand. His niece couldn't help laughin', to save her; she said the old gentleman died as methodical as he lived. She didn't expect he had any money, an' was prepared to pay for everything herself; she's very well off.'

"'T was funny, certain,' said Miss Pendexter. 'I expect he felt comfortable, knowin' he had that money by him. 'T is a comfort, when all's said and done, 'specially to folks that's gettin' old.'

A sad look shadowed her face for an instant, and then she smiled and rose to take leave, looking expectantly at her hostess to see if there were anything more to be said.

'I hope to come out square myself,' she said, by way of farewell pleasantry; 'but there are times when I feel doubtful.'

Mrs. Hand was evidently considering something, and waited a moment or two before she spoke. 'Suppose we both walk up to see your aunt Dallett, New Year's Day, if it ain't too windy and the snow keeps off?' she proposed. 'I couldn't rise the hill if 't was a windy day. We could take a hearty breakfast an' start in good season; I'd rather walk than ride, the road's so rough this time o' year.'

AUNT CYNTHY DALLETT

'Oh, what a person you are to think o' things! I did so dread goin' 'way up there all alone,' said Abby Pendexter. 'I'm no hand to go off alone, an' I had it before me, so I really got to dread it. I do so enjoy it after I get there, seein' Aunt Cynthy, an' she's always so much better than I expect to find her.'

'Well, we'll start early,' said Mrs. Hand cheerfully; and so they parted. As Miss Pendexter went down the foot-path to the gate, she sent grateful thoughts back to the little sitting-room she had just left.

'How doors are opened!' she exclaimed to herself. 'Here I've been so poor an' distressed at beginnin' the year with nothin', as it were, that I couldn't think o' even goin' to make poor old Aunt Cynthy a friendly call. I'll manage to make some kind of a little pleasure too, an' somethin' for dear Mis' Hand. "Use what you've got," mother always used to say when every sort of an emergency come up, an' I may only have wishes to give, but I'll make 'em good ones!'

II

The first day of the year was clear and bright, as if it were a New Year's pattern of what winter can be at its very best. The two friends were prepared for changes of weather, and met each other well wrapped in their winter cloaks and shawls, with sufficient brown barége veils tied securely over their bonnets. They ignored for some time the plain truth that each carried something under her arm; the shawls were rounded out suspiciously, especially Miss Pendexter's, but each respected the other's air of secrecy. The narrow road was frozen in deep ruts, but a smooth-trodden little foot-path that ran along its edge was very inviting to the wayfarers. Mrs. Hand walked first and Miss Pendexter followed, and they were talking busily nearly all the way, so that they had to stop for breath now and then at the tops of the little hills. It was not a hard walk; there were a good many almost level stretches through the woods, in spite of the fact that they should be a very great deal higher when they reached Mrs. Dallett's door.

'I do declare, what a nice day 't is, an' such pretty footin'!' said Mrs. Hand, with satisfaction. 'Seems to me as if my feet went o' themselves; gener'lly I have to toil so when I walk that I can't enjoy nothin' when I get to a place.'

'It's partly this beautiful bracin' air,' said Abby Pendexter. 'Sometimes such nice air comes just before a fall of snow. Don't it seem to make anybody feel young again and to take all your troubles away?'

Mrs. Hand was a comfortable, well-to-do soul, who seldom worried about anything, but something in her companion's tone touched her heart, and she glanced sidewise and saw a pained look in Abby Pendexter's thin face. It was a moment for confidence.

'Why, you speak as if something distressed your mind, Abby,' said the elder woman kindly.

'I ain't one that has myself on my mind as a usual thing, but it does seem now as if I was goin' to have it very hard,' said Abby. 'Well, I've been anxious before.'

'Is it anything wrong about your property?' Mrs. Hand ventured to ask.

'Only that I ain't got any,' answered Abby, trying to speak gayly. "T was all I could do to pay my last quarter's rent,

AUNT CYNTHY DALLETT

twelve dollars. I sold my hens, all but this one that had run away at the time, an' now I'm carryin' her up to Aunt Cynthy, roasted just as nice as I know how.'

'I thought you was carrying somethin',' said Mrs. Hand, in her usual tone. 'For me, I've got a couple o' my mince pies. I thought the old lady might like 'em; one we can eat for our dinner, and one she shall have to keep. But weren't you unwise to sacrifice your poultry, Abby? You always need eggs, and hens don't cost much to keep.'

'Why, yes, I shall miss 'em,' said Abby; 'but, you see, I had to do every way to get my rent-money. Now the shop's shut down I haven't got any way of earnin' anything, and I spent what little I've saved through the summer.'

'Your aunt Cynthy ought to know it an' ought to help you,' said Mrs. Hand. 'You're a real foolish person, I must say. I expect you do for her when she ought to do for you.'

'She's old, an' she's all the near relation I've got,' said the little woman. 'I've always felt the time would come when she'd need me, but it's been her great pleasure to live alone an' feel free. I shall get along somehow, but I shall have it hard. Somebody may want help for a spell this winter, but I'm afraid I shall have to give up my house. 'T ain't as if I owned it. I don't know just what to do, but there'll be a way.'

Mrs. Hand shifted her two pies to the other arm, and stepped across to the other side of the road where the ground looked a little smoother.

'No, I wouldn't worry if I was you, Abby,' she said. "There, I suppose if 't was me I should worry a good deal more! I expect I should lay awake nights.' But Abby answered nothing, and they came to a steep place in the road and found another subject for conversation at the top.

'Your aunt don't know we're coming?' asked the chief guest of the occasion.

'Oh, no, I never send her word,' said Miss Pendexter. 'She'd be so desirous to get everything ready, just as she used to.'

'She never seemed to make any trouble o' havin' company; she always appeared so easy and pleasant, and let you set with her while she made her preparations,' said Mrs. Hand, with great approval. 'Some has such a dreadful way of making you feel inopportune, and you can't always send word you're comin'. I did have a visit once that's always been a lesson to me; 't was years ago; I don't know's I ever told you?'

'I don't believe you ever did,' responded the listener to this somewhat indefinite prelude.

'Well, 't was one hot summer afternoon. I set forth an' took a great long walk 'way over to Mis' Eben Fulham's, on the crossroad between the cranberry ma'sh and Staples's Corner. The doctor was drivin' that way, an' he give me a lift that shortened it some at the last; but I never should have started, if I'd known 't was so far. I had been promisin' all summer to go, and every time I saw Mis' Fulham, Sundays, she'd say somethin' about it. We wa'n't very well acquainted, but always friendly. She moved here from Bedford Hill.'

'Oh, yes; I used to know her,' said Abby, with interest.

'Well, now, she did give me a beautiful welcome when I got there,' continued Mrs. Hand. "T was about four o'clock in the afternoon, an' I told her I'd come to accept her invitation if 't was convenient, an' the doctor had been called several

AUNT CYNTHY DALLETT

miles beyond and expected to be detained, but he was goin' to pick me up as he returned about seven; 't was very kind of him. She took me right in, and she did appear so pleased, an' I must go right into the best room where 't was cool, and then she said she'd have tea early, and I should have to excuse her a short time. I asked her not to make any difference, and if I couldn't assist her; but she said no, I must just take her as I found her; and she give me a large fan, and off she went.

'There. I was glad to be still and rest where 't was cool, an' I set there in the rockin'-chair an' enjoyed it for a while, an' I heard her clacking at the oven door out beyond, an' gittin' out some dishes. She was a brisk-actin' little woman, an' I thought I'd caution her when she come back not to make up a great fire, only for a cup o' tea, perhaps. I started to go right out in the kitchen, an' then somethin' told me I'd better not, we never'd been so free together as that; I didn't know how she'd take it, an' there I set an' set. 'T was sort of a greenish light in the best room, an' it begun to feel a little damp to me, – the s'rubs outside grew close up to the windows. Oh, it did seem dreadful long! I could hear her busy with the dishes an' beatin' eggs an' stirrin', an' I knew she was puttin' herself out to get up a great supper, and I kind o' fidgeted about a little an' even stepped to the door, but I thought she'd expect me to remain where I was. I saw everything in that room forty times over, an' I did divert myself killin' off a brood o' moths that was in a worsted-work mat on the table. It all fell to pieces. I never saw such a sight o' moths to once. But occupation failed after that, an' I begun to feel sort o' tired an' numb. There was one o' them late crickets got into the room an' begun to chirp, an' it sounded kind o' fallish. I couldn't help sayin' to myself that Mis' Fulham had forgot all about my bein' there. I thought of all the beauties of hospitality that ever I see! –'

'Didn't she ever come back at all, not whilst things was in the oven, nor nothin'?' inquired Miss Pendexter, with awe.

'I never see her again till she come beamin' to the parlour door an' invited me to walk out to tea,' said Mrs. Hand. "T was 'most a quarter past six by the clock; I thought 't was seven. I'd thought o' everything, an' I'd counted, an' I'd trotted my foot, an' I'd looked more'n twenty times to see if there was any more moth-millers."

'I s'pose you did have a very nice tea?' suggested Abby, with interest.

'Oh, a beautiful tea! She couldn't have done more if I'd been the Queen,' said Mrs. Hand. 'I don't know how she could ever have done it all in the time, I'm sure. The table was loaded down; there was cup-custards and custard pie, an' cream pie, an' two kinds o' hot biscuits, an' black tea as well as green, an' elegant cake, – one kind she'd just made new, and called it quick cake; I've often made it since – an' she'd opened her best preserves, two kinds. We set down together, an' I'm sure I appreciated what she'd done; but 't wa'n't no time for real conversation whilst we was to the table, and before we got quite through the doctor come hurryin' along, an' I had to leave. He asked us if we'd had a good talk, as we come out, an' I couldn't help laughing to myself; but she said quite hearty that she'd had a nice visit from me. She appeared well satisfied, Mis' Fulham did; but for me, I was disappointed; an' early that fall she died.'

AUNT CYNTHY DALLETT

Abby Pendexter was laughing like a girl; the speaker's tone had grown more and more complaining. 'I do call that a funny experience,' she said. ' "Better a dinner o' herbs." I guess that text must ha' risen to your mind in connection. You must tell that to Aunt Cynthy, if conversation seems to fail.' And she laughed again, but Mrs. Hand still looked solemn and reproachful.

'Here we are; there's Aunt Cynthy's lane right ahead, there by the great yellow birch,' said Abby. 'I must say, you've made the way seem very short, Mis' Hand.'

III

Old Aunt Cynthia Dallett sat in her high-backed rocking-chair by the little north window, which was her favourite dwelling-place.

'New Year's Day again,' she said, aloud, – 'New Year's Day again!' And she folded her old bent hands, and looked out at the great woodland view and the hills without really seeing them, she was lost in so deep a reverie. 'I'm gittin' to be very old,' she added, after a little while.

It was perfectly still in the small grey house. Outside in the apple-trees there were some blue-jays flitting about and calling noisily, like schoolboys fighting at their games. The kitchen was full of pale winter sunshine. It was more like late October than the first of January, and the plain little room seemed to smile back into the sun's face. The outer door was standing open into the green dooryard, and a fat small dog lay asleep on the step. A capacious cupboard stood behind Mrs. Dallett's chair and kept the wind away from her corner. Its doors and drawers were painted a clean lead-colour, and there were places round the knobs and buttons where the touch of hands had worn deep into the wood. Every braided rug was straight on the floor. The square clock on its shelf between the front windows looked as if it had just had its face washed and been wound up for a whole year to come. If Mrs. Dallett turned her head she could look into the bedroom, where her plump feather bed was covered with its dark blue homespun winter quilt. It was all very peaceful and comfortable, but it was very lonely. By her side, on a light-stand, lay the religious newspaper of her denomination, and a pair of spectacles whose jointed silver bows looked like a funny two-legged beetle cast helplessly upon its back.

'New Year's Day again,' said old Cynthia Dallett. Time had left nobody in her house to wish her a Happy New Year, – she was the last one left in the old nest. 'I'm gittin' to be very old,' she said for the second time; it seemed to be all there was to say.

She was keeping a careful eye on her friendly clock, but it was hardly past the middle of the morning, and there was no excuse for moving; it was the long hour between the end of her slow morning work and the appointed time for beginning to get dinner. She was so stiff and lame that this hour's rest was usually most welcome, but to-day she sat as if it were Sunday, and did not take up her old shallow splint basket of braiding-rags from the side of her footstool.

'I do hope Abby Pendexter 'll make out to git up to see me this afternoon as usual,' she continued. 'I know 't ain't so easy for her to get up the hill as it used to be, but I do seem to want to see some o' my own folks. I wish 't I'd thought to send her word I expected her when Jabez Hooper went back

AUNT CYNTHY DALLETT

after he came up here with the flour. I'd like to have had her come prepared to stop two or three days.'

A little chickadee perched on the windowsill outside and bobbed his head sideways to look in, and then pecked impatiently at the glass. The old woman laughed at him with childish pleasure and felt companioned; it was pleasant at that moment to see the life in even a bird's bright eye.

'Sign of a stranger,' she said, as he whisked his wings and flew away in a hurry. 'I must throw out some crumbs for 'em; it's getting to be hard pickin' for the stayin'-birds.' She looked past the trees of her little orchard now with seeing eyes, and followed the long forest slopes that led downward to the lowland country. She could see the two white steeples of Fairfield Village, and the map of fields and pastures along the valley beyond, and the great hills across the valley to the westward. The scattered houses looked like toys that had been scattered by children. She knew their lights by night, and watched the smoke of their chimneys by day. Far to the northward were higher mountains, and these were already white with snow. Winter was already in sight, but to-day the wind was in the south, and the snow seemed only part of a great picture.

'I do hope the cold 'll keep off a while longer,' thought Mrs. Dallett. 'I don't know how I'm going to get along after the deep snow comes.'

The little dog suddenly waked, as if he had had a bad dream, and after giving a few anxious whines he began to bark outrageously. His mistress tried, as usual, to appeal to his better feelings.

"T ain't nobody, Tiger,' she said. 'Can't you have some

patience? Maybe it's some foolish boys that's rangin' about with their guns.' But Tiger kept on, and even took the trouble to waddle in on his short legs, barking all the way. He looked warningly at her, and then turned and ran out again. Then she saw him go hurrying down to the bars, as if it were an occasion of unusual interest.

'I guess somebody is comin'; he don't act as if 't were a vagrant kind o' noise; must really be somebody in our lane.' And Mrs. Dallett smoothed her apron and gave an anxious housekeeper's glance round the kitchen. None of her state visitors, the minister or the deacons, ever came in the morning. Country people are usually too busy to go visiting in the forenoons.

Presently two figures appeared where the road came out of the woods, – the two women already known to the story, but very surprising to Mrs. Dallett; the short, thin one was easily recognized as Abby Pendexter, and the taller, stout one was soon discovered to be Mrs. Hand. Their old friend's heart was in a glow. As the guests approached they could see her pale face with its thin white hair framed under the close black silk handkerchief.

'There she is at her window smilin' away!' exclaimed Mrs. Hand; but by the time they reached the doorstep she stood waiting to meet them.

'Why, you two dear creatur's!' she said, with a beaming smile. 'I don't know when I've ever been so glad to see folks comin'. I had a kind of left-all-alone feelin' this mornin', an' I didn't even make bold to be certain o' you, Abby, though it looked so pleasant. Come right in an' set down. You're all out o' breath, ain't you, Mis' Hand?'

AUNT CYNTHY DALLETT

Mrs. Dallett led the way with eager hospitality. She was the tiniest little bent old creature, her handkerchiefed head was quick and alert, and her eyes were bright with excitement and feeling, but the rest of her was much the worse for age; she could hardly move, poor soul, as if she had only a make-believe framework of a body under a shoulder-shawl and thick petticoats. She got back to her chair again, and the guests took off their bonnets in the bedroom, and returned discreet and sedate in their black woollen dresses. The lonely kitchen was blest with society at last, to its mistress's heart's content. They talked as fast as possible about the weather, and how warm it had been walking up the mountain, and how cold it had been a year ago, that day when Abby Pendexter had been kept at home by a snowstorm and missed her visit. 'And I ain't seen you now, aunt, since the twenty-eighth of September, but I've thought of you a great deal, and looked forward to comin' more'n usual,' she ended, with an affectionate glance at the pleased old face by the window.

'I've been wantin' to see you, dear, and wonderin' how you was gettin' on,' said Aunt Cynthy kindly. 'And I take it as a great attention to have you come to-day, Mis' Hand,' she added, turning again towards the more distinguished guest. 'We have to put one thing against another. I should hate dreadfully to live anywhere except on a high hill farm, 'cordin' as I was born an' raised. But there ain't the chance to neighbour that townfolks has, an' I do seem to have more lonely hours than I used to when I was younger. I don't know but I shall soon be gittin' too old to live alone.' And she turned to her niece with an expectant, lovely look, and Abby smiled back.

'I often wish I could run in an' see you every day, aunt,' she answered. 'I have been sayin' so to Mrs. Hand.'

'There, how anybody does relish company when they don't have but a little of it!' exclaimed Aunt Cynthia. 'I am all alone to-day; there is going to be a shootin'-match somewhere the other side o' the mountain, an' Johnny Foss, that does my chores, begged off to go when he brought the milk unusual early this mornin'. Gener'lly he's about here all the fore part of the day; but he don't go off with the boys very often, and I like to have him have a little sport; 't was New Year's Day, anyway; he's a good stiddy boy for my wants.'

'Why, I wish you Happy New Year, aunt!' said Abby, springing up with unusual spirit. 'Why, that's just what we come to say, and we like to have forgot all about it!' She kissed her aunt, and stood a minute holding her hand with a soft affectionate touch. Mrs. Hand rose and kissed Mrs. Dallett too, and it was a moment of ceremony and deep feeling.

'I always like to keep the day,' said the old hostess, as they seated themselves and drew their splint-bottomed chairs a little nearer together than before. 'You see, I was brought up to it, and father made a good deal of it; he said he liked to make it pleasant and give the year a fair start. I can see him now, how he used to be standing there by the fireplace when we came out o' the two bedrooms early in the morning, an' he always made out, poor's he was, to give us some little present, and he'd heap 'em up on the corner o' the mantelpiece, an' we'd stand front of him in a row, and mother be bustling about gettin' breakfast. One year he give me a beautiful copy o' the *Life o' General Lafayette*, in a green cover, – I've got it now, but we child'n 'bout read it to pieces, – an' one year a nice piece o'

AUNT CYNTHY DALLETT

blue ribbon, an' Abby – that was your mother, Abby – had a pink one. Father was real kind to his child'n. I thought o' them early days when I first waked up this mornin', and I couldn't help lookin' up then to the corner o' the shelf just as I used to look.'

'There's nothin' so beautiful as to have a bright childhood to look back to,' said Mrs. Hand. 'Sometimes I think child'n has too hard a time now, – all the responsibility is put on to 'em, since they take the lead o' what to do an' what they want, and get to be so toppin' an' knowin'. 'T was happier in the old days, when the fathers an' mothers done the rulin'.'

'They say things have changed,' said Aunt Cynthy; 'but staying right here, I don't know much of any world but my own world.'

Abby Pendexter did not join in this conversation, but sat in her straight-backed chair with folded hands and the air of a good child. The little old dog had followed her in, and now lay sound asleep again at her feet. The front breadth of her black dress looked rusty and old in the sunshine that slanted across it, and the aunt's sharp eyes saw this and saw the careful darns. Abby was as neat as wax, but she looked as if the frost had struck her. 'I declare, she's gittin' along in years,' thought Aunt Cynthia compassionately. 'She begins to look sort o' set and dried up, Abby does. She oughtn't to live all alone; she's one that needs company.'

At this moment Abby looked up with new interest. 'Now, aunt,' she said, in her pleasant voice, 'I don't want you to forget to tell me if there ain't some sewin' or mendin' I can do whilst I'm here. I know your hands trouble you some, an' I may's well tell you we're bent on stayin' all day an' makin' a good visit, Mis' Hand an' me.'

'Thank ye kindly,' said the old woman; 'I do want a little sewin' done before long, but 't ain't no use to spile a good holiday.' Her face took a resolved expression. 'I'm goin' to make other arrangements,' she said. 'No, you needn't come up here to pass New Year's Day an' be put right down to sewin'. I make out to do what mendin' I need, an' to sew on my hooks an' eyes. I get Johnny Ross to thread me up a good lot o' needles every little while, an' that helps me a good deal. Abby, why can't you step into the best room an' bring out the rockin'-chair? I seem to want Mis' Hand to have it.'

'I opened the window to let the sun in awhile,' said the niece, as she returned. 'It felt cool in there an' shut up.'

'I thought of doin' it not long before you come,' said Mrs. Dallett, looking gratified. Once the taking of such a liberty would have been very provoking to her. 'Why, it does seem good to have somebody think o' things an' take right hold like that!'

'I'm sure you would, if you were down at my house,' said Abby, blushing. 'Aunt Cynthy, I don't suppose you could feel as if 't would be best to come down an' pass the winter with me, — just durin' the cold weather, I mean. You'd see more folks to amuse you, an' — I do think of you so anxious these long winter nights.'

There was a terrible silence in the room, and Miss Pendexter felt her heart begin to beat very fast. She did not dare to look at her aunt at first.

Presently the silence was broken. Aunt Cynthia had been

AUNT CYNTHY DALLETT

gazing out of the window, and she turned towards them a little paler and older than before, and smiling sadly.

'Well, dear, I'll do just as you say,' she answered. 'I'm beat by age at last, but I've had my own way for eighty-five years, come the month o' March, an' last winter I did use to lay awake an' worry in the long storms. I'm kind o' humble now about livin' alone to what I was once.' At this moment a new light shone in her face. 'I don't expect you'd be willin' to come up here an' stay till spring, — not if I had Foss's folks stop for you to ride to meetin' every pleasant Sunday, an' take you down to the Corners plenty o' other times besides?' she said beseechingly. 'No, Abby, I'm too old to move now; I should be homesick down to the village. If you'll come an' stay with me, all I have shall be yours. Mis' Hand hears me say it.'

'Oh, don't you think o' that; you're all I've got near to me in the world, an' I'll come an' welcome,' said Abby, though the thought of her own little home gave a hard tug at her heart. 'Yes, Aunt Cynthy, I'll come, an' we'll be real comfortable together. I've been lonesome sometimes —'

"'T will be best for both,' said Mrs. Hand judicially. And so the great question was settled, and suddenly, without too much excitement, it became a thing of the past.

'We must be thinkin' o' dinner,' said Aunt Cynthia gayly. 'I wish I was better prepared; but there's nice eggs an' pork an' potatoes, an' you girls can take hold an' help.' At this moment the roast chicken and the best mince pies were offered and kindly accepted, and before another hour had gone they were sitting at their New Year feast, which Mrs. Dallett decided to be quite proper for the Queen.

Before the guests departed, when the sun was getting low, Aunt Cynthia called her niece to her side and took hold of her hand.

'Don't you make it too long now, Abby,' said she. 'I shall be wantin' ye every day till you come; but you mustn't forgit what a set old thing I be.'

Abby had the kindest of hearts, and was always longing for somebody to love and care for; her aunt's very age and helplessness seemed to beg for pity.

'This is Saturday; you may expect me the early part of the week; and thank you, too, aunt,' said Abby.

Mrs. Hand stood by with deep sympathy. 'It's the proper thing,' she announced calmly. 'You'd both of you be a sight happier; and truth is, Abby's wild an' reckless, an' needs somebody to stand right over her, Mis' Dallett. I guess she'll try an' behave, but there – there's no knowin'!' And they all laughed. Then the New Year guests said farewell and started off down the mountain road. They looked back more than once to see Aunt Cynthia's face at the window as she watched them out of sight. Miss Abby Pendexter was full of excitement; she looked as happy as a child.

'I feel as if we'd gained the battle of Waterloo,' said Mrs. Hand. 'I've really had a most beautiful time. You an' your aunt mustn't forgit to invite me up some time again to spend another day.'

MISS TEMPY'S WATCHERS

★

THE time of year was April; the place was a small farming town in New Hampshire, remote from any railroad. One by one the lights had been blown out in the scattered houses near Miss Tempy Dent's; but as her neighbours took a last look out-of-doors, their eyes turned with instinctive curiosity toward the old house, where a lamp burned steadily. They gave a little sigh. 'Poor Miss Tempy!' said more than one bereft acquaintance; for the good woman lay dead in her north chamber, and the light was a watcher's light. The funeral was set for the next day, at one o'clock.

The watchers were two of the oldest friends, Mrs. Crowe and Sarah Ann Binson. They were sitting in the kitchen, because it seemed less awesome than the unused best room, and they beguiled the long hours by steady conversation. One would think that neither topics nor opinions would hold out, at that rate, all through the long spring night; but there was a certain degree of excitement just then, and the two women had risen to an unusual level of expressiveness and confidence. Each had already told the other more than one fact that she had determined to keep secret; they were again and again tempted into statements that either would have found impossible by daylight. Mrs. Crowe was knitting a blue yarn stocking for her husband; the foot was already so long that it seemed as if she must have forgotten to narrow it at the proper time. Mrs. Crowe knew exactly what she was about, however; she was of a much cooler disposition than Sister Binson, who made futile attempts at some sewing, only to drop her work into her lap whenever the talk was most engaging.

Their faces were interesting, – of the dry, shrewd, quick-witted New England type, with thin hair twisted neatly back out of the way. Mrs. Crowe could look vague and benignant, and Miss Binson was, to quote her neighbours, a little too sharp-set; but the world knew that she had need to be, with the load she must carry of supporting an inefficient widowed sister and six unpromising and unwilling nieces and nephews. The eldest boy was at last placed with a good man to learn the mason's trade. Sarah Ann Binson, for all her sharp, anxious aspect, never defended herself, when her sister whined and fretted. She was told every week of her life that the poor children never would have had to lift a finger if their father had lived, and yet she had kept her steadfast way with the little farm, and patiently taught the young people many useful things, for which, as everybody said, they would live to thank her. However pleasureless her life appeared to outward view, it was brimful of pleasure to herself.

Mrs. Crowe, on the contrary, was well to do, her husband being a rich farmer and an easy-going man. She was a stingy woman, but for all that she looked kindly; and when she gave away anything, or lifted a finger to help anybody, it was thought a great piece of beneficence, and a compliment, indeed, which the recipient accepted with twice as much gratitude as double the gift that came from a poorer and more generous acquaintance. Everybody liked to be on good terms with Mrs. Crowe. Socially she stood much higher than Sarah Ann Binson. They were both old schoolmates and friends of Temperance Dent, who had asked them, one day, not long

MISS TEMPY'S WATCHERS

before she died, if they would not come together and look after the house, and manage everything, when she was gone. She may have had some hope that they might become closer friends in this period of intimate partnership, and that the richer woman might better understand the burdens of the poorer. They had not kept the house the night before; they were too weary with the care of their old friend, whom they had not left until all was over.

There was a brook which ran down the hillside very near the house, and the sound of it was much louder than usual. When there was silence in the kitchen, the busy stream had a strange insistence in its wild voice, as if it tried to make the watchers understand something that related to the past.

'I declare, I can't begin to sorrow for Tempy yet. I am so glad to have her at rest,' whispered Mrs. Crowe. 'It is strange to set here without her, but I can't make it clear that she has gone. I feel as if she had got easy and dropped off to sleep, and I'm more scared about waking her up than knowing any other feeling.'

'Yes,' said Sarah Ann, 'it's just like that, ain't it? But I tell you we are goin' to miss her worse than we expect. She's helped me through with many a trial, has Temperance. I ain't the only one who says the same, neither.'

These words were spoken as if there were a third person listening; somebody beside Mrs. Crowe. The watchers could not rid their minds of the feeling that they were being watched themselves. The spring wind whistled in the window crack, now and then, and buffeted the little house in a gusty way that had a sort of companionable effect. Yet, on the whole, it was a very still night, and the watchers spoke in a half-whisper.

'She was the freest-handed woman that ever I knew,' said Mrs. Crowe, decidedly. 'According to her means, she gave away more than anybody. I used to tell her 't wa'n't right. I used really to be afraid that she went without too much, for we have a duty to ourselves.'

Sister Binson looked up in a half-amused, unconscious way, and then recollected herself.

Mrs. Crowe met her look with a serious face. 'It ain't so easy for me to give as it is for some,' she said simply, but with an effort which was made possible only by the occasion. 'I should like to say, while Tempy is laying here yet in her own house, that she has been a constant leason to me. Folks are too kind, and shame me with thanks for what I do. I ain't such a generous woman as poor Tempy was, for all she had nothin' to do with, as one may say.'

Sarah Binson was much moved at this confession, and was even pained and touched by the unexpected humility. 'You have a good many calls on you' — she began, and then left her kind little compliment half finished.

'Yes, yes, but I've got means enough. My disposition's more of a cross to me as I grow older, and I made up my mind this morning that Tempy's example should be my pattern henceforth.' She began to knit faster than ever.

''T ain't no use to get morbid; that's what Tempy used to say herself,' said Sarah Ann, after a minute's silence. 'Ain't it strange to say "used to say"?' and her own voice choked a little. 'She never did like to hear folks git goin' about themselves.'

MISS TEMPY'S WATCHERS

"'T was only because they're apt to do it so as other folks will say 't wasn't so, an' praise 'em up,' humbly replied Mrs. Crowe, 'and that ain't my object. There wa'n't a child but what Tempy set herself to work to see what she could do to please it. One time my brother's folks had been stopping here in the summer, from Massachusetts. The children was all little, and they broke up a sight of toys, and left 'em when they were going away. Tempy come right up after they rode by, to see if she couldn't help me set the house to rights, and she caught me just as I was going to fling some of the clutter into the stove. I was kind of tired out, starting 'em off in season. "Oh, give me them!" says she, real pleading; and she wropped 'em up and took 'em home with her when she went, and she mended 'em up and stuck 'em together, and made some young one or other happy with every blessed one. You'd thought I'd done her the biggest favour. "No thanks to me. I should ha' burnt 'em, Tempy," says I.'

'Some of 'em came to our house, I know,' said Miss Binson. 'She'd take a lot o' trouble to please a child, 'stead o' shoving of it out o' the way, like the rest of us when we're drove.'

'I can tell you the biggest thing she ever done, and I don't know 's there's anybody left but me to tell it. I don't want it forgot,' Sarah Binson went on, looking up at the clock to see how the night was going. 'It was that pretty-looking Trevor girl, who taught the Corners school, and married so well afterwards, out in New York State. You remember her, I dare say?'

'Certain,' said Mrs. Crowe, with an air of interest.

'She was a splendid scholar, folks said, and give the school a great start; but she'd overdone herself getting her education,

THE ONLY ROSE AND OTHER TALES

and working to pay for it, and she all broke down one spring, and Tempy made her come and stop with her a while, – you remember that? Well, she had an uncle, her mother's brother, out in Chicago, who was well off and friendly, and used to write to Lizzie Trevor, and I dare say make her some presents; but he was a lively, driving man, and didn't take time to stop and think about his folks. He hadn't seen her since she was a little girl. Poor Lizzie was so pale and weakly that she just got through the term o' school. She looked as if she was just going straight off in a decline. Tempy, she cosseted her up a while, and then, next thing folks knew, she was tellin' round how Miss Trevor had gone to see her uncle, and meant to visit Niagary Falls on the way, and stop over night. Now I happened to know, in ways I won't dwell on to explain, that the poor girl was in debt for her schoolin' when she come here, and her last quarter's pay had just squared it off at last, and left her without a cent ahead, hardly; but it had fretted her thinking of it, so she paid it all; those might have dunned her that she owed it to. An' I taxed Tempy about the girl's goin' off on such a journey till she owned up, rather 'n have Lizzie blamed, that she'd given her sixty dollars, same 's if she was rolling in riches, and sent her off to have a good rest and vacation.'

'Sixty dollars!' exclaimed Mrs. Crowe. 'Tempy only had ninety dollars a year that came in to her; rest of her livin' she got by helpin' about, with what she raised off this little piece o' ground, sand one side an' clay the other. An' how often I've heard her tell, years ago, that she'd rather see Niagary than any other sight in the world!'

The women looked at each other in silence; the magnitude

MISS TEMPY'S WATCHERS

of the generous sacrifice was almost too great for their comprehension.

'She was just poor enough to do that!' declared Mrs. Crowe at last, in an abandonment of feeling. 'Say what you may, I feel humbled to the dust,' and her companion ventured to say nothing. She never had given away sixty dollars at once, but it was simply because she never had it to give. It came to her very lips to say in explanation, 'Tempy was so situated'; but she checked herself in time, for she would not betray her own loyal guarding of a dependent household.

'Folks say a great deal of generosity, and this one's being public-sperited, and that one free-handed about giving,' said Mrs. Crowe, who was a little nervous in the silence. 'I suppose we can't tell the sorrow it would be to some folks not to give, same 's 't would be to me not to save. I seem kind of made for that, as if 't was what I'd got to do. I should feel sights better about it if I could make it evident what I was savin' for. If I had a child, now, Sarah Ann,' and her voice was a little husky, – 'if I had a child, I should think I was heapin' of it up because he was the one trained by the Lord to scatter it again for good. But here's Mr. Crowe and me, we can't do anything with money, and both of us like to keep things same's they've always been. Now Priscilla Dance was talking away like a mill-clapper, week before last. She'd think I would go right off and get one o' them new-fashioned gilt-and-white papers for the best room, and some new furniture, an' a marble-top table. And I looked at her, all struck up. "Why," says I, "Priscilla, that nice old velvet paper ain't hurt a mite. I shouldn't feel 't was my best room without it. Dan'el says 't is the first thing he can remember, rubbin' his little baby fingers on to it, and how splendid he thought them red roses was." I maintain,' continued Mrs. Crowe stoutly, 'that folks wastes sights o' good money doin' just such foolish things. Tearin' out the insides o' meetin'-houses, and fixin' the pews different; 't was good enough as 't was with mendin'; then times come, an' they want to put it all back same's 't was before.'

This touched upon an exciting subject to active members of that parish. Miss Binson and Mrs. Crowe belonged to opposite parties, and had at one time come as near hard feelings as they could, and yet escape them. Each hastened to speak of other things and to show her untouched friendliness.

'I do agree with you,' said Sister Binson, ' that few of us know what use to make of money, beyond every-day necessities. You've seen more o' the world than I have, and know what's expected. When it comes to taste and judgment about such things, I ought to defer to others;' and with this modest avowal the critical moment passed when there might have been an improper discussion.

In the silence that followed, the fact of their presence in a house of death grew more clear than before. There was something disturbing in the noise of a mouse gnawing at the dry boards of a closet wall near by. Both the watchers looked up anxiously at the clock; it was almost the middle of the night, and the whole world seemed to have left them alone with their solemn duty. Only the brook was awake.

'Perhaps we might give a look upstairs now,' whispered Mrs. Crowe, as if she hoped to hear some reason against their going just then to the chamber of death; but Sister Binson

MISS TEMPY'S WATCHERS

rose, with a serious and yet satisfied countenance, and lifted the small lamp from the table. She was much more used to watching than Mrs. Crowe, and much less affected by it. They opened the door into a small entry with a steep stairway; they climbed the creaking stairs, and entered the cold upper room on tiptoe. Mrs. Crowe's heart began to beat very fast as the lamp was put on a high bureau, and made long, fixed shadows about the walls. She went hesitatingly toward the solemn shape under its white drapery, and felt a sense of remonstrance as Sarah Ann gently, but in a business-like way, turned back the thin sheet.

'Seems to me she looks pleasanter and pleasanter,' whispered Sarah Ann Binson impulsively, as they gazed at the white face with its wonderful smile. ' To-morrow 't will all have faded out. I do believe they kind of wake up a day or two after they die, and it's then they go.' She replaced the light covering, and they both turned quickly away; there was a chill in this upper room.

"'T is a great thing for anybody to have got through, ain't it?' said Mrs. Crowe softly, as she began to go down the stairs on tiptoe. The warm air from the kitchen beneath met them with a sense of welcome and shelter.

'I don' know why it is, but I feel as near again to Tempy down here as I do up there,' replied Sister Binson. 'I feel as if the air was full of her, kind of. I can sense things, now and then, that she seems to say. Now I never was one to take up with no nonsense of sperits and such, but I declare I felt as if she told me just now to put some more wood into the stove.'

Mrs. Crowe preserved a gloomy silence. She had suspected

before this that her companion was of a weaker and more credulous disposition than herself. "'T is a great thing to have got through,' she repeated, ignoring definitely all that had last been said. 'I suppose you know as well as I that Tempy was one that always feared death. Well, it's all put behind her now; she knows what 't is.' Mrs. Crowe gave a little sigh, and Sister Binson's quick sympathies were stirred toward this other old friend, who also dreaded the great change.

'I'd never like to forgit almost those last words Tempy spoke plain to me,' she said gently, like the comforter she truly was. 'She looked up at me once or twice, that last afternoon after I come to set by her, and let Mis' Owen go home; and I says, "Can I do anything to ease you, Tempy?" and the tears come into my eyes so I couldn't see what kind of a nod she give me. "No, Sarah Ann, you can't, dear," says she; and then she got her breath again, and says she, looking at me real meanin', "I'm only a-gettin' sleepier and sleepier; that's all there is," says she, and smiled up at me kind of wishful, and shut her eyes. I knew well enough all she meant. She'd been lookin' out for a chance to tell me, and I don' know's she ever said much afterwards.'

Mrs. Crowe was not knitting; she had been listening too eagerly. 'Yes, 't will be a comfort to think of that sometimes,' she said, in acknowledgment.

'I know that old Dr. Prince said once, in evenin' meetin', that he'd watched by many a dyin' bed, as we well knew, and enough o' his sick folks had been scared o' dyin' their whole lives through; but when they come to the last, he'd never seen one but was willin', and most were glad, to go. "'T is as natural as bein' born or livin' on," he said. I don't

MISS TEMPY'S WATCHERS

know what had moved him to speak that night. You know he wa'n't in the habit of it, and 't was the monthly concert of prayer for foreign missions anyways,' said Sarah Ann; 'but 't was a great stay to the mind to listen to his words of experience.'

'There never was a better man,' responded Mrs. Crowe, in a really cheerful tone. She had recovered from her feeling of nervous dread, the kitchen was so comfortable with lamp-light and firelight; and just then the old clock began to tell the hour of twelve with leisurely whirring strokes.

Sister Binson laid aside her work, and rose quickly and went to the cupboard. 'We'd better take a little to eat,' she explained. 'The night will go fast after this. I want to know if you went and made some o' your nice cupcake, while you was home to-day?' she asked, in a pleased tone; and Mrs. Crowe acknowledged such a gratifying piece of thoughtfulness for this humble friend who denied herself all luxuries. Sarah Ann brewed a generous cup of tea, and the watchers drew their chairs up to the table presently, and quelled their hunger with good country appetites. Sister Binson put a spoon into a small, old-fashioned glass of preserved quince, and passed it to her friend. She was most familiar with the house, and played the part of hostess. 'Spread some o' this on your bread and butter,' she said to Mrs. Crowe. 'Tempy wanted me to use some three or four times, but I never felt to. I know she'd like to have us comfortable now, and would urge us to make a good supper, poor dear.'

'What excellent preserves she did make!' mourned Mrs. Crowe. 'None of us has got her light hand at doin' things tasty. She made the most o' everything, too. Now, she only had that one old quince-tree down in the far corner of the piece, but she'd go out in the spring and tend to it, and look at it so pleasant, and kind of expect the old thorny thing into bloomin'.'

'She was just the same with folks,' said Sarah Ann. 'And she'd never git more'n a little apernful o' quinces, but she'd have every mite o' goodness out o' those, and set the glasses up onto her best-room closet shelf, *so* pleased. 'T wa'n't but a week ago to-morrow mornin' I fetched her a little taste o' jelly in a teaspoon; and she says "Thank ye," and took it, an' the minute she tasted it she looked up at me as worried as could be. "Oh, I don't want to eat that," says she. "I always keep that in case o' sickness." "You're goin' to have the good o' one tumbler yourself," says I. "I'd just like to know who's sick now, if you ain't!" An' she couldn't help laughin', I spoke up so smart. Oh, dear me, how I shall miss talkin' over things with her! She always sensed things, and got just the p'int you meant.'

'She didn't begin to age until two or three years ago, did she?' asked Mrs. Crowe. 'I never saw anybody keep her looks as Tempy did. She looked young long after I begun to feel like an old woman. The doctor used to say 't was her young heart, and I don't know but what he was right. How she did do for other folks! There was one spell she wasn't at home a day to a fortnight. She got most of her livin' so, and that made her own potatoes and things last her through. None o' the young folks could get married without her, and all the old ones was disappointed if she wa'n't round when they was down with sickness and had to go. An' cleanin', or tailorin' for boys, or rug-hookin', – there was nothin' but

MISS TEMPY'S WATCHERS

what she could do as handy as most. "I do love to work," — ain't you heard her say that twenty times a week?'

Sarah Ann Binson nodded, and began to clear away the empty plates. 'We may want a taste o' somethin' more towards mornin',' she said. 'There's plenty in the closet here; and in case some comes from a distance to the funeral, we'll have a little table spread after we get back to the house.'

'Yes, I was busy all the mornin'. I've cooked up a sight o' things to bring over,' said Mrs. Crowe. 'I felt 't was the last I could do for her.'

They drew their chairs near the stove again, and took up their work. Sister Binson's rocking-chair creaked as she rocked; the brook sounded louder than ever. It was more lonely when nobody spoke, and presently Mrs. Crowe returned to her thoughts of growing old.

'Yes, Tempy aged all of a sudden. I remember I asked her if she felt as well as common, one day, and she laughed at me good. There, when Mr. Crowe begun to look old, I couldn't help feeling as if somethin' ailed him, and like as not 't was somethin' he was goin' to git right over, and I dosed him for it stiddy, half of one summer.'

'How many things we shall be wanting to ask Tempy!' exclaimed Sarah Ann Binson, after a long pause. 'I can't make up my mind to doin' without her. I wish folks could come back just once, and tell us how 't is where they've gone. Seems then we could do without 'em better.'

The brook hurried on, the wind blew about the house now and then; the house itself was a silent place, and the supper, the warm fire, and an absence of any new topics for conversation made the watchers drowsy. Sister Binson closed her eyes first, to rest them for a minute; and Mrs. Crowe glanced at her compassionately, with a new sympathy for the hard-worked little woman. She made up her mind to let Sarah Ann have a good rest, while she kept watch alone; but in a few minutes her own knitting was dropped, and she, too, fell asleep. Overhead, the pale shape of Tempy Dent, the out-worn body of that generous, loving-hearted, simple soul, slept on also in its white raiment. Perhaps Tempy herself stood near, and saw her own life and its surroundings with new understanding. Perhaps she herself was the only watcher.

Later, by some hours, Sarah Ann Binson woke with a start. There was a pale light of dawn outside the small windows. Inside the kitchen, the lamp burned dim. Mrs. Crowe awoke, too.

'I think Tempy'd be the first to say 't was just as well we both had some rest,' she said, not without a guilty feeling.

Her companion went to the outer door, and opened it wide. The fresh air was none too cold, and the brook's voice was not nearly so loud as it had been in the midnight darkness. She could see the shapes of the hills, and the great shadows that lay across the lower country. The east was fast growing bright.

"'T will be a beautiful day for the funeral,' she said, and turned again, with a sigh, to follow Mrs. Crowe up the stairs.

THE DULHAM LADIES

★

To be leaders of society in the town of Dulham was as satisfactory to Miss Dobin and Miss Lucinda Dobin as if Dulham were London itself. Of late years, though they would not allow themselves to suspect such treason, the most ill-bred of the younger people in the village made fun of them behind their backs, and laughed at their treasured summer mantillas, their mincing steps, and the shape of their parasols.

They were always conscious of the fact that they were the daughters of a once eminent Dulham minister; but beside this unanswerable claim to the respect of the First Parish, they were aware that their mother's social position was one of superior altitude. Madam Dobin's grandmother was a Greenaple of Boston. In her younger days she had often visited her relatives, the Greenaples and Hightrees, and in seasons of festivity she could relate to a select and properly excited audience her delightful experiences of town life. Nothing could be finer than her account of having taken tea at Governor Clovenfoot's, on Beacon Street, in company with an English lord, who was indulging himself in a brief vacation from his arduous duties at the Court of St. James.

'He exclaimed that he had seldom seen in England so beautiful and intelligent a company of ladies,' Madam Dobin would always say in conclusion. 'He was decorated with the blue ribbon of the Knights of the Garter.' Miss Dobin and Miss Lucinda thought for many years that this famous blue ribbon was tied about the noble gentleman's leg. One day they even discussed the question openly; Miss Dobin placing the decoration at his knee, and Miss Lucinda locating it much lower down, according to the length of the short grey socks with which she was familiar.

'You have no imagination, Lucinda,' the elder sister replied impatiently. 'Of course, those were the days of small-clothes and long silk stockings!' – whereat Miss Lucinda was rebuked, but not persuaded.

'I wish that my dear girls could have the outlook upon society which fell to my portion,' Madam Dobin sighed, after she had set these ignorant minds to rights, and enriched them by communicating the final truth about the blue ribbon. 'I must not chide you for the absence of opportunities, but if our cousin Harriet Greenaple were only living, you would not lack enjoyment or social education.'

Madam Dobin had now been dead a great many years. She seemed an elderly woman to her daughters some time before she left them; they thought later that she had really died comparatively young, since their own years had come to equal the record of hers. When they visited her tall white tombstone in the orderly Dulham burying-ground, it was a strange thought to both the daughters that they were older women than their mother had been when she died. To be sure, it was the fashion to appear older in her day, – they could remember the sober effect of really youthful married persons in cap and frisette; but, whether they owed it to the changed times or to their own qualities, they felt no older themselves than ever they had. Beside upholding the ministerial dignity of their father, they were obliged to give a lenient sanction to the ways of the world

THE DULHAM LADIES

for their mother's sake; and they combined the two duties with reverence and impartiality.

Madam Dobin was, in her prime, a walking example of refinement and courtesy. If she erred in any way, it was by keeping too strict watch and rule over her small kingdom. She acted with great dignity in all matters of social administration and etiquette, but, while it must be owned that the parishioners felt a sense of freedom for a time after her death, in their later years they praised and valued her more and more, and often lamented her generously and sincerely.

Several of her distinguished relatives attended Madam Dobin's funeral, which was long considered the most dignified and elegant pageant of that sort which had ever taken place in Dulham. It seemed to mark the close of a famous epoch in Dulham history, and it was increasingly difficult for ever afterward to keep the tone of society up to the old standard. Somehow, the distinguished relatives had one by one disappeared, though they all had excellent reasons for the discontinuance of their visits. A few had left this world altogether, and the family circle of the Greenaples and Hightrees was greatly reduced in circumference. Sometimes, in summer, a stray connection drifted Dulham-ward, and was displayed to the townspeople (not to say paraded) by the gratified hostesses. It was a disappointment if the guest could not be persuaded to remain over Sunday and appear at church. When household antiquities became fashionable, the ladies remarked upon a surprising interest in their corner cupboard and best chairs, and some distant relatives revived their almost forgotten custom of paying a summer visit to Dulham. They were not long in finding out with what desperate affection

Miss Dobin and Miss Lucinda clung to their mother's wedding china and other inheritances, and were allowed to depart without a single teacup. One graceless descendant of the Hightrees prowled from garret to cellar, and admired the household belongings diligently, but she was not asked to accept even the dislocated cherry-wood footstool that she had discovered in the far corner of the parsonage pew.

Some of the Dulham friends had always suspected that Madame Dobin made a social misstep when she chose the Reverend Edward Dobin for her husband. She was no longer young when she married, and though she had gone through the wood and picked up a crooked stick at last, it made a great difference that her stick possessed an ecclesiastical bark. The Reverend Edward was, moreover, a respectable graduate of Harvard College, and to a woman of her standards a clergyman was by no means insignificant. It was impossible not to respect his office, at any rate, and she must have treated him with proper veneration for the sake of that, if for no other reason, though his early advantages had been insufficient, and he was quite insensible to the claims of the Greenaple pedigree, and preferred an Indian pudding to pie crust that was, without exaggeration, half a quarter high. The delicacy of Madam Dobin's touch and preference in everything, from hymns to cookery, was quite lost upon this respected preacher, yet he was not without pride or complete confidence in his own decisions.

The Reverend Mr. Dobin was never very enlightening in his discourses, and was providentially stopped short by a stroke of paralysis in the middle of his clerical career. He lived on and on through many dreary years, but his children

THE DULHAM LADIES

never accepted the fact that he was a tyrant, and served him humbly and patiently. He fell at last into a condition of great incapacity and chronic trembling, but was able for nearly a quarter of a century to be carried to the meeting-house from time to time to pronounce farewell discourses. On high days of the church he was always placed in the pulpit, and held up his shaking hands when the benediction was pronounced, as if the divine gift were exclusively his own, and the other minister did but say empty words. Afterward he was usually tired and displeased and hard to cope with, but there was always a proper notice taken of these too often recurring events. For old times' and for pity's sake and from natural goodness of heart, the elder parishioners rallied manfully about the Reverend Mr. Dobin; and whoever his successor or colleague might be, the Dobins were always called the minister's folks, while the active labourer in that vineyard was only Mr. Smith or Mr. Jones, as the case might be. At last the poor old man died, to everybody's relief and astonishment; and after he was properly preached about and lamented, his daughters, Miss Dobin and Miss Lucinda, took a good look at life from a new standpoint, and decided that, now they were no longer constrained by home duties, they must make themselves of a great deal more use to the town.

Sometimes there is such a household as this (which has been perhaps too minutely described), where the parents linger until their children are far past middle age, and always keep them in a too childish and unworthy state of subjection. The Misses Dobin's characters were much influenced by such an unnatural prolongation of the filial relationship, and they were amazingly slow to suspect that they were not so young as they used to be. There was nothing to measure themselves by but Dulham people and things. The elm trees were growing yet, and many of the ladies of the First Parish were older than they, and called them, with pleasant familiarity, the Dobin girls. These elderly persons seemed really to be growing old, and Miss Lucinda frequently lamented the change in society; she thought it a freak of nature and too sudden blighting of earthly hopes that several charming old friends of her mother's were no longer living. They were advanced in age when Miss Lucinda was a young girl, though time and space are but relative, after all.

Their influence upon society would have made a great difference in many ways. Certainly, the new parishioners, who had often enough been instructed to pronounce their pastor's name as if it were spelled with one 'b,' would not have boldly returned again and again to their obnoxious habit of saying Dobbin. Miss Lucinda might carefully speak to the neighbour and new-comers of 'my sister, Miss Do-bin'; only the select company of intimates followed her lead, and at last there was something humiliating about it, even though many persons spoke of them only as 'the ladies.'

'The name was originally *D'Aubigne*, we think,' Miss Lucinda would say coldly and patiently, as if she had already explained this foolish mistake a thousand times too often. It was like the sorrows in many a provincial château in the Reign of Terror. The ladies looked on with increasing dismay at the retrogression in society. They felt as if they were a feeble garrison, to whose lot it had fallen to repulse a noisy, irreverent mob, an increasing band of marauders who would overthrow all landmarks of the past, all etiquette and social

THE DULHAM LADIES

rank. The new minister himself was a round-faced, unspiritual-looking young man, whom they would have instinctively ignored if he had not been a minister. The new people who came to Dulham were not like the older residents, and they had no desire to be taught better. Little they cared about the Greenaples or the Hightrees; and once, when Miss Dobin essayed to speak of some detail of her mother's brilliant experiences in Boston high life, she was interrupted, and the new-comer who sat next her at the parish sewing society began to talk about something else. We cannot believe that it could have been the tea-party at Governor Clovenfoot's which the rude creature so disrespectfully ignored, but some persons are capable of showing any lack of good taste.

The ladies had an unusual and most painful sense of failure, as they went home together that evening. 'I have always made it my object to improve and interest the people at such times; it would seem so possible to elevate their thoughts and direct them into higher channels,' said Miss Dobin sadly. 'But as for that Woolden woman, there is no use in casting pearls before swine!'

Miss Lucinda murmured an indignant assent. She had a secret suspicion that the Woolden woman had heard the story in question oftener than had pleased her. She was but an ignorant creature; though she had lived in Dulham twelve or thirteen years, she was no better than when she came. The mistake was in treating sister Harriet as if she were on a level with the rest of the company. Miss Lucinda had observed more than once, lately, that her sister sometimes repeated herself, unconsciously, a little oftener than was agreeable. Perhaps they were getting a trifle dull; towards spring it might be well to pass a few days with some of their friends, and have a change.

'If I have tried to do anything,' said Miss Dobin in an icy tone, 'it has been to stand firm in my lot and place, and to hold the standard of cultivated mind and elegant manners as high as possible. You would think it had been a hundred years since our mother's death, so completely has the effect of her good breeding and exquisite hospitality been lost sight of, here in Dulham. I could wish that our father had chosen to settle in a larger and more appreciative place. They would like to put us on the shelf, too. I can see that plainly.'

'I am sure we have our friends,' said Miss Lucinda anxiously, but with a choking voice. 'We must not let them think we do not mean to keep up with the times, as we always have. I do feel as if perhaps – our hair –'

And the sad secret was out at last. Each of the sisters drew a long breath of relief at this beginning of a confession.

It was certain that they must take some steps to retrieve their lost ascendency. Public attention had that evening been called to their fast-disappearing locks, poor ladies; and Miss Lucinda felt the discomfort most, for she had been the inheritor of the Hightree hair, long and curly, and chestnut in colour. There used to be a waviness about it, and sometimes pretty escaping curls, but these were gone long ago. Miss Dobin resembled her father, and her hair had not been luxuriant, so that she was less changed by its absence than one might suppose. The straightness and thinness had increased so gradually that neither sister had quite accepted the thought that other persons would particularly notice their altered appearance.

THE DULHAM LADIES

They had shrunk, with the reticence born of close family association, from speaking of the cause even to each other, when they made themselves pretty little lace and dotted muslin caps. Breakfast caps, they called them, and explained that these were universally worn in town; the young Princess of Wales originated them, or at any rate adopted them. The ladies offered no apology for keeping the breakfast caps on until bedtime, and in spite of them a forward child had just spoken, loud and shrill, an untimely question in the ears of the for once silent sewing society. 'Do Miss Dobinses wear them great caps because their heads is cold?' the little beast had said; and everybody was startled and dismayed.

Miss Dobin had never shown better her good breeding and valour, the younger sister thought.

'No, little girl,' replied the stately Harriet, with a chilly smile. 'I believe that our headdresses are quite in the fashion for ladies of all ages. And you must remember that it is never polite to make such personal remarks.' It was after this that Miss Dobin had been reminded of Madam Somebody's unusual headgear at the evening entertainment in Boston. Nobody but the Woolden woman could have interrupted her under such trying circumstances.

Miss Lucinda, however, was certain that the time had come for making some effort to replace her lost adornment. The child had told an unwelcome truth, but had paved the way for further action, and now was the time to suggest something that had slowly been taking shape in Miss Lucinda's mind. A young grand-nephew of their mother and his bride had passed a few days with them, two or three summers before, and the sisters had been quite shocked to find that the pretty young woman wore a row of frizzes, not originally her own, over her smooth forehead. At the time, Miss Dobin and Miss Lucinda had spoken severely with each other of such bad taste, but now it made a great difference that the wearer of the frizzes was not only a relative by marriage and used to good society, but also that she came from town, and might be supposed to know what was proper in the way of toilet.

'I really think, sister, that we had better see about having some – arrangements, next time we go anywhere,' Miss Dobin said unexpectedly, with a slight tremble in her voice, just as they reached their own door. 'There seems to be quite a fashion for them nowadays. For the parish's sake we ought to recognize' – and Miss Lucinda responded with instant satisfaction. She did not like to complain, but she had been troubled with neuralgic pains in her forehead on suddenly meeting the cold air. The sisters felt a new bond of sympathy in keeping this secret with and for each other; they took pains to say to several acquaintances that they were thinking of going to the next large town to do a few errands for Christmas.

A bright, sunny morning seemed to wish the ladies good-fortune. Old Hetty Downs, their faithful maid-servant and protector, looked after them in affectionate foreboding. 'Dear sakes, what devil's wiles may be played on them blessed innocents afore they're safe home again?' she murmured, as they vanished round the corner of the street that led to the railway station.

Miss Dobin and Miss Lucinda paced discreetly side by side down the main street of Westbury. It was nothing like Boston, of course, but the noise was slightly confusing, and the passers-by sometimes roughly pushed against them. West-

THE DULHAM LADIES

bury was a consequential manufacturing town, but a great convenience at times like this. The trifling Christmas gifts for their old neighbours and Sunday-school scholars were purchased and stowed away in their neat Fayal basket before the serious commission of the day was attended to. Here and there, in the shops, disreputable frizzes were displayed in unblushing effrontery, but no such vulgar shopkeeper merited the patronage of the Misses Dobin. They pretended not to observe the unattractive goods, and went their way to a low, one-storied building on a side street, where an old tradesman lived. He had been useful to the minister while he still remained upon the earth and had need of a wig, sandy in hue and increasingly sprinkled with grey, as if it kept pace with other changes of existence. But old Paley's shutters were up, and a bar of rough wood was nailed firmly across the one that had lost its fastening and would rack its feeble hinges in the wind. Old Paley had always been polite and bland; they really had looked forward to a little chat with him; they had heard a year or two before of his wife's death, and meant to offer sympathy. His business of hair-dressing had been carried on with that of parasol and umbrella mending, and the condemned umbrella which was his sign flapped and swung in the rising wind, a tattered skeleton before the closed door. The ladies sighed and turned away; they were beginning to feel tired; the day was long, and they had not met with any pleasures yet. 'We might walk up the street a little farther,' suggested Miss Lucinda; 'that is, if you are not tired,' as they stood hesitating on the corner after they had finished a short discussion of Mr. Paley's disappearance. Happily it was only a few minutes before they came to a stop together in front of a new, shining shop, where smirking waxen heads all in a row were decked with the latest fashions of wigs and frizzes. One smiling fragment of a gentleman stared so straight at Miss Lucinda with his black eyes that she felt quite coy and embarrassed, and was obliged to feign not to be conscious of his admiration. But Miss Dobin, after a brief delay, boldly opened the door and entered; it was better to be sheltered in the shop than exposed to public remark as they gazed in at the windows. Miss Lucinda felt her heart beat and her courage give out; she, coward like, left the transaction of their business to her sister, and turned to contemplate the back of the handsome model. It was a slight shock to find that he was not so attractive from this point of view. The wig he wore was well made all round, but his shoulders were roughly finished in a substance that looked like plain plaster of Paris.

'What can I have ze pleasure of showing you, young ladees?' asked a person who advanced; and Miss Lucinda faced about to discover a smiling, middle-aged Frenchman, who rubbed his hands together and looked at his customers, first one and then the other, with delightful deference. He seemed a very civil nice person, the young ladies thought.

'My sister and I were thinking of buying some little arrangements to wear above the forehead,' Miss Dobin explained, with pathetic dignity; but the Frenchman spared her any further words. He looked with eager interest at the bonnets, as if no lack had attracted his notice before. 'Ah, yes. *Je comprends;* ze high foreheads are not now ze mode. Je prefer them, **moi**, yes, yes, but ze ladees must accept ze fashion; zay must now cover ze forehead with ze frizzes, ze bangs, you say. As you wis', as you wis'!' and the tactful little man, with many shrugs and merry gestures at such girlish fancies, pulled down one box after another.

It was a great relief to find that this was no worse, to say the least, than any other shopping, though the solemnity and secrecy of the occasion were infringed upon by the great supply of 'arrangements' and the loud discussion of the colour of some crimps a noisy girl was buying from a young saleswoman the other side of the shop.

Miss Dobin waved aside the wares which were being displayed for her approval. 'Something – more simple, if you please,' – she did not like to say 'older.'

'But these are *très simple*,' protested the Frenchman. 'We have nothing younger'; and Miss Dobin and Miss Lucinda blushed, and said no more. The Frenchman had his own way; he persuaded them that nothing was so suitable as some conspicuous forelocks that matched their hair as it used to be. They would have given anything rather than leave their breakfast caps at home, if they had known that their proper winter bonnets must come off. They hardly listened to the wig merchant's glib voice as Miss Dobin stood revealed before the merciless mirror at the back of the shop.

He made everything as easy as possible, the friendly creature, and the ladies were grateful to him. Besides, now that the bonnet was on again there was a great improvement in Miss Dobin's appearance. She turned to Miss Lucinda, and saw a gleam of delight in her eager countenance. 'It really is very becoming. I like the way it parts over your forehead,' said the younger sister, 'but if it were long enough to go behind the ears' – '*Non, non,*' entreated the Frenchman. 'To make her the old woman at once would be cruelty!' And Lucinda, who was wondering how well she would look in her turn, succumbed promptly to such protestations. Yes, there was no use in being old before their time. Dulham was not quite keeping pace with the rest of the world in these days, but they need not drag behind everybody else just because they lived there.

The price of the little arrangements was much less than the sisters expected, and the uncomfortable expense of their reverend father's wigs had been, it was proved, a thing of the past. Miss Dobin treated her polite Frenchman with great courtesy; indeed, Miss Lucinda had more than once whispered to her to talk French, and as they were bowed out of the shop the gracious *Bongsure* of the elder lady seemed to act like the string of a showerbath, and bring down an awesome torrent of foreign phrases upon the two guileless heads. It was impossible to reply; the ladies bowed again, however, and Miss Lucinda caught a last smile from the handsome wax countenance in the window. He appeared to regard her with fresh approval, and she departed down the street with mincing steps.

'I feel as if anybody might look at me now, sister,' said gentle Miss Lucinda. 'I confess, I have really suffered sometimes, since I knew I looked so distressed.'

'Yours is lighter than I thought it was in the shop,' remarked Miss Dobin doubtfully, but she quickly added that perhaps it would change a little. She was so perfectly satisfied with her own appearance that she could not bear to dim the pleasure of anyone else. The truth remained that she never would have let Lucinda choose that particular arrangement if she had seen it first in a good light. And Lucinda was thinking exactly the same of her companion.

THE DULHAM LADIES

'I am sure we shall have no more neuralgia,' said Miss Dobin. 'I am sorry we waited so long, dear,' and they tripped down the main street of Westbury, confident that nobody would suspect them of being over thirty. Indeed, they felt quite girlish, and unconsciously looked sideways as they went along, to see their satisfying reflections in the windows. The great panes made excellent mirrors, with not too clear or lasting pictures of these comforted passers-by.

The Frenchman in the shop was making merry with his assistants. The two great frisettes had long been out of fashion; he had been lying in wait with them for two unsuspecting country ladies, who could be cajoled into such a purchase.

'Sister,' Miss Lucinda was saying, 'you know there is still an hour to wait before our train goes. Suppose we take a little longer walk down the other side of the way'; and they strolled slowly back again. In fact, they nearly missed the train, naughty girls! Hetty would have been so worried, they assured each other, but they reached the station just in time.

'Lutie,' said Miss Dobin, 'put up your hand and part it from your forehead; it seems to be getting a little out of place'; and Miss Lucinda, who had just got breath enough to speak, returned the information that Miss Dobin's was almost covering her eyebrows. They might have to trim them a little shorter; of course it could be done. The darkness was falling; they had taken an early dinner before they started, and now they were tired and hungry after the exertion of the afternoon, but the spirit of youth flamed afresh in their hearts, and they were very happy. If one's heart remains young, it is a sore trial to have the outward appearance entirely at variance. It was the ladies' nature to be girlish, and they found it impossible not to be grateful to the flimsy, ineffectual disguise which seemed to set them right with the world. The old conductor, who had known them for many years, looked hard at them as he took their tickets, and, being a man of humour and compassion, affected not to notice anything remarkable in their appearance. 'You ladies never mean to grow old, like the rest of us,' he said gallantly, and the sisters fairly quaked with joy. Their young hearts would forever keep them truly unconscious of the cruel thievery of time.

'Bless us!' the obnoxious Mrs. Woolden was saying, at the other end of the car. 'There's the old maid Dobbinses, and they've bought 'em some bangs. I expect they wanted to get thatched in a little before real cold weather; but don't they look just like a pair o' poodle dogs.'

The little ladies descended wearily from the train. Somehow they did not enjoy a day's shopping as much as they used. They were certainly much obliged to Hetty for sending her niece's boy to meet them, with a lantern; also for having a good warm supper ready when they came in. Hetty took a quick look at her mistresses, and returned to the kitchen. 'I knew somebody would be foolin' of 'em,' she assured herself angrily, but she had to laugh. Their dear, kind faces were wrinkled and pale, and the great frizzes had lost their pretty curliness, and were hanging down, almost straight and very ugly, into the ladies' eyes. They could not tuck them up under their caps, as they were sure might be done.

Then came a succession of rainy days, and nobody visited the rejuvenated household. The frisettes looked very bright chestnut by the light of day, and it must be confessed that Miss

THE DULHAM LADIES

Dobin took the scissors and shortened Miss Lucinda's half an inch, and Miss Lucinda returned the compliment quite secretly, because each thought her sister's forehead lower than her own. Their dear grey eyebrows were honestly displayed, as if it were the fashion not to have them match with wigs. Hetty at last spoke out, and begged her mistresses, as they sat at breakfast, to let her take the frizzes back and change them. Her sister's daughter worked in that very shop, and though in the workroom, would be able to oblige them, Hetty was sure.

But the ladies looked at each other in pleased assurance, and then turned together to look at Hetty, who stood already a little apprehensive near the table, where she had just put down a plateful of smoking drop-cakes. The good creature really began to look old.

'They are worn very much in town,' said Miss Dobin. 'We think it was quite fortunate that the fashion came in just as our hair was growing a trifle thin. I dare say we may choose those that are a shade duller in colour when these are a little past. Oh, we shall not want tea this evening, you remember, Hetty. I am glad there is likely to be such a good night for the sewing circle.' And Miss Dobin and Miss Lucinda nodded and smiled.

'Oh, my sakes alive!' the troubled handmaiden groaned. 'Going to the circle, be they, to be snickered at! Well, the Dobbin girls they was born, and the Dobbin girls they will remain till they die; but if they ain't innocent Christian babes to those that knows 'em well, mark me down for an idjit myself! They believe them front-pieces has set the clock back forty year or more, but if they're pleased to think so, let 'em!'

Away paced the Dulham ladies, late in the afternoon, to grace the parish occasion, and face the amused scrutiny of their neighbours. 'I think we owe it to society to observe the fashions of the day,' said Miss Lucinda. 'A lady cannot afford to be unattractive. I feel now as if we were prepared for anything!'

MISS PECK'S PROMOTION
★

Miss Peck had spent a lonely day in her old farm-house, high on a long Vermont hillside that sloped toward the west. She was able for an hour at noon to overlook the fog in the valley below, and pitied the people in the village whose location she could distinguish only by means of the church steeple which pricked through the grey mist, like a buoy set over a dangerous reef. During this brief time, when the sun was apparently shining for her benefit alone, she reflected proudly on the advantage of living on high land, but in the early afternoon, when the fog began to rise slowly, and at last shut her in, as well as the rest of the world, she was conscious of uncommon depression of spirits.

'I might as well face it now as any time,' she said aloud, as she lighted her clean kerosene lamp and put it on the table. 'Eliza Peck! just set down and make it blazing clear how things stand with you, and what you're going to do in regard to 'em! 'T ain't no use matching your feelin's to the weather, without you've got reason for it.' And she twitched the short curtains across the windows so that their brass rings squeaked on the wires, opened the door for the impatient cat that was mewing outside, and then seated herself in the old rocking-chair at the table end.

It is quite a mistake to believe that people who live by themselves find every day a lonely one. Miss Peck and many other solitary persons could assure us that it is very seldom that they feel their lack of companionship. As the habit of living alone grows more fixed, it becomes confusing to have other people about, and seems more or less bewildering to be interfered with by other people's plans and suggestions. Only once in a while does the feeling of solitariness become burdensome, or a creeping dread and sense of defencelessness assail one's comfort. But when Miss Peck was aware of the approach of such a mood she feared it, and was prepared to fight it with her best weapon of common sense.

She was much given to talking aloud, as many solitary persons are; not merely talking to herself in the usual half-conscious way, but making her weaker self listen to severe comment and pointed instruction. Miss Peck the less was frequently brought to trial in this way by Miss Peck the greater, and when it was once announced that justice must be done, no amount of quailing or excuse averted the process of definite conviction.

This evening she turned the light up to its full brightness, reached for her knitting-work, lifted it high above her lap for a moment, as her favourite cat jumped up to its evening quarters; then she began to rock to and fro with regularity and decision. "'T is all nonsense,' she said, as if she were addressing someone greatly her inferior, — "t is all nonsense for you to go on this way, Elizy Peck! You're better off than you've been this six year, if you only had sense to feel so.'

There was no audible reply, and the speaker evidently mistook the silence for unconvinced stubbornness.

'If ever there was a woman who was determined to live by other people's wits, and to eat other folks' dinners, 't was and is your lamented brother's widder, Harri't Peck — Harri't White that was. She's claimed the town's compassion till it's good as run dry, and she's thought that you, Elizy Peck,

MISS PECK'S PROMOTION

a hard-workin' and self-supportin' woman, was made for nothin' but her use and comfort. Ever since your father died and you've been left alone you've had her for a clog to your upward way. Six years you've been at her beck and call, and now that a respectable man, able an' willing to do for her, has been an' fell in love with her, and shouldered her and all her whims, and promised to do for the children as if they was his own, you've been grumpin' all day, an' *I'd* like to know what there is to grump about!'

There was a lack of response even to this appeal to reason, and the knitting-needles clicked in dangerous nearness to the old cat's ears, so that they twitched now and then, and one soft paw unexpectedly revealed its white curving claws.

'Yes,' said Miss Peck presently, in a more lenient tone, 'I s'pose 't is the children you're thinking of most. I declare I should like to see that Tom's little red head, and feel it warm with my two hands this minute! There's always somethin' hopeful in havin' to do with children, 'less they come of *too* bad a stock. Grown folks – well, you can make out to grin an' bear 'em if you must; but like 's not young ones 'll turn out to be somebody, and what you do for 'em may count towards it. There's that Tom, he looks just as his father used to, and there ain't a day he won't say somethin' real pleasant, and never sees the difference betwixt you and somebody handsome. I expect they'll spile him – you don't know what kind o' young ones they'll let him play with, nor how they'll let him murder the King's English, and never think o' boxin' his ears. Them big factory towns is all for eatin' and clothes. I'm glad you was raised in a good old academy town, if 't was the Lord's will to plant you in the fur outskirts. Land, how Harri't did smirk at that man! I will say she looked pretty – 't is hard work and worry makes folks plain like me – I believe she's fared better to be left a widder with three child'n, and everybody saying how hard it was, an' takin' holt, than she would if brother had lived and she'd had to stir herself to keep house and do for him. You've been the real widder that Tom left – you've mourned him, and had your way to go alone – not she! The colonel's lady,' repeated Miss Peck scornfully – 'that's what spi'lt her. She never could come down to common things, Mis' Colonel Peck! Well, she may have noble means now, but she's got to be spoke of as Mis' Noah Pigley all the rest of her days. Not that I'm goin' to fling at any man's accident of name,' said the just Eliza, in an apologetic tone. 'I did want to adopt little Tom, but 't was to be expected he'd object – a boy's goin' to be useful in his business, and poor Tommy's the likeliest. I would have 'dopted him out an' out, and he shall have the old farm anyway. But oh dear me, he's all spoilt for farming now, is little Tom, unless I can make sure of him now and then for a good long visit in summer time.

'Summer an' winter; I s'pose you're likely to live a great many years, Elizy,' sighed the good woman. 'All sole alone, too! There! I've landed right at the startin' point,' – and the kitchen was very still while some dropped stitches in a belated stocking for the favourite nephew were obscured by a mist of tears like the fog outside. There was no more talking aloud, for Miss Peck fell into a reverie about old days and the only brother who had left his little household in her care and marched to the war whence for him there was to

MISS PECK'S PROMOTION

be no return. She had remembered very often, with a great sense of comfort, a message in one of his very last letters. 'Tell Eliza that she's more likely to be promoted than I am,' he said (when he had just got his step of Major); 'she's my superior officer, however high I get, and now I've heard what luck she's had with the haying, I appoint her Brigadier-General for gallantry in the field.' How poor Tom's jokes had kept their courage up even when they were most anxious! Yes, she had made many sacrifices of personal gain, as every good soldier must. She had meant to be a schoolteacher. She had the gift for it, and had studied hard in her girlhood. One thing after another had kept her at home, and now she must stay here – her ambitions were at an end. She would do what good she could among her neighbours, and stand in her lot and place. It was the first time she had found to think soberly about her life, for her sister-in-law and the children had gone to their new home within a few days, and since then she had stifled all power of proper reflection by hard work at setting the house in order and getting in her winter supplies. 'Thank Heaven the house and place belong to me,' she said in a decisive tone, ''t was wise o' father to leave it so – and let her have the money. She'd left me no peace till I moved off if I'd only been half-owner; she's always meant to get to a larger place – but what I want is real promotion.'

The Peck farm-house was not only on a by-road that wandered among the slopes of the hills, but it was at the end of a long lane of its own. There was rarely any sound at night except from the winds of heaven or the soughing of the neighbouring pine-trees. By day, there was a beautiful inspiriting outlook over the wide country from the farm-house windows, but on such a night as this the darkness made an impenetrable wall. Miss Peck was not afraid of it; on the contrary, she had a sense of security in being shut safe into the very heart of the night. By day she might be vexed by intruders, by night they could scarcely find her – her bright light could not be seen from the road. If she were to wither away in the old grey house like an unplanted kernel in its shell, she would at least wither undisturbed. Her sorrow of loneliness was not the fear of molestation. She was fearless enough at the thought of physical dangers.

The evening did not seem so long as she expected – a glance at her reliable timekeeper told her at last that it was already past eight o'clock, and her eyes began to feel heavy. The fire was low, the fog was making its presence felt even in the house, for the autumn night was chilly, and Miss Peck decided that when she came to the end of the stitches on a certain needle she would go to bed. To-morrow, she meant to cut her apples for drying, a duty too long delayed. She had sent away some of her best fruit that day to make the annual barrel of cider with which she provided herself, more from habit than from real need of either the wholesome beverage or its resultant vinegar. 'If this fog lasts, I've got to dry my apples by the stove,' she thought, doubtfully, and was conscious of a desire to survey the weather from the outer doorway before she slept. How she missed Harriet and the children! – though they had been living with her only for a short time before the wedding, and since the half-house they had occupied in the village had been let. The thought of bright-eyed, red-headed little Tom still brought the warm

MISS PECK'S PROMOTION

tears very near to falling. He had cried bitterly when he went away. So had his mother – at least, she held up her pocket-handkerchief. Miss Peck never had believed in Harriet's tears.

Out of the silence of the great hillslope came the dull sound of a voice, and as Miss Peck sprang from her chair to the window, dropping the sleeping cat in a solid mass on the floor, she recognized the noise of a carriage. Her heart was beating provokingly; she was tired by the excitement of the last few days. She did not remember this, but was conscious of being startled in an unusual way. It must be some strange crisis in her life; she turned and looked about the familiar kitchen as if it were going to be altogether swept away. 'Now, you needn't be afraid that Pigley's comin' to bring her back, Elizy Peck!' she assured herself with grim humour in that minute's apprehension of disaster.

A man outside spoke sternly to his horse. Eliza stepped quickly to the door and opened it wide. She was not afraid of the messenger, only of the message.

'Hold the light so's I can see to tie this colt,' said a familiar voice; 'it's as dark as a pocket, 'Liza. I'll be right in. You must put on a good warm shawl; 't is as bad as rain, this fog is. The minister wants you to come down to his house; he's at his wit's end, and there was nobody we could think of that's free an' able except you. His wife's gone, died at a quarter to six, and left a mis'able baby, but the doctor expects 't will live. The nurse they bargained with 's failed 'em, and 't is an awful state o' things as you ever see. Half the women in town are there, and the minister's overcome; he's sort of fainted away two or three times, and they don't know who else to get, till the doctor said your name, and he groaned right out you was the one. 'T ain't right to refuse, as I view it. Mis' Spence an' Mis' Corbell is going to watch with the dead, but there needs a head.'

Eliza Peck felt for once as if she lacked that useful possession herself, and sat down, with amazing appearance of calmness, in one of her splint-bottomed chairs to collect her thoughts. The messenger was a good deal excited; so was she; but in a few moments she rose, cutting short his inconsequent description of affairs at the parsonage.

'You just put out the fire as best you can,' she said. 'We'll talk as we go along. There's plenty o' ashes there, I'm sure; I let the stove cool off considerable, for I was meanin' to go to bed in another five minutes. The cat'll do well enough. I'll leave her plenty for to-morrow, and she's got a place where she can crep in an' out of the wood-shed. I'll just slip on another dress and put the nails over the windows, an' we'll be right off.' She was quite herself again now; and, true to her promise, it was not many minutes before the door was locked, the house left in darkness, and Ezra Weston and Miss Peck were driving comfortably down the lane. The fog had all blown away, suddenly the stars were out, and the air was sweet with the smell of the wet bark of black birches and cherry- and apple-trees that grew by the fences. The leaves had fallen fast through the day, weighted by the dampness until their feeble stems could keep them in place no longer; for the bright colours of the foliage there had come at night sweet odours and a richness of fragrance in the soft air.

"'T is an unwholesome streak o' weather, ain't it?' asked

MISS PECK'S PROMOTION

Ezra Weston. 'Feels like a dog-day evening now, don't it ? Come this time o' year you want bracin' up.'

Miss Peck did not respond; her sympathetic heart was dwelling on the thought that she was going, not only to a house of mourning, but to a bereft parsonage. She would not have felt so unequal to soothing the sorrows of her every-day acquaintances, but she could hardly face the duty of consoling the new minister. But she never once wished that she had not consented so easily to respond to his pitiful summons.

There was a strangely festive look in the village, for the exciting news of Mrs. Elbury's death had flown from house to house — lights were bright everywhere, and in the parsonage brightest of all. It looked as if the hostess were receiving her friends, and helping them to make merry, instead of being white and still, and done with this world, while the busy women of the parish were pulling open her closets and bureau drawers in search of household possessions. Nobody stopped to sentimentalize over the poor soul's delicate orderliness, or the simple, loving preparations she had made for the coming of the baby which fretfully wailed in the next room.

'Here's a nice black silk that never was touched with the scissors!' said one good dame, as if a kind Providence ought to have arranged for the use of such a treasure in setting the bounds of the good woman's life.

'Does seem too bad, don't it? I always heard her folks was well off,' replied somebody in a loud whisper; 'she had everything to live for.' There was great eagerness to be of service to the stricken pastor, and the kind neighbours did their best to prove the extent of their sympathy. One after another went to the room where he was, armed with various excuses, and the story of his sad looks and distress was repeated again and again to a grieved audience.

When Miss Peck came in she had to listen to a full description of the day's events, and was decorously slow in assuming her authority; but at last the house was nearly empty again, and only the watchers and one patient little mother of many children, who held this motherless child in loving arms, were left with Miss Peck in the parsonage. It seemed a year since she had sat in her quiet kitchen, a solitary woman whose occupations seemed too few and too trivial for her eager capacities and ambitions.

The autumn days went by, winter set in early, and Miss Peck was still mistress of the parsonage housekeeping. Her own cider was brought to the parsonage, and so were the potatoes and the apples; even the cat was transferred to a dull village existence, far removed in every way from her happy hunting grounds among the snow-birds and plump squirrels. The minister's pale little baby loved Miss Peck and submitted to her rule already. She clung fast to the good woman with her little arms, and Miss Peck, who had always imagined that she did not care for infants, found herself watching the growth of this spark of human intelligence and affection with intense interest. After all, it was good to be spared the long winter at the farm; it had never occurred to her to dread it, but she saw now that it was a season to be dreaded, and one by one forgot the duties which at first beckoned her homeward and seemed so unavoidable. The farm-house seemed cold and empty when she paid it an occasional visit. She would not have believed that she could content herself so well away from the dear old home. If she could have had her favourite little Tom within reach, life would have been perfectly happy.

The minister proved at first very disappointing to her imaginary estimate and knowledge of him. If it had not been for her sturdy loyalty to him as pastor and employer, she could sometimes have joined more or less heartily in the expressions of the disaffected faction which forms a difficult element in every parish. Her sense of humour was deeply gratified when the leader of the opposition remarked that the minister was beginning to take notice a little, and was wearing his best hat every day, like every other widower since the world was made. Miss Peck's shrewd mind had already made sure that Mr. Elbury's loss was not so great as she had at first sympathetically believed; she knew that his romantic, ease-loving, self-absorbed, and self-admiring nature had been curbed and held in check by the literal, prosaic, faithful-in-little-things disposition of his dead wife. She was self-denying, he was self-indulgent; she was dutiful, while he was given to indolence – and the unfounded plea of ill-health made his only excuse. Miss Peck soon fell into the way of putting her shoulder to the wheel, and unobtrusively, even secretly, led the affairs of the parish. She never was deaf to the explanation of the wearing effect of brain-work, but accepted the weakness as well as the power of the ministerial character; and nobody listened more respectfully to his somewhat flowery and inconsequent discourses on Sunday than Miss Peck. The first Sunday they went to church together Eliza slipped into her own pew, half way up the side aisle, and thought well of herself for her prompt decision afterward, though she regretted the act for a moment as she saw the minister stop to let her into the empty pew of the parsonage. He had been sure she was just behind him, and gained much sympathy from the congregation as he sighed and wended his lonely way up the pulpit stairs. Even Mrs. Corbell, who had been averse to settling the Rev. Mr. Elbury, was moved by this incident, but directly afterward whispered to her next neighbour that 'Lizy Peck would be sitting there before the year was out if she had the business head they had all given her credit for.'

It gives rise to melancholy reflections when one sees how quickly those who have suffered most cruel and disturbing bereavements learn to go their way alone. The great plan of our lives is never really broken nor suffers accidents. However stunning the shock, one can almost always understand gratefully that it was best for the vanished friend to vanish just when he did; that this world held no more duties or satisfactions for him; that his earthly life was in fact done and ended. Our relations with him must be lifted to a new plane. Miss Peck thought often of the minister's loss, and always with tender sympathy, yet she could not help seeing that he was far from being unresigned or miserable in his grief. She was ready to overlook the fact that he depended upon his calling rather than upon his own character and efforts. The only way in which she made herself uncongenial to the minister was by persistent suggestions that he should take more exercise and 'stir about outdoors a little.' Once, when she had gone so far as to briskly inform him that he was getting logy, Mr. Elbury showed entire displeasure; and a little later, in the privacy of the kitchen, she voiced the opinion that Elizy Peck knew very well that she never did think ministers were

MISS PECK'S PROMOTION

angels – only human beings, like herself, in great danger of being made fools of. But the two good friends made up their little quarrel at supper-time.

'I have been looking up the derivation of that severe word you applied to me this noon,' said the Rev. Mr. Elbury pleasantly. 'It is a localism; but it comes from the Dutch word *log*, which means heavy or unwieldy.'

These words were pronounced plaintively, with evident consciousness that they hardly applied to his somewhat lank figure; and Miss Peck felt confused and rebuked, and went on pouring tea until both cup and saucer were full, and she scalded the end of her thumb. She was very weak in the hands of such a scholar as this, but later she had a reassuring sense of not having applied the epithet unjustly. With a feminine reverence for his profession, and for his attainments, she had a keen sense of his human fallibility; and neither his grief, nor his ecclesiastical halo, nor his considerate idea of his own value, could blind her sharp eyes to certain shortcomings. She forgave them readily, but she knew them all by sight and name.

If there were any gift of Mr. Elbury's which could sincerely be called perfectly delightful by many people, it was his voice. When he was in a hurry, and gave hasty directions to his housekeeper about some mislaid possession, or called her downstairs to stop the baby's vexatious crying, the tones were entirely different from those best known to the parish. Nature had gifted him with a power of carrying his voice into the depths of sympathetic being and recovering it again gallantly. He had been considered the superior, in some respects, of that teacher of elocution who led the students of the theological seminary toward the glorious paths of oratory. There was a mellow middle-tone, most suggestive of tender feeling; but though it sounded sweet to other feminine ears, Miss Peck was always annoyed by it and impatient of a certain artificial quality in its cadences. To hear Mr. Elbury talk to his child in this tone, and address her as 'my motherless babe,' however affecting to other ears, was always unpleasant to Miss Peck. But she thought very well of his preaching; and the more he let all the decisions and responsibilities of every-day life fall to her share, the more she enjoyed life and told her friends that Mr. Elbury was a most amiable man to live with. And when spring was come the hillside farm was let on shares to one of Miss Peck's neighbours whom she could entirely trust. It was not the best of bargains for its owner, who had the reputation of being an excellent farmer, and the agreement cost her many sighs and not a little wakefulness. She felt too much shut in by this village life; but the minister pleaded his hapless lot, the little child was even more appealing in her babyhood, and so the long visit from little Tom and his sisters, the familiar garden, the three beehives, and the glory of the sunsets in the great, unbroken, western sky were all given up together for that year.

It was not so hard as it might have been. There was one most rewarding condition of life – the feast of books, which was new and bewilderingly delightful to the minister's housekeeper. She had made the most of the few well-chosen volumes of the farmhouse, but she never had known the joy of having more books than she could read, or their exquisite power of temptation, the delight of their friendly company. She was oftenest the student, the brain-wearied member, of

MISS PECK'S PROMOTION

the parsonage family, but she never made it an excuse, or really recognized the new stimulus either. Life had never seemed so full to her; she was working with both hands earnestly, and no half-heartedness. She was filled with reverence in the presence of the minister's books; to her his calling, his character, and his influence were all made positive and respectable by this foundation of learning on his library-shelves. He was to her a man of letters, a critic, and a philosopher, besides being an experienced theologian from the very nature of his profession. Indeed, he had an honest liking for books, and was fond of reading aloud or being read to; and many an evening went joyfully by in the presence of the great English writers, whose best thoughts were rolled out in Mr. Elbury's best tones, and Miss Peck listened with delight, and cast many an affectionate glance at the sleeping child in the cradle at her feet, filled with gratitude as she was for all her privileges.

Mr. Elbury was most generous in his appreciation of Miss Peck's devotion, and never hesitated to give expression to sincere praise of her uncommon power of mind. He was led into paths of literature, otherwise untrod, by her delight; and sometimes, to rest his brain and make him ready for a good night's sleep, he asked his companion to read him a clever story. It was all a new world to the good woman, whose schooling and reading had been sound, but restricted; and if ever a mind waked up with joy to its possession of the world of books, it was hers. She became ambitious for the increase of her own little library; and it was in reply to her outspoken plan for larger crops and more money from the farm another year, for the sake of book-buying, that Mr. Elbury once said, earnestly, that his books were hers now. This careless expression was the spark which lit a new light for Miss Peck's imagination. For the first time a thrill of personal interest in the man made itself felt, through her devoted capacity for service and appreciation. He had ceased to be simply himself; he stood now for a widened life, a suggestion of added good and growth, a larger circle of human interests; in fact, his existence had made all the difference between her limited rural home and that connection with the great world which even the most contracted parsonage is sure to hold.

And that very night, while Mr. Elbury had gone, somewhat ruefully and ill-prepared, to his Bible class, Miss Peck's conscience set her womanly weakness before it for a famous arraigning. It was so far successful that words failed the defendant completely, and the session was dissolved in tears. For some days Miss Peck was not only stern with herself, but even with the minister, and was entirely devoted to her domestic affairs.

The very next Sunday it happened that Mr. Elbury exchanged pulpits with a brother-clergyman in the next large town, a thriving manufacturing centre, and he came home afterward in the best of spirits. He never had seemed so appreciative of his comfortable home, or Miss Peck's motherly desire to shield his weak nature from these practical cares of life to which he was entirely inadequate. He was unusually gay and amusing, and described, not with the best taste, the efforts of two of his unmarried lady-parishioners to make themselves agreeable. He had met them on the short journey, and did not hesitate to speak of himself lightly as a widower; in fact he recognized his own popularity and attractions in a

MISS PECK'S PROMOTION

way that was not pleasing to Miss Peck, yet she was used to his way of speaking and unaffectedly glad to have him at home again. She had been much disturbed and grieved by her own thoughts in his absence. She could not be sure whether she was wise in drifting toward a nearer relation to the minister. She was not exactly shocked at finding herself interested in him, but, with her usual sense of propriety and justice, she insisted upon taking everybody's view of the question before the weaker Miss Peck was accorded a hearing. She was enraged with herself for feeling abashed and liking to avoid the direct scrutiny of her fellow-parishioners. Mrs. Corbell and she had always been the best of friends, but for the first time Miss Peck was annoyed by such freedom of comment and opinion. And Sister Corbell had never been so forward about spending the afternoon at the parsonage, or running in for half-hours of gossip in the morning, as in these latter days. At last she began to ask the coy Eliza about her plans for the wedding, in a half-joking, half-serious tone which was hard to bear.

'You're a sight too good for him,' was the usual conclusion, 'and so I tell everybody. The whole parish has got it settled for you; and there's as many as six think hard of you, because you've given 'em no chance, bein' right here on the spot.'

It seemed as if a resistless torrent of fate were sweeping our independent friend toward the brink of a great change. She insisted to the quailing side of her nature that she did not care for the minister himself, that she was likely to age much sooner than he, with his round, boyish face and plump cheeks. 'They'll be takin' you for his mother, Lizy, when you go amongst strangers, little and dried up as you're gettin' to be a'ready; you're three years older anyway, and look as if 't was nine.' Yet the capable, clear-headed woman was greatly enticed by the high position and requirements of mistress of the parsonage. She liked the new excitement and authority, and grew more and more happy in the exercise of powers which a solitary life at the farm would hardly arouse or engage. There was a vigorous growth of independence and determination in Miss Peck's character, and she had not lived alone so many years for nothing. But there was no outward sign yet of capitulation. She was firmly convinced that the minister could not get on without her, and that she would rather not get on without him and the pleasure of her new activities. If possible, she grew a little more self-contained and reserved in manner and speech, while carefully anticipating his wants and putting better and better dinners on the parochial table.

As for Mr. Elbury himself, he became more cheerful every day, and was almost demonstrative in his affectionate gratitude. He spoke always as if they were one in their desire to interest and benefit the parish; he had fallen into a pleasant home-like habit of saying 'we' whenever household or parish affairs were under discussion. Once, when somebody had been remarking the too-evident efforts of one of her sister-parishioners to gain Mr. Elbury's affection, he had laughed leniently; but when this gossiping caller had gone away the minister said, gently, 'We know better, don't we, Miss Peck?' and Eliza could not help feeling that his tone meant a great deal. Yet she took no special notice of him, and grew much more taciturn than was natural. Her heart beat

MISS PECK'S PROMOTION

warmly under her prim alpaca dress; she already looked younger and a great deal happier than when she first came to live at the parsonage. Her executive ability was made glad by the many duties that fell upon her, and those who knew her and Mr. Elbury best thought nothing could be wiser than their impending marriage. Did not the little child need Miss Peck's motherly care? did not the helpless minister need the assistance of a clear-sighted business woman and good housekeeper? did not Eliza herself need and deserve a husband? but even with increasing certainty she still gave no outward sign of their secret understanding. It was likely that Mr. Elbury thought best to wait a year after his wife's death, and when he spoke right out was the time to show what her answer would be. But somehow the thought of the dear old threadbare farm in the autumn weather was always a sorrowful thought; and on the days when Mr. Elbury hired a horse and wagon, and invited her and the baby to accompany him on a series of parochial visits, she could not bear to look at the home-fields and the pasture-slopes. She was thankful that the house itself was not in sight from the main road. The crops that summer had been unusually good; something called her thoughts back continually to the old home, and accused her of disloyalty. Yet she consoled herself by thinking that it was very natural to have such regrets, and to consider the importance of such a step at her sensible time of life. So it drew near winter again, and she grew more and more unrelenting and scornful whenever her acquaintances suggested the idea that her wedding ought to be drawing near.

Mr. Elbury seemed to have taken a new lease of youthful hope and ardour. He was busy in the parish and very popular, particularly among his women-parishioners. Miss Peck urged him on with his good works, and it seemed as if they expressed their interest in each other by their friendliness to the parish in general. Mr. Elbury had joined a ministers' club in the large town already spoken of, and spent a day there now and then, besides his regular Monday-night attendance at the club-meeting. He was preparing a series of sermons on the history of the Jews, and was glad to avail himself of a good free-library, the lack of which he frequently lamented in his own village. Once he said, eagerly, that he had no idea of ending his days here, and this gave Miss Peck a sharp pang. She could not bear to think of leaving her old home, and the tears filled her eyes. When she had reached the shelter of the kitchen, she retorted to the too-easily ruffled element of her character that there was no need of crossing that bridge till she came to it; and, after an appealing glance at the academy-steeple above the maple trees, she returned to the study to finish dusting. She saw, without apprehension, that the minister quickly pushed something under the leaves of his blotting-paper and frowned a little. It was not his usual time for writing – she had a new proof of her admiring certainty that Mr. Elbury wrote for the papers at times under an assumed name.

One Monday evening he had not returned from the ministers' meeting until later than usual, and she began to be slightly anxious. The baby had not been very well all day, and she particularly wished to have an errand done before night, but did not dare to leave the child alone, while, for a wonder, nobody had been in. Mr. Elbury had shown a great deal of feeling before he went away in the morning,

MISS PECK'S PROMOTION

and as she was admiringly looking at his well-fitting clothes and neat clerical attire, a thrill of pride and affection had made her eyes shine unwontedly. She was really beginning to like him very much. For the first and last time in his life the minister stepped quickly forward and kissed her on the forehead.

'My good, kind friend!' he exclaimed, in that deep tone which the whole parish loved; then he hurried away. Miss Peck felt a strange dismay, and stood by the breakfast-table like a statue. She even touched her forehead with trembling fingers. Somehow she inwardly rebelled, but kissing meant more to her than to some people. She never had been used to it except with little Tom – though the last brotherly kiss his father gave her before he went to the war had been one of the treasures of her memory. All that day she was often reminded of the responsible and darker side, the inspected and criticized side, of the high position of minister's wife. It was clearly time for proper rebuke when evening came; and as she sat by the light, mending Mr. Elbury's stockings, she said over and over again that she had walked into this with her eyes wide open, and if the experience of forty years hadn't put any sense into her it was too late to help it now.

Suddenly she heard the noise of wheels in the side yard. Could anything have happened to Mr. Elbury? were they bringing him home hurt, or dead even? He never drove up from the station unless it were bad weather. She rushed to the door with a flaring light, and was bewildered at the sight of trunks and, most of all, at the approach of Mr. Elbury, for he wore a most sentimental expression, and led a young person by the hand.

'Dear friend,' he said, in that mellow tone of his, 'I hope you, too, will love my little wife.'

Almost any other woman would have dropped the kerosene lamp on the doorstep, but not Miss Eliza Peck. Luckily a gust of autumn wind blew it out, and the bride had to fumble her way into her new home. Miss Peck quickly procured one of her own crinkly lamplighters, and bent toward the open fire to kindle a new light.

'You've taken me by surprise,' she managed to say, in her usual tone of voice, though she felt herself shaking with excitement.

At that moment the ailing stepdaughter gave a forlorn little wail from the wide sofa, where she had been put to sleep with difficulty. Miss Peck's kind heart felt the pathos of the situation; she lifted the little child and stilled it, then she held out a kindly hand to the minister's new wife, while Mr. Elbury stood beaming by.

'I wish you may be very happy here, as I have been,' said the good woman, earnestly. 'But, Mr. Elbury, you ought to have let me know. I could have kept a secret' – and satisfaction filled Eliza Peck's heart that she never, to use her own expression, had made a fool of herself before the First Parish. She had kept her own secret, and in this earthquake of a moment was clearly conscious that she was heroine enough to behave as if there never had been any secret to keep. And indignation with the Rev. Mr. Elbury, who had so imprudently kept his own counsel, threw down the sham temple of Cupid which a faithless god call Propinquity had succeeded in rearing.

Miss Peck made a feast, and for the last time played the

MISS PECK'S PROMOTION

part of hostess at the minister's table. She had remorselessly inspected the conspicuous bad taste of the new Mrs. Elbury's dress, the waving, cheap-looking feather of her hat, the make-believe richness of her clothes, and saw, with dire compassion, how unused she was to young children. The brave Eliza tried to make the best of things – but one moment she found herself thinking how uncomfortable Mr. Elbury's home would be henceforth with this poor reed to lean upon, a townish, empty-faced, tiresomely pretty girl; the next moment she pitied the girl herself, who would have the hard task before her of being the wife of an indolent preacher in a country town. Miss Peck had generally allowed her farm to supplement the limited salary of the First Parish; in fact, she had been a silent partner in the parsonage establishment rather than a dependant. Would the First Parish laugh at her now? It was a stinging thought; but she honestly believed that the minister himself would be most commiserated when the parish opinion had found time to simmer down.

The next day our heroine, whose face was singularly free from disappointment, told the minister that she would like to leave at once, for she was belated about many things, not having had notice in season of his change of plan.

'I've been telling your wife all about the house and parish interests as best I can, and it's likely she wants to take everything into her own hands right away,' added the uncommon housekeeper, with a spice of malice; but Mr. Elbury flushed, and looked down at the short, capable Eliza appealingly. He knew her virtues so well that this announcement was a crushing blow.

'Why, I thought of course you would continue here as

usual,' he said in a strange, harsh voice that would have been perfectly surprising in the pulpit. 'Mrs. Elbury has never known any care. We count upon your remaining.'

Whereupon Miss Peck looked him disdainfully in the face, and, for a moment, mistook him for that self so often reproved and now sunk into depths of ignominy.

'If you thought that, you ought to have known better,' she said. 'You can't expect a woman who has property and relations of her own to give up her interests for yours altogether. I got a letter this morning from my brother's boy, little Tom, and he's got leave from his mother and her husband to come and stop with me a good while – he says all winter. He's been sick, and they've had to take him out of school. I never supposed that such stived-up air would agree with him,' concluded Miss Peck, triumphantly. She was full of joy and hope at this new turn of affairs, and the minister was correspondingly hopeless. 'I'll take the baby home for a while, if 't would be a convenience for you,' she added, more leniently. 'That is, after I get my house well warmed, and there's something in it to eat. I wish you could have spoken to me a fortnight ago; but I saw Joe Farley to-day – that boy that lived with me quite a while – he's glad to come back. He only engaged to stop till after cider time where he's been this summer, and he's promised to look about for a good cow for me. I always thought well of Joe.'

The minister turned away ruefully, and Miss Peck went about her work. She meant to leave the house in the best of order; but the whole congregation came trooping in that day and the next, and she hardly had time to build a fire in her own kitchen before Joe Farley followed her from the

MISS PECK'S PROMOTION

station with the beloved little Tom. He looked tall and thin and pale, and largely freckled under his topknot of red hair. Bless his heart! how his lonely aunt kissed him and hugged him, and how thankful he was to get back to her, though she never would have suspected it if she had not known him so well. A shy boy-fashion of reserve and stolidity had replaced his early demonstrations, but he promptly went to the shelf of books to find the familiar old *Robinson Crusoe*. Miss Peck's heart leaped for joy as she remembered how much more she could teach the child about books. She felt a great wave of gratitude fill her cheerful soul as she remembered the pleasure and gain of those evenings when she and Mr. Elbury had read together.

There was a great deal of eager discussion in the village; and much amused scrutiny of Eliza's countenance as she walked up the side aisle that first Sunday after the minister was married. She led little Tom by the hand, but he opened the pew-door and ushered her in handsomely, and she looked smilingly at her neighbours and nodded her head sideways at the boy in a way that made them suspect she was much more in love with him, freckles and all, than she had ever been with Mr. Elbury. A few minutes later she frowned at Tom sternly for greeting his old acquaintances over the pew-rail in a way that did not fit the day or place. There was no chance to laugh at her disappointment; for nobody could help understanding that her experience at the parsonage had been merely incidental in her life, and that she had returned willingly to her old associations. The dream of being a minister's wife had been only a dream, and she was surprised to find herself waking from it with such resignation to her lot.

'I'd just like to know what sort of a breakfast they had,' she said to herself as the bride's topknot went waving and bobbing up to the parsonage pew. 'If ever there was a man who was fussy about his cup o' coffee, 't is Reverend Wilbur Elbury! There now, Elizy Peck, don't you wish it was you a-setting there up front and feeling the eyes of the whole parish sticking in your back? You could have had him, you know, if you'd set right about it. I never did think you had proper ideas of what gettin' promoted is; but if you ain't discovered a new world for yourself like C'lumbus, I miss my guess. If you'd stayed on the farm all alone last year you'd had no thoughts but hens and rutabagys, and as 't is you've been livin' amon'st books. There's nothin' to regret if you did just miss makin' a fool o' yourself.'

At this moment Mr. Elbury's voice gently sounded from the pulpit, and Miss Peck sprang to her feet with the agility of a jack-in-the-box – she had forgotten her surroundings in the vividness of her reverie. She hardly knew what the minister said in that first prayer; for many reasons this was an exciting day.

A little later our heroine accepted the invitation of her second cousin, Mrs. Corbell, to spend an hour or two between morning and afternoon services. They had agreed that it seemed like old times, and took pleasure in renewing this custom of the Sunday visit. Little Tom was commented upon as to health and growth and freckles and family resemblance; and when he strayed out of doors, after such a dinner as only a growing boy can make vanish with the enchanter's wand of his appetite, the two women indulged in a good talk.

'I don't know how you viewed it this morning,' began

MISS PECK'S PROMOTION

Cousin Corbell; 'but, to my eyes, the minister looked as if he felt cheap as a broom. There, I never was one o' his worshippers, you well know. To speak plain, Elizy, I was really concerned at one time for fear you would be over-persuaded. I never said one word to warp your judgment, but I did feel as if 't would be a shame. I –'

But Miss Peck was not ready yet to join in the opposition, and she interrupted at once in an amiable but decided tone. 'We'll let bygones be bygones; it's just as well, and a good deal better. Mr. Elbury always treated me the best he knew how; and I knew he wa'n't perfect, but 't was full as much his misfortune as his fault. I declare I don't know what else he could ha' done if he hadn't taken to preaching; and he has very kind feelings, specially if anyone's in trouble. Talk of "leading about silly captive women," there are some cases where we've got to turn round and say it right the other way – 't is the silly women that do the leadin' themselves. And I tell you,' concluded Miss Peck, with apparent irrelevancy, 'I was glad last night to have a good honest look at a yellow sunset. If ever I do go and set my mind on a minister, I'm going to hunt for one that's well settled in a hill parish. I used to feel as if I was shut right in, there at the parsonage; it's a good house enough, if it only stood where you could see anything out of the windows. I can't carry out my plans o' life in any such situation.'

'I expect to hear that you've blown right off the top of your hill some o' these windy days,' said Mrs. Corbell, without resentment, though she was very dependent, herself, on seeing the passing.

The church bell began to ring, and our friends rose to put

on their bonnets and answer its summons. Miss Peck's practical mind revolted at the possibility of there having been a decent noonday meal at the parsonage. 'Maria Corbell!' she said, with dramatic intensity, 'mark what I'm goin' to say – it ain't I that's goin' to reap the whirlwind; it's your pastor, the Reverend Mr. Elbury, of the First Parish.'

THE FLIGHT OF BETSEY LANE

★

I

ONE windy morning in May, three old women sat together near an open window in the shed chamber of Byfleet Poor-house. The wind was from the north-west, but their window faced the south-east, and they were only visited by an occasional pleasant waft of fresh air. They were close together, knee to knee, picking over a bushel of beans, and commanding a view of the dandelion-starred, green yard below, and of the winding, sandy road that led to the village, two miles away. Some captive bees were scolding among the cobwebs of the rafters overhead, or thumping against the upper panes of glass; two calves were bawling from the barnyard, where some of the men were at work loading a dump-cart and shouting as if every one were deaf. There was a cheerful feeling of activity, and even an air of comfort, about the Byfleet Poor-house. Almost everyone was possessed of a most interesting past, though there was less to be said about the future. The inmates were by no means distressed or unhappy; many of them retired to this shelter only for the winter season, and would go out presently, some to begin such work as they could still do, others to live in their own small houses; old age had impoverished most of them by limiting their power of endurance; but far from lamenting the fact that they were town charges, they rather liked the change and excitement of a winter residence on the poor-farm. There was a sharp-faced, hard-worked young widow with seven children, who was an exception to the general level of society, because she deplored the change in her fortunes. The older women regarded her with suspicion, and were apt to talk about her in moments like this, when they happened to sit together at their work.

The three bean-pickers were dressed alike in stout brown ginghams, checked by a white line, and all wore great faded aprons of blue drilling, with sufficient pockets convenient to the right hand. Miss Peggy Bond was a very small, belligerent-looking person, who wore a huge pair of steel-bowed spectacles, holding her sharp chin well up in air, as if to supplement an inadequate nose. She was more than half blind, but the spectacles seemed to face upward instead of square ahead, as if their wearer were always on the sharp lookout for birds. Miss Bond had suffered much personal damage from time to time, because she never took heed where she planted her feet, and so was always tripping and stubbing her bruised way through the world. She had fallen down hatchways and cellarways, and stepped composedly into deep ditches and pasture brooks; but she was proud of stating that she was upsighted, and so was her father before her. At the poor-house, where an unusual malady was considered a distinction, upsightedness was looked upon as a most honourable infirmity. Plain rheumatism, such as afflicted Aunt Lavina Dow, whose twisted hands found even this light work difficult and tiresome, – plain rheumatism was something of every-day occurrence, and nobody cared to hear about it. Poor Peggy was a meek and friendly soul, who never put herself forward; she was just like other folks, as she always loved to say, but Mrs. Lavina Dow was a different sort of person altogether, of great dignity and, occasionally, almost aggressive behaviour. The time had been when she could do a good day's work with anybody: but for

THE FLIGHT OF BETSEY LANE

many years now she had not left the town-farm, being too badly crippled to work; she had no relations or friends to visit, but from an innate love of authority she could not submit to being one of those who are forgotten by the world. Mrs. Dow was the hostess and social lawgiver here, where she remembered every inmate and every item of interest for nearly forty years, besides an immense amount of town history and biography for three or four generations back.

She was the dear friend of the third woman, Betsey Lane; together they led thought and opinion – chiefly opinion – and held sway, not only over Byfleet Poor-farm, but also the selectmen and all others in authority. Betsey Lane had spent most of her life as aid-in-general to the respected household of old General Thornton. She had been much trusted and valued, and, at the breaking up of that once large and flourishing family, she had been left in good circumstances, what with legacies and her own comfortable savings; but by sad misfortune and lavish generosity everything had been scattered, and after much illness, which ended in a stiffened arm and more uncertainty, the good soul had sensibly decided that it was easier for the whole town to support her than for a part of it. She had always hoped to see something of the world before she died; she came of an adventurous, seafaring stock, but had never made a longer journey than to the towns of Danby and Northville, thirty miles away.

They were all old women; but Betsey Lane, who was sixty-nine, and looked much older, was the youngest. Peggy Bond was far on in the seventies, and Mrs. Dow was at least ten years older. She made a great secret of her years; and as she sometimes spoke of events prior to the Revolution with the assertion of having been an eye-witness, she naturally wore an air of vast antiquity. Her tales were an inexpressible delight to Betsey Lane, who felt younger by twenty years because her friend and comrade was so unconscious of chronological limitations.

The bushel basket of cranberry beans was within easy reach, and each of the pickers had filled her lap from it again and again. The shed chamber was not an unpleasant place in which to sit at work, with its traces of seed corn hanging from the brown crossbeams, its spare churns, and dusty loom, and rickety wool-wheels, and a few bits of old furniture. In one far corner was a wide board of dismal use and suggestion, and close beside it an old cradle. There was a battered chest of drawers where the keeper of the poor-house kept his garden-seeds, with the withered remains of three seed cucumbers ornamenting the top. Nothing beautiful could be discovered, nothing interesting, but there was something usable and homely about the place. It was the favourite and untroubled bower of the bean-pickers, to which they might retreat unmolested from the public apartments of this rustic institution.

Betsey Lane blew away the chaff from her handful of beans. The spring breeze blew the chaff back again, and sifted it over her face and shoulders. She rubbed it out of her eyes impatiently, and happened to notice old Peggy holding her own handful high, as if it were an oblation, and turning her queer, up-tilted head this way and that, to look at the beans sharply, as if she were first cousin to a hen.

'There, Miss Bond, 't is kind of botherin' work for you, ain't it?' Betsey inquired compassionately.

'I feel to enjoy it, anything that I can do my own way

THE FLIGHT OF BETSEY LANE

so,' responded Peggy. 'I like to do my part. Ain't that old Mis' Fales comin' up the road? It sounds like her step.'

The others looked, but they were not far-sighted, and for a moment Peggy had the advantage. Mrs. Fales was not a favourite.

'I hope she ain't comin' here to put up this spring. I guess she won't now, it's gettin' so late,' said Betsey Lane. 'She likes to go rovin' soon as the roads is settled.'

''T is Mis' Fales!' said Peggy Bond, listening with solemn anxiety. 'There, do let's pray her by!'

'I guess she's headin' for her cousin's folks up Beech Hill way,' said Betsey presently. 'If she'd left her daughter's this mornin', she'd have got just about as far as this. I kind o' wish she had stepped in just to pass the time o' day, long 's she wa'n't going to make no stop.'

There was a silence as to further speech in the shed chamber; and even the calves were quiet in the barnyard. The men had all gone away to the field where corn-planting was going on. The beans clicked steadily into the wooden measure at the pickers' feet. Betsey Lane began to sing a hymn, and the others joined in as best they might, like autumnal crickets; their voices were sharp and cracked, with now and then a few low notes of plaintive tone. Betsey herself could sing pretty well, but the others could only make a kind of accompaniment. Their voices ceased altogether at the higher notes.

'Oh my! I wish I had the means to go to the Centennial,' mourned Betsey Lane, stopping so suddenly that the others had to go on croaking and shrilling without her for a moment before they could stop. 'It seems to me as if I can't die happy

THE ONLY ROSE AND OTHER TALES

'less I do,' she added; 'I ain't never seen nothin' of the world, an' here I be.'

'What if you was as old as I be?' suggested Mrs. Dow pompously. 'You've got time enough yet, Betsey; don't you go an' despair. I knowed of a woman that went clean round the world four times when she was past eighty, an' enjoyed herself real well. Her folks followed the sea; she had three sons an' a daughter married, – all ship-masters, and she'd been with her own husband when they was young. She was left a widder early, and fetched up her family herself, – a real stirrin', smart woman. After they'd got married off, an' settled, an' was doing well, she come to be lonesome; and first she tried to stick it out alone, but she wa'n't one that could; an' she got a notion she hadn't nothin' before her but her last sickness, and she wa'n't a person that enjoyed havin' other folks do for her. So one on her boys – I guess 't was the oldest – said he was going to take her to sea; there was ample room, an' he was sailin' a good time o' year for the Cape o' Good Hope an' way up to some o' them tea-ports in the Chiny Seas. She was all high to go, but it made a sight o' talk at her age; an' the minister made it a subject o' prayer the last Sunday, and all the folks took a last leave; but she said to some she'd fetch 'em home something real pritty, and so did. An' then they come home t' other way, round the Horn, an' she done so well, an' was such a sight o' company, the other child'n was jealous, an' she promised she'd go a v'y'ge long o' each on 'em. She was as sprightly a person as ever I see; an' could speak well o' what she'd seen.'

'Did she die to sea?' asked Peggy, with interest.

'No, she died to home between v'y'ges, or she'd gone to sea again. I was to her funeral. She liked her son George's ship

THE FLIGHT OF BETSEY LANE

the best; 't was the one she was going on to Callao. They said the men aboard all called her "gran'ma'am," an' she kep' 'em mended up, an' would go below and tend to 'em if they was sick. She might 'a' been alive an' enjoyin' of herself a good many years but for the kick of a cow; 't was a new cow out of a drove, a dreadful unruly beast.'

Mrs. Dow stopped for breath, and reached down for a new supply of beans; her empty apron was grey with soft chaff. Betsey Lane, still pondering on the Centennial, began to sing another verse of her hymn, and again the old women joined her. At this moment some strangers came driving round into the yard from the front of the house. The turf was soft, and our friends did not hear the horses' steps. Their voices cracked and quavered; it was a funny little concert, and a lady in an open carriage just below listened with sympathy and amusement.

II

'Betsey! Betsey! Miss Lane!' a voice called eagerly at the foot of the stairs that led up from the shed. 'Betsey! There's a lady here wants to see you right away.'

Betsey was dazed with excitement, like a country child who knows the rare pleasure of being called out of school. 'Lor', I ain't fit to go down, be I?' she faltered, looking anxiously at her friends; but Peggy was gazing even nearer to the zenith than usual, in her excited effort to see down into the yard, and Mrs. Dow only nodded somewhat jealously, and said that she guessed 't was nobody would do her any harm. She rose ponderously, while Betsey hesitated, being, as they would have said, all of a twitter. 'It is a lady, certain,' Mrs. Dow assured her; ''t ain't often there's a lady comes here.'

'While there was any of Mis' Gen'ral Thornton's folks left, I wa'n't without visits from the gentry,' said Betsey Lane, turning back proudly at the head of the stairs, with a touch of old-world pride and sense of high station. Then she disappeared, and closed the door behind her at the stair-foot with a decision quite unwelcome to the friends above.

'She needn't 'a' been so dreadful 'fraid anybody was goin' to listen. I guess we've got folks to ride an' see us, or had once, if we hain't now,' said Miss Peggy Bond, plaintively.

'I expect 't was only the wind shoved it to,' said Aunt Lavina. 'Betsey is one that gits flustered easier than some. I wish 't was somebody to take her off an' give her a kind of a good time; she's young to settle down 'long of old folks like us. Betsey's got a notion o' rovin' such as ain't my natur', but I should like to see her satisfied. She'd been a very understandin' person, if she had the advantages that some does.'

"T is so,' said Peggy Bond, tilting her chin high. 'I suppose you can't hear nothin' they're saying? I feel my hearin' ain't up to what it was. I can hear things close to me well as ever; but there, hearin' ain't everything; 't ain't as if we lived where there was more goin' on to hear. Seems to me them folks is stoppin' a good while.'

'They surely be,' agreed Lavina Dow.

'I expect it's somethin' particular. There ain't none of the Thornton folks left, except one o' the gran'darters, an' I've often heard Betsey remark that she should never see her more, for she lives to London. Strange how folks feels contented in them strayaway places off to the ends of the airth.'

The flies and bees were buzzing against the hot windowpanes; the handfuls of beans were clicking into the brown

THE FLIGHT OF BETSEY LANE

wooden measure. A bird came and perched on the window-sill, and then flitted away toward the blue sky. Below, in the yard, Betsey Lane stood talking with the lady. She had put her blue drilling apron over her head, and her face was shining with delight.

'Lor', dear,' she said, for at least the third time, 'I remember ye when I first see ye; an awful pritty baby you was, an' they all said you looked just like the old gen'ral. Be you goin' back to foreign parts right away?'

'Yes, I'm going back; you know that all my children are there. I wish I could take you with me for a visit,' said the charming young guest. 'I'm going to carry over some of the pictures and furniture from the old house; I didn't care half so much for them when I was younger as I do now. Perhaps next summer we shall all come over for a while. I should like to see my girls and boys playing under the pines.'

'I wish you re'lly was livin' to the old place,' said Betsey Lane. Her imagination was not swift; she needed time to think over all that was being told her, and she could not fancy the two strange houses across the sea. The old Thornton house was to her mind the most delightful and elegant in the world.

'Is there anything I can do for you?' asked Mrs. Strafford kindly, – 'anything that I can do for you myself, before I go away? I shall be writing to you, and sending some pictures of the children, and you must let me know how you are getting on.'

'Yes, there is one thing, darlin'. If you could stop in the village an' pick me out a pritty, little, small lookin'-glass, that I can keep for my own an' have to remember you by. 'T ain't that I want to set me above the rest o' the folks, but I was always used to havin' my own when I was to your grandma's. There's very nice folks here, some on 'em, and I'm better off than if I was able to keep house; but sence you ask me, that's the only thing I feel cropin' about. What be you goin' right back for? ain't you goin' to see the great fair to Pheladelphy, that everybody talks about?'

'No,' said Mrs. Strafford, laughing at this eager and almost convicting question. 'No; I'm going back next week. If I were, I believe that I should take you with me. Good-bye, dear old Betsey; you make me feel as if I were a little girl again; you look just the same.'

For full five minutes the old woman stood out in the sunshine, dazed with delight, and majestic with a sense of her own consequence. She held something tight in her hand, without thinking what it might be; but just as the friendly mistress of the poor-farm came out to hear the news, she tucked the roll of money into the bosom of her brown gingham dress. '"T was my dear Mis' Katy Strafford,' she turned to say proudly. 'She come way over from London; she's been sick; they thought the voyage would do her good. She said most the first thing she had on her mind was to come an' find me, and see how I was, an' if I was comfortable; an' now she's goin' right back. She's got two splendid houses; an' said how she wished I was there to look after things, – she remembered I was always her gran'ma's right hand. Oh, it does so carry me back, to see her! Seems if all the rest on 'em must be there together to the old house. There, I must go right up an' tell Mis' Dow an' Peggy.'

'Dinner's all ready; I was just goin' to blow the horn for the

THE FLIGHT OF BETSEY LANE

men-folks,' said the keeper's wife. 'They'll be right down. I expect you've got along smart with them beans, – all three of you together'; but Betsey's mind roved so high and so far at that moment that no achievements of bean-picking could lure it back.

III

The long table in the great kitchen soon gathered its company of waifs and strays, – creatures of improvidence and misfortune, and the irreparable victims of old age. The dinner was satisfactory, and there was not much delay for conversation. Peggy Bond and Mrs. Dow and Betsey Lane always sat together at one end, with an air of putting the rest of the company below the salt. Betsey was still flushed with excitement; in fact, she could not eat as much as usual, and she looked up from time to time expectantly, as if she were likely to be asked to speak of her guest; but everybody was hungry, and even Mrs. Dow broke in upon some attempted confidences by asking inopportunely for a second potato. There were nearly twenty at the table, counting the keeper and his wife and two children, noisy little persons who had come from school with the small flock belonging to the poor widow, who sat just opposite our friends. She finished her dinner before anyone else, and pushed her chair back; she always helped with the housework, – a thin, sorry, bad-tempered-looking poor soul, whom grief had sharpened instead of softening. 'I expect you feel too fine to set with common folks,' she said enviously to Betsey.

'Here I be a-settin',' responded Betsey calmly. 'I don' know's I behave more unbecomin' than usual.' Betsey prided herself upon her good and proper manners; but the rest of the company, who would have liked to hear the bit of morning news, were now defrauded of that pleasure. The wrong note had been struck; there was a silence after the clatter of knives and plates, and one by one the cheerful town charges disappeared. The bean-picking had been finished, and there was a call for any of the women who felt like planting corn; so Peggy Bond, who could follow the line of hills pretty fairly, and Betsey herself, who was still equal to anybody at that work, and Mrs. Dow, all went out to the field together. Aunt Lavina laboured slowly up the yard, carrying a light splint-bottomed kitchen chair and her knitting-work, and sat near the stone wall on a gentle rise, where she could see the pond and the green country, and exchange a word with her friends as they came and went up and down the rows. Betsey vouchsafed a word now and then about Mrs. Strafford, but you would have thought that she had been suddenly elevated to Mrs. Strafford's own cares and the responsibilities attending them, and had little in common with her old associates. Mrs. Dow and Peggy knew well that these high-feeling times never lasted long, and so they waited with as much patience as they could muster. They were by no means without that true tact which is only another word for unselfish sympathy.

The strip of corn land ran along the side of a great field; at the upper end of it was a field-corner thicket of young maples and walnut saplings, the children of a great nut-tree that marked the boundary. Once, when Betsey Lane found herself alone near this shelter at the end of her row, the other planters having lagged behind beyond the rising ground, she

THE FLIGHT OF BETSEY LANE

looked stealthily about, and then put her hand inside her gown, and for the first time took out the money that Mrs. Strafford had given her. She turned it over and over with an astonished look: there were new bank-bills for a hundred dollars. Betsey gave a funny little shrug of her shoulders, came out of the bushes, and took a step or two on the narrow edge of turf, as if she were going to dance; then she hastily tucked away her treasure, and stepped discreetly down into the soft harrowed and hoed land, and began to drop corn again, five kernels to a hill. She had seen the top of Peggy Bond's head over the knoll, and now Peggy herself came entirely into view, gazing upward to the skies, and stumbling more or less, but counting the corn by touch and twisting her head about anxiously to gain advantage over her uncertain vision. Betsey made a friendly, inarticulate little sound as they passed; she was thinking that somebody said once that Peggy's eyesight might be remedied if she could go to Boston to the hospital; but that was so remote and impossible an undertaking that no one had ever taken the first step. Betsey Lane's brown old face suddenly worked with excitement, but in a moment more she regained her usual firm expression, and spoke carelessly to Peggy as she turned and came alongside.

The high spring wind of the morning had quite fallen; it was a lovely May afternoon. The woods about the field to the northward were full of birds, and the young leaves scarcely hid the solemn shapes of a company of crows that patiently attended the corn-planting. Two of the men had finished their hoeing, and were busy with the construction of a scarecrow; they knelt in the furrows, chuckling, and looking over some forlorn, discarded garments. It was a time-honoured custom to make the scarecrow resemble one of the poor-house family; and this year they intended to have Mrs. Lavina Dow protect the field in effigy; last year it was the counterfeit of Betsey Lane who stood on guard, with an easily recognized quilted hood and the remains of a valued shawl that one of the calves had found airing on a fence and chewed to pieces. Behind the men was the foundation for this rustic attempt at statuary, — an upright stake and bar in the form of a cross. This stood on the highest part of the field; and as the men knelt near it, and the quaint figures of the corn-planters went and came, the scene gave a curious suggestion of foreign life. It was not like New England; the presence of the rude cross appealed strangely to the imagination.

IV

Life flowed so smoothly, for the most part, at the Byfleet Poor-farm, that nobody knew what to make, later in the summer, of a strange disappearance. All the elder inmates were familiar with illness and death, and the poor pomp of a town-pauper's funeral. The comings and goings and the various misfortunes of those who composed this strange family, related only through its disasters, hardly served for the excitement and talk of a single day. Now that the June days were at their longest, the old people were sure to wake earlier than ever; but one morning, to the astonishment of everyone, Betsey Lane's bed was empty; the sheets and blankets, which were her own, and guarded with jealous care, were carefully folded and placed on a chair not too near the window, and Betsey had flown. Nobody had heard her go down the creaking stairs. The kitchen door was unlocked, and the old watch-

THE FLIGHT OF BETSEY LANE

dog lay on the step outside in the early sunshine, wagging his tail and looking wise, as if he were left on guard and meant to keep the fugitive's secret.

'Never knowed her to do nothin' afore 'thout talking it over a fortnight, and paradin' off when we could all see her,' ventured a spiteful voice. 'Guess we can wait till night to hear 'bout it.'

Mrs. Dow looked sorrowful and shook her head. 'Betsey had an aunt on her mother's side that went and drownded of herself; she was a pritty-appearing woman as ever you see.'

'Perhaps she's gone to spend the day with Decker's folks,' suggested Peggy Bond. 'She always takes an extra early start; she was speakin' lately o' going up their way'; but Mrs. Dow shook her head with a most melancholy look. 'I'm impressed that something's befell her,' she insisted. 'I heard her a-groanin' in her sleep. I was wakeful the forepart o' the night, – 't is very unusual with me, too.'

"'T wa'n't like Betsey not to leave us any word,' said the other old friend, with more resentment than melancholy. They sat together almost in silence that morning in the shed chamber. Mrs. Dow was sorting and cutting rags, and Peggy braided them into long ropes, to be made into mats at a later date. If they had only known where Betsey Lane had gone, they might have talked about it until dinner-time at noon; but failing this new subject, they could take no interest in any of their old ones. Out in the field the corn was well up, and the men were hoeing. It was a hot morning in the shed chamber, and the woollen rags were dusty and hot to handle.

THE ONLY ROSE AND OTHER TALES

V

Byfleet people knew each other well, and when this mysteriously absent person did not return to the town-farm at the end of a week, public interest became much excited; and presently it was ascertained that Betsey Lane was neither making a visit to her friends the Deckers on Birch Hill, nor to any nearer acquaintances; in fact, she had disappeared altogether from her wonted haunts. Nobody remembered to have seen her pass, hers had been such an early flitting; and when somebody thought of her having gone away by train, he was laughed at for forgetting that the earliest morning train from South Byfleet, the nearest station, did not start until long after eight o'clock; and if Betsey had designed to be one of the passengers, she would have started along the road at seven, and been seen and known of all women. There was not a kitchen in that part of Byfleet that did not have windows toward the road. Conversation rarely left the level of the neighbourhood gossip: to see Betsey Lane, in her best clothes, at that hour in the morning, would have been the signal for much exercise of imagination; but as day after day went by without news, the curiosity of those who knew her best turned slowly into fear, and at last Peggy Bond again gave utterance to the belief that Betsey had either gone out in the early morning and put an end to her life, or that she had gone to the Centennial. Some of the people at table were moved to loud laughter, – it was at supper-time on a Sunday night, – but others listened with great interest.

'She never'd put on her good clothes to drownd herself,' said the widow. 'She might have thought 't was good as takin' 'em

THE FLIGHT OF BETSEY LANE

with her, though. Old folks has wandered off an' got lost in the woods afore now.'

Mrs. Dow and Peggy resented this impertinent remark, but deigned to take no notice of the speaker. 'She wouldn't have wore her best clothes to the Centennial, would she?' mildly inquired Peggy, bobbing her head toward the ceiling. ''T would be a shame to spoil your best things in such a place. An' I don't know of her havin' any money; there's the end o' that.'

'You're bad as old Mis' Bland, that used to live neighbour to our folks,' said one of the old men. 'She was dreadful precise; an' she so begretched to wear a good alapaca dress that was left to her, that it hung in a press forty year, an' baited the moths at last.'

'I often seen Mis' Bland a-goin' in to meetin' when I was a young girl,' said Peggy Bond approvingly. 'She was a good-appearin' woman, an' she left property.'

'Wish she'd left it to me, then,' said the poor soul opposite, glancing at her pathetic row of children: but it was not good manners at the farm to deplore one's situation, and Mrs. Dow and Peggy only frowned. 'Where do you suppose Betsey can be?' said Mrs. Dow, for the twentieth time. 'She didn't have no money. I know she ain't gone far, if it's so that she's yet alive. She's be'n real pinched all the spring.'

'Perhaps that lady that come one day give her some,' the keeper's wife suggested mildly.

'Then Betsey would have told me,' said Mrs. Dow, with injured dignity.

THE ONLY ROSE AND OTHER TALES

VI

On the morning of her disappearance, Betsey rose even before the pewee and the English sparrow, and dressed herself quietly, though with trembling hands, and stole out of the kitchen door like a plunderless thief. The old dog licked her hand and looked at her anxiously; the tortoise-shell cat rubbed against her best gown, and trotted away up the yard, then she turned anxiously and came after the old woman, following faithfully until she had to be driven back. Betsey was used to long country excursions afoot. She dearly loved the early morning; and finding that there was no dew to trouble her, she began to follow pasture paths and short cuts across the fields, surprising here and there a flock of sleepy sheep, or a startled calf that rustled out from the bushes. The birds were pecking their breakfast from bush and turf; and hardly any of the wild inhabitants of that rural world were enough alarmed by her presence to do more than flutter away if they chanced to be in her path. She stepped along, lightfooted and eager as a girl, dressed in her neat old straw bonnet and black gown, and carrying a few belongings in her best bundle-handkerchief, one that her only brother had brought home from the East Indies fifty years before. There was an old crow perched as sentinel on a small, dead pine-tree, where he could warn friends who were pulling up the sprouted corn in a field close by; but he only gave a contemptuous caw as the adventurer appeared, and she shook her bundle at him in revenge, and laughed to see him so clumsy as he tried to keep his footing on the twigs.

'Yes, I be,' she assured him. 'I'm a-goin' to Pheladelphy,

THE FLIGHT OF BETSEY LANE

to the Centennial, same 's other folks. I'd jest as soon tell ye 's not, old crow'; and Betsey laughed aloud in pleased content with herself and her daring, as she walked along. She had only two miles to go to the station at South Byfleet, and she felt for the money now and then, and found it safe enough. She took great pride in the success of her escape, and especially in the long concealment of her wealth. Not a night had passed since Mrs. Strafford's visit that she had not slept with the roll of money under her pillow by night, and buttoned safe inside her dress by day. She knew that everybody would offer advice and even commands about the spending or saving of it; and she brooked no interference.

The last mile of the foot-path to South Byfleet was along the railway track; and Betsey began to feel in haste, though it was still nearly two hours to train time. She looked anxiously forward and back along the rails every few minutes, for fear of being run over; and at last she caught sight of an engine that was apparently coming toward her, and took flight into the woods before she could gather courage to follow the path again. The freight train proved to be at a standstill, waiting at a turnout; and some of the men were straying about, eating their early breakfast comfortably in this time of leisure. As the old woman came up to them, she stopped too, for a moment of rest and conversation.

'Where be ye goin'?' she asked pleasantly; and they told her. It was to the town where she had to change cars and take the great through train; a point of geography which she had learned from evening talks between the men at the farm.

'What'll ye carry me there for?'

'We don't run no passenger cars,' said one of the young fellows, laughing. 'What makes you in such a hurry?'

'I'm startin' for Pheladelphy, an' it's a gre't ways to go.'

'So 't is; but you're consid'able early, if you're makin' for the eight-forty train. See here! you haven't got a needle an' thread 'long of you in that bundle, have you? If you'll sew me on a couple o' buttons, I'll give ye a free ride. I'm in a sight o' distress, an' none o' the fellows is provided with as much as a bent pin.'

'You poor boy! I'll have you seen to, in half a minute. I'm troubled with a stiff arm, but I'll do the best I can.'

The obliging Betsey seated herself stiffly on the slope of the embankment, and found her thread and needle with utmost haste. Two of the train-men stood by and watched the careful stitches, and even offered her a place as spare brakeman, so that they might keep her near; and Betsey took the offer with considerable seriousness, only thinking it necessary to assure them that she was getting most too old to be out in all weathers. An express went by like an earthquake, and she was presently hoisted on board an empty box-car by two of her new and flattering acquaintances, and found herself before noon at the end of the first stage of her journey, without having spent a cent, and furnished with any amount of thrifty advice. One of the young men, being compassionate of her unprotected state as a traveller, advised her to find out the widow of an uncle of his in Philadelphia, saying despairingly that he couldn't tell her just how to find the house; but Miss Betsey Lane said that she had an English tongue in her head, and should be sure to find whatever she was looking for. This unexpected incident of the freight train was the reason why

THE FLIGHT OF BETSEY LANE

everybody about the South Byfleet station insisted that no such person had taken passage by the regular train that same morning, and why there were those who persuaded themselves that Miss Betsey Lane was probably lying at the bottom of the poor-farm pond.

VII

'Land sakes!' said Miss Betsey Lane, as she watched a Turkish person parading by in his red fez, 'I call the Centennial somethin' like the day o' judgment! I wish I was goin' to stop a month, but I dare say 't would be the death o' my poor old bones.'

She was leaning against the barrier of a patent pop-corn establishment, which had given her a sudden reminder of home, and of the winter nights when the sharp-kernelled little red and yellow ears were brought out, and Old Uncle Eph Flanders sat by the kitchen stove, and solemnly filled a great wooden chopping-tray for the refreshment of the company. She had wandered and loitered and looked until her eyes and head had grown numb and unreceptive; but it is only unimaginative persons who can be really astonished. The imagination can always outrun the possible and actual sights and sounds of the world; and this plain old body from Byfleet rarely found anything rich and splendid enough to surprise her. She saw the wonders of the West and the splendours of the East with equal calmness and satisfaction; she had always known that there was an amazing world outside the boundaries of Byfleet. There was a piece of paper in her pocket on which was marked, in her clumsy handwriting, 'If Betsey Lane should meet with accident, notify the selectmen of

Byfleet'; but having made this slight provision for the future, she had thrown herself boldly into the sea of strangers, and then had made the joyful discovery that friends were to be found at every turn.

There was something delightfully companionable about Betsey; she had a way of suddenly looking up over her big spectacles with a reassuring and expectant smile, as if you were going to speak to her, and you generally did. She must have found out where hundreds of people came from, and whom they had left at home, and what they thought of the great show, as she sat on a bench to rest, or leaned over the railings where free luncheons were afforded by the makers of hot waffles and molasses candy and fried potatoes; and there was not a night when she did not return to her lodgings with a pocket crammed with samples of spool cotton and nobody knows what. She had already collected small presents for almost everybody she knew at home, and she was such a pleasant, beaming old country body, so unmistakably appreciative and interested, that nobody ever thought of wishing that she would move on. Nearly all the busy people of the Exhibition called her either Aunty or Grandma at once, and made little pleasures for her as best they could. She was a delightful contrast to the indifferent, stupid crowd that drifted along, with eyes fixed at the same level, and seeing, even on that level, nothing for fifty feet at a time. 'What be you making here, dear?' Betsey Lane would ask joyfully, and the most perfunctory guardian hastened to explain. She squandered money as she had never had the pleasure of doing before, and this hastened the day when she must return to Byfleet. She was always inquiring if there were any spectacle-sellers at hand,

THE FLIGHT OF BETSEY LANE

and received occasional directions; but it was a difficult place for her to find her way about in, and the very last day of her stay arrived before she found an exhibitor of the desired sort, an oculist and instrument-maker.

'I called to get some specs for a friend that's upsighted,' she gravely informed the salesman, to his extreme amusement. 'She's dreadful troubled, and jerks her head up like a hen a-drinkin'. She's got a blur a-growin' an' spreadin', an' sometimes she can see out to one side on 't, and more times she can't.'

'Cataracts,' said a middle-aged gentleman at her side; and Betsey Lane turned to regard him with approval and curiosity.

''T is Miss Peggy Bond I was mentioning, of Byfleet Poor-farm,' she explained. 'I count on gettin' some glasses to relieve her trouble, if there's any to be found.'

'Glasses won't do her any good,' said the stranger. 'Suppose you come and sit down on this bench, and tell me all about it. First, where is Byfleet?' and Betsey gave the directions at length.

'I thought so,' said the surgeon. 'How old is this friend of yours?'

Betsey cleared her throat decisively, and smoothed her gown over her knees as if it were an apron; then she turned to take a good look at her new acquaintance as they sat on the rustic bench together. 'Who be you, sir, I should like to know?' she asked, in a friendly tone.

'My name's Dunster.'

'I take it you're a doctor,' continued Betsey, as if they had overtaken each other walking from Byfleet to South Byfleet on a summer morning.

'I'm a doctor; part of one at least,' said he. 'I know more or less about eyes; and I spend my summers down on the shore at the mouth of your river; some day I'll come up and look at this person. How old is she?'

'Peggy Bond is one that never tells her age; 't ain't come quite up to where she'll begin to brag of it, you see,' explained Betsey reluctantly; 'but I know her to be nigh to seventy-six, one way or t'other. Her an' Mrs. Mary Ann Chick was same year's child'n, and Peggy knows I know it, an' two or three times when we've be'n in the buryin'-ground where Mary Ann lays an' has her dates right on her headstone, I couldn't bring Peggy to take no sort o' notice. I will say she makes, at times, a convenience of being upsighted. But there, I feel for her, – everybody does; it keeps her stubbin' an' trippin' against everything, beakin' and gazin' up the way she has to.'

'Yes, yes,' said the doctor, whose eyes were twinkling. 'I'll come and look after her, with your town doctor, this summer, – some time in the last of July or first of August.'

'You'll find occupation,' said Betsey, not without an air of patronage. 'Most of us to the Byfleet Farm has got our ails, now I tell ye. You ain't got no bitters that'll take a dozen years right off an ol' lady's shoulders?'

The busy man smiled pleasantly, and shook his head as he went away. 'Dunster,' said Betsey to herself, soberly committing the new name to her sound memory. 'Yes, I mustn't forget to speak of him to the doctor, as he directed. I do' know now as Peggy would vally herself quite so much accordin' to, if she had her eyes fixed same as other folks. I expect there wouldn't been a smarter woman in town, though, if she'd had a proper chance. Now I've done what I set to do for her, I do

THE FLIGHT OF BETSEY LANE

believe, an' 't wa'n't glasses, neither. I'll git her a pritty little shawl with that money I laid aside. Peggy Bond ain't got a pritty shawl. I always wanted to have a real good time, an' now I'm havin' it.'

VIII

Two or three days later, two pathetic figures might have been seen crossing the slopes of the poor-farm field, toward the low shores of Byfield pond. It was early in the morning, and the stubble of the lately mown grass was wet with rain and hindering to old feet. Peggy Bond was more blundering and liable to stray in the wrong direction than usual; it was one of the days when she could hardly see at all. Aunt Lavina Dow was unusually clumsy of movement, and stiff in the joints; she had not been so far from the house for three years. The morning breeze filled the gathers of her wide gingham skirt, and aggravated the size of her unwieldy figure. She supported herself with a stick, and trusted beside to the fragile support of Peggy's arm. They were talking together in whispers.

'Oh, my sakes!' exclaimed Peggy, moving her small head from side to side. 'Hear you wheeze, Mis' Dow! This may be the death o' you; there, do go slow! You set here on the side-hill, an' le' me go try if I can see.'

'It needs more eyesight than you've got,' said Mrs. Dow, panting between the words. 'Oh! to think how spry I was in my young days, an' here I be now, the full of a door, an' all my complaints so aggravated by my size. 'T is hard! 't is hard! but I'm a-doin' of all this for pore Betsey's sake. I know they've all laughed, but I look to see her ris' to the top o 'the pond this day, — 't is just nine days since she departed; an' say what they may, I know she hove herself in. It run in her family; Betsey had an aunt that done just so, an' she ain't be'n like herself, a-broodin' an' hivin' away alone, an' nothin' to say to you an' me that was always such good company all together. Somethin' sprung her mind, now I tell ye, Mis' Bond.'

'I feel to hope we sha'n't find her, I must say,' faltered Peggy. It was plain that Mrs. Dow was the captain of this doleful expedition. 'I guess she ain't never thought o' drowndin' of herself, Mis' Dow; she's gone off a-visitin' way over to the other side o' South Byfleet; some thinks she's gone to the Centennial even now!'

'She hadn't no proper means, I tell ye,' wheezed Mrs. Dow indignantly; 'an' if you prefer that others should find her floatin' to the top this day, instid of us that's her best friends, you can step back to the house.'

They walked on in aggrieved silence. Peggy Bond trembled with excitement, but her companion's firm grasp never wavered, and so they came to the narrow, gravelly margin and stood still. Peggy tried in vain to see the glittering water and the pond-lilies that starred it; she knew that they must be there; once, years ago, she had caught fleeting glimpses of them, and she never forgot what she had once seen. The clear blue sky overhead, the dark pine-woods beyond the pond, were all clearly pictured in her mind. 'Can't you see nothin'?' she faltered; 'I believe I'm wuss'n upsighted this day. I'm going to be blind.'

'No,' said Lavina Dow solemnly; 'no, there ain't nothin' whatever, Peggy. I hope to mercy she ain't' —

THE FLIGHT OF BETSEY LANE

'Why, whoever'd expected to find you 'way out here!' exclaimed a brisk and cheerful voice. There stood Betsey Lane herself, close behind them, having just emerged from a thicket of alders that grew close by. She was following the short way homeward from the railroad.

'Why, what's the matter, Mis' Dow? You ain't overdoin', be ye? an' Peggy's all of a flutter. What in the name o' natur' ails ye?'

'There ain't nothin' the matter, as I knows on,' responded the leader of this fruitless expedition. 'We only thought we'd take a stroll this pleasant mornin',' she added, with sublime self-possession. 'Where've you be'n, Betsey Lane?'

'To Pheladelphy, ma'am,' said Betsey, looking quite young and gay, and wearing a townish and unfamiliar air that upheld her words. 'All ought to go that can; why, you feel's if you'd be'n all round the world. I guess I've got enough to think of and tell ye for the rest o' my days. I've always wanted to go somewheres. I wish you'd be'n there, I do so. I've talked with folks from Chiny an' the back o' Pennsylvany; and I see folks way from Austraaly that 'peared as well as anybody; an' I see how they made spool cotton, an' sights o' other things; an' I spoke with a doctor that lives down to the beach in the summer, an' he offered to come up 'long in the first of August, an' see what he can do for Peggy's eyesight. There was di'monds there as big as pigeon's eggs; an' I met with Mis' Abby Fletcher from South Byfleet depot; an' there was hogs there that weighed risin' thirteen hunderd –'

'I want to know,' said Mrs. Lavina Dow and Peggy Bond, together.

'Well, 't was a great exper'ence for a person,' added Lavina, turning ponderously, in spite of herself, to give a last wistful look at the smiling waters of the pond.

'I don't know how soon I be goin' to settle down,' proclaimed the rustic sister of Sindbad. 'What's for the good o' one's for the good of all. You just wait till we're setting together up in the old shed chamber! You know, my dear Mis' Katy Strafford give me a han'some present o' money that day she come to see me; and I'd be'n a-dreamin' by night an' day o' seein' that Centennial; and when I come to think on 't I felt sure somebody ought to go from this neighbourhood, if 't was only for the good o' the rest; and I thought I'd better be the one. I wa'n't goin' to ask the selec'men neither. I've come back with one-thirty-five in money, and I see everything there, an' I fetched ye all a little somethin'; but I'm full o' dust now, an' pretty nigh beat out. I never see a place more friendly then Pheladelphy; but 't ain't natural to a Byfleet person to be always walkin' on a level. There, now, Peggy, you take my bundle-handkercher and the basket, and let Mis' Dow sag on to me. I'll git her along twice as easy.'

With this the small elderly company set forth triumphant toward the poor-house, across the wide green field.

THE HILTONS' HOLIDAY

★

I

THERE was a bright, full moon in the clear sky, and the sunset was still shining faintly in the west. Dark woods stood all about the old Hilton farmhouse, save down the hill, westward, where lay the shadowy fields which John Hilton, and his father before him, had cleared and tilled with much toil, – the small fields to which they had given the industry and even affection of their honest lives.

John Hilton was sitting on the doorstep of his house. As he moved his head in and out of the shadows, turning now and then to speak to his wife, who sat just within the doorway, one could see his good face, rough and somewhat unkempt, as if he were indeed a creature of the shady woods and brown earth, instead of the noisy town. It was late in the long spring evening, and he had just come from the lower field as cheerful as a boy, proud of having finished the planting of his potatoes.

'I had to do my last row mostly by feelin',' he said to his wife. 'I'm proper glad I pushed through, an' went back an' ended off after supper. 'T would have taken me a good part o' to-morrow mornin', an' broke my day.'

''T ain't no use for ye to work yourself all to pieces, John,' answered the woman quickly. 'I declare it does seem harder than ever that we couldn't have kep' our boy; he'd been comin' fourteen years old this fall, most a grown man, and he'd work right 'longside of ye now the whole time.'

''T was hard to lose him; I do seem to miss little John,' said the father sadly. 'I expect there was reasons why 't was best.

I feel able an' smart to work; my father was a girt strong man, an' a monstrous worker afore me. 'T ain't that; but I was thinkin' by myself to-day what a sight o' company the boy would ha' been. You know, small's he was, how I could trust to leave him anywheres with the team, and how he'd beseech to go with me wherever I was goin'; always right in my tracks I used to tell 'em. Poor little John, for all he was so young he had a great deal o' judgment; he'd ha' made a likely man.'

The mother sighed heavily as she sat within the shadow.

'But then there's the little girls, a sight o' help an' company,' urged the father eagerly, as if it were wrong to dwell upon sorrow and loss. 'Katy, she's most as good as a boy, except that she ain't very rugged. She's a real little farmer, she's helped me a sight this spring; an' you've got Susan Ellen, that makes a complete little housekeeper for ye as far as she's learnt. I don't see but we're better off than most folks, each on us having a workmate.'

'That's so, John,' acknowledged Mrs. Hilton wistfully, beginning to rock steadily in her straight, splint-bottomed chair. It was always a good sign when she rocked.

'Where be the little girls so late?' asked their father. "T is gettin' long past eight o'clock. I don't know when we've all set up so late, but it's so kind o' summer-like an' pleasant. Why, where be they gone?'

'I've told ye; only over to Becker's folks,' answered the mother. 'I don't see myself what keeps 'em so late; they beseeched me after supper till I let 'em go. They're all in a dazzle with the new teacher; she asked 'em to come over. They say she's unusual smart with 'rethmetic, but she has a

THE HILTONS' HOLIDAY

kind of a gorpen look to me. She's goin' to give Katy some pieces for her doll, but I told Katy she ought to be ashamed wantin' dolls' pieces, big as she's gettin' to be. I don't know's she ought, though; she ain't but nine this summer.'

'Let her take her comfort,' said the kind-hearted man. 'Them things draws her to the teacher, an' makes them acquainted. Katy's shy with new folks, more so 'n Susan Ellen, who's of the business kind. Katy's shy-feelin' and wishful.'

'I don't know but she is,' agreed the mother slowly. 'Ain't it sing'lar how well acquainted you be with that one, an' I with Susan Ellen? 'T was always so from the first. I'm doubtful sometimes our Katy ain't one that'll be like to get married – anyways not about here. She lives right with herself, but Susan Ellen ain't nothin' when she's alone, she's always after company; all the boys is waitin' on her a'ready. I ain't afraid but she'll take her pick when the time comes. I expect to see Susan Ellen well settled, – she feels grown up now, – but Katy don't care one mite 'bout none o' them things. She wants to be rovin' out o' doors. I do believe she'd stand an' hark to a bird the whole forenoon.'

'Perhaps she'll grow up to be a teacher,' suggested John Hilton. 'She takes to her book more'n the other one. I should like one on 'em to be a teacher same 's my mother was. They're good girls as anybody's got.'

'So they be,' said the mother, with unusual gentleness, and the creak of her rocking-chair was heard, regular as the ticking of a clock. The night breeze stirred in the great woods, and the sound of a brook that went falling down the hillside grew louder and louder. Now and then one could hear the plaintive chirp of a bird. The moon glittered with whiteness like a winter moon, and shone upon the low-roofed house until its small window-panes gleamed like silver, and one could almost see the colours of a blooming bush of lilac that grew in a sheltered angle by the kitchen door. There was an incessant sound of frogs in the lowlands.

'Be you sound asleep, John?' asked the wife presently.

'I don't know but what I was a'most,' said the tired man, starting a little. 'I should laugh if I was to fall sound asleep right here on the step; 't is the bright night, I expect, makes my eyes feel heavy, an' 't is so peaceful. I was up an' dressed a little past four an' out to work. Well, well!' and he laughed sleepily and rubbed his eyes. 'Where's the little girls? I'd better step along an' meet 'em.'

'I wouldn't just yet; they'll get home all right, but 't is late for 'em certain. I don't want 'em keepin' Mis' Becker's folks up neither. There, le' 's wait a few minutes,' urged Mrs. Hilton.

'I've be'n a-thinkin' all day I'd like to give the child'n some kind of a treat,' said the father, wide awake now. 'I hurried up my work 'cause I had it so in mind. They don't have the opportunities some do, an' I want 'em to know the world, an' not stay right here on the farm like a couple o' bushes.'

'They're a sight better off not to be so full o' notions as some is,' protested the mother suspiciously.

'Certain,' answered the farmer; 'but they're good, bright child'n, an' commencin' to take a sight o' notice. I want 'em to have all we can give 'em. I want 'em to see how other folks does things.'

THE HILTONS' HOLIDAY

'Why, so do I,' — here the rocking-chair stopped ominously, — 'but so long 's they're contented —'

'Contented ain't all in this world; hopper-toads may have that quality an' spend all their time a-blinkin'. I don't know 's bein' contented is all there is to look for in a child. Ambition 's somethin' to me.'

'Now you've got your mind on to some plot or other.' (The rocking-chair began to move again.) 'Why can't you talk right out?'

"T ain't nothin' special,' answered the good man, a little ruffled; he was never prepared for his wife's mysterious powers of divination. 'Well there, you do find things out the master! I only thought perhaps I'd take 'em to-morrow, an' go off somewhere if 't was a good day. I've been promisin' for a good while I'd take 'em to Topham Corners; they've never been there since they was very small.'

'I believe you want a good time yourself. You ain't never got over bein' a boy.' Mrs. Hilton seemed much amused. 'There, go if you want to an' take 'em; they've got their summer hats an' new dresses. I don't know o' nothin' that stands in the way. I should sense it better if there was a circus or anythin' to go to. Why don't you wait an' let the girls pick 'em some strawberries or nice ros'berries, and then they could take an' sell 'em to the stores?'

John Hilton reflected deeply. 'I should like to get me some good yellow-turnip seed to plant late. I ain't more'n satisfied with what I've been gettin' o' late years o' Ira Speed. An' I'm goin' to provide me with a good hoe; mine 's gettin' wore out an' all shackly. I can't seem to fix it good.'

'Them's excuses,' observed Mrs. Hilton, with friendly tolerance. 'You just cover up the hoe with somethin', if you get it – I would. Ira Speed's so jealous he'll remember it of you this twenty year, your goin' an' buyin' a new hoe o' anybody but him.'

'I've always thought 't was a free country,' said John Hilton soberly. 'I don't want to vex Ira neither; he favours us all he can in trade. 'T is difficult for him to spare a cent, but he's as honest as daylight.'

At this moment there was a sudden sound of young voices, and a pair of young figures came out from the shadow of the woods into the moonlighted open space. An old cock crowed loudly from his perch in the shed, as if he were a herald of royalty. The little girls were hand in hand, and a brisk young dog capered about them as they came.

'Wa'n't it dark gittin' home through the woods this time o' night?' asked the mother hastily, and not without reproach.

'I don't love to have you gone so late; mother an' me was timid about ye, and you've kep' Mis' Becker's folks up, I expect,' said their father regretfully. 'I don't want to have it said that my little girls ain't got good manners.'

'The teacher had a party,' chirped Susan Ellen, the elder of the two children. 'Goin' home from school she asked the Grover boys, an' Mary an' Sarah Speed. An' Mis' Becker was real pleasant to us: she passed round some cake, an' handed us sap sugar on one of her best plates, an' we played games an' sung some pieces too. Mis' Becker thought we did real well. I can pick out most of a tune on the cabinet organ; teacher says she'll give me lessons.'

'I want to know, dear!' exclaimed John Hilton.

THE HILTONS' HOLIDAY

'Yes, an' we played Copenhagen, an' took sides spellin', an' Katy beat everybody spellin' there was there.'

Katy had not spoken; she was not so strong as her sister, and while Susan Ellen stood a step or two away addressing her eager little audience, Katy had seated herself close to her father on the doorstep. He put his arm around her shoulders, and drew her close to his side, where she stayed.

'Ain't you got nothin' to tell, daughter?' he asked, looking down fondly; and Katy gave a pleased little sigh for answer.

'Tell 'em what 's goin' to be the last day o' school, and about our trimmin' the schoolhouse,' she said; and Susan Ellen gave the programme in most spirited fashion.

"T will be a great time,' said the mother, when she had finished. 'I don't see why folks wants to go trapesin' off to strange places when such things is happenin' right about 'em.' But the children did not observe her mysterious air. 'Come, you must step yourselves right to bed!'

They all went into the dark, warm house; the bright moon shone upon it steadily all night, and the lilac flowers were shaken by no breath of wind until the early dawn.

II

The Hiltons always waked early. So did their neighbours, the crows and song-sparrows and robins, the light-footed foxes and squirrels in the woods. When John Hilton waked, before five o'clock, an hour later than usual because he had sat up so late, he opened the house door and came out into the yard, crossing the short green turf hurriedly as if the day were too far spent for any loitering. The magnitude of the plan for taking a whole day of pleasure confronted him seriously, but the weather was fair, and his wife, whose disapproval could not have been set aside, had accepted and even smiled upon the great project. It was inevitable now, that he and the children should go to Topham Corners. Mrs. Hilton had the pleasure of waking them, and telling the news.

In a few minutes they came frisking out to talk over the great plans. The cattle were already fed, and their father was milking. The only sign of high festivity was the wagon pulled out into the yard, with both seats put in as if it were Sunday; but Mr. Hilton still wore his every-day clothes, and Susan Ellen suffered instantly from disappointment.

'Ain't we goin', father?' she asked complainingly; but he nodded and smiled at her, even though the cow, impatient to get to pasture, kept whisking her rough tail across his face. He held his head down and spoke cheerfully, in spite of this vexation.

'Yes, sister, we're goin' certain', an' goin' to have a great time too.' Susan Ellen thought that he seemed like a boy at that delightful moment, and felt new sympathy and pleasure at once. 'You go an' help mother about breakfast an' them things; we want to get off quick's we can. You coax mother now, both on ye, an' see if she won't go with us.'

'She said she wouldn't be hired to,' responded Susan Ellen. 'She says it's goin' to be hot, an' she's laid out to go over an' see how her aunt Tamsen Brooks is this afternoon.'

The father gave a little sigh; then he took heart again. The truth was that his wife made light of the contemplated pleasure, and, much as he usually valued her companionship and approval, he was sure that they should have a better time without her. It was impossible, however, not to feel guilty of

THE HILTONS' HOLIDAY

disloyalty at the thought. Even though she might be completely unconscious of his best ideals, he only loved her and the ideals the more, and bent his energies to satisfying her indefinite expectations. His wife still kept much of that youthful beauty which Susan Ellen seemed likely to reproduce.

An hour later the best wagon was ready, and the great expedition set forth. The little dog sat apart, and barked as if it fell entirely upon him to voice the general excitement. Both seats were in the wagon, but the empty place testified to Mrs. Hilton's unyielding disposition. She had wondered why one broad seat would not do, but John Hilton meekly suggested that the wagon looked better with both. The little girls sat on the back seat dressed alike in their Sunday hats of straw with blue ribbons, and their little plaid shawls pinned neatly about their small shoulders. They wore grey thread gloves, and sat very straight. Susan Ellen was half a head the taller, but otherwise, from behind, they looked much alike. As for their father, he was in his Sunday best, – a plain black coat, and a winter hat of felt, which was heavy and rusty-looking for that warm early summer day. He had it in mind to buy a new straw hat at Topham, so that this with the turnip seed and the hoe made three important reasons for going.

'Remember an' lay off your shawls when you get there, an' carry them over your arms,' said the mother, clucking like an excited hen to her chickens. 'They'll do to keep the dust off your new dresses goin' an' comin'. An' when you eat your dinners don't get spots on you, an' don't point at folks as you ride by, an' stare, or they'll know you come from the country. An', John, you call into Cousin Ad'line Marlow's an' see how they all be, an' tell her I expect her over certain to stop awhile before hayin'. It always eases her phthisic to git up here on the high land, an' I've got a new notion about doin' over her best-room carpet sence I see her that'll save rippin' one breadth. An' don't come home all wore out; an', John, don't you go an' buy me no kickshaws to fetch home. I ain't a child, an' you ain't got no money to waste. I expect you'll go, like 's not, an' buy you some kind of a foolish boy's hat; do look an' see if it's reasonable good straw, an' won't splinter all off round the edge. An' you mind, John –'

'Yes, yes, hold on!' cried John impatiently; then he cast a last affectionate, reassuring look at her face, flushed with the hurry and responsibility of starting them off in proper shape. 'I wish you was goin' too,' he said, smiling. 'I do so!' Then the old horse started, and they went out at the bars, and began the careful long descent of the hill. The young dog, tethered to the lilac-bush, was frantic with piteous appeals; the little girls piped their eager good-byes again and again, and their father turned many times to look back and wave his hand. As for their mother, she stood alone and watched them out of sight.

There was one place far out on the high-road where she could catch a last glimpse of the wagon, and she waited what seemed a very long time until it appeared and then was lost to sight again behind a low hill. 'They're nothin' but a pack o' child'n together,' she said aloud; and then felt lonelier than she expected. She even stooped and patted the unresigned little dog as she passed him, going into the house.

The occasion was so much more important than anyone had foreseen that both the little girls were speechless. It seemed at first like going to church in new clothes, or to a

THE HILTONS' HOLIDAY

funeral; they hardly knew how to behave at the beginning of a whole day of pleasure. They made grave bows at such persons of their acquaintance as happened to be straying in the road. Once or twice they stopped before a farmhouse, while their father talked an inconsiderately long time with someone about the crops and the weather, and even dwelt upon town business and the doings of the selectmen, which might be talked of at any time. The explanations that he gave of their excursion seemed quite unnecessary. It was made entirely clear that he had a little business to do at Topham Corners, and thought he had better give the little girls a ride; they had been very steady at school, and he had finished planting, and could take the day as well as not. Soon, however, they all felt as if such an excursion were an every-day affair, and Susan Ellen began to ask eager questions, while Katy silently sat apart enjoying herself as she never had done before. She liked to see the strange houses, and the children who belonged to them; it was delightful to find flowers that she knew growing all along the road, no matter how far she went from home. Each small homestead looked its best and pleasantest, and shared the exquisite beauty that early summer made, – shared the luxury of greenness and floweriness that decked the rural world. There was an early peony or a late lilac in almost every dooryard.

It was seventeen miles to Topham. After a while they seemed very far from home, having left the hills far behind, and descended to a great level country with fewer tracts of woodland, and wider fields where the crops were much more forward. The houses were all painted, and the roads were smoother and wider. It had been so pleasant driving along that Katy dreaded going into the strange town when she first caught sight of it, though Susan Ellen kept asking with bold fretfulness if they were not almost there. They counted the steeples of four churches, and their father presently showed them the Topham Academy, where their grandmother once went to school, and told them that perhaps some day they would go there too. Katy's heart gave a strange leap; it was such a tremendous thing to think of, but instantly the suggestion was transformed for her into one of the certainties of life. She looked with solemn awe at the tall belfry, and the long rows of windows in the front of the academy, there where it stood high and white among the clustering trees. She hoped that they were going to drive by, but something forbade her taking the responsibility of saying so.

Soon the children found themselves among the crowded village houses. Their father turned to look at them with affectionate solicitude.

'Now sit up straight and appear pretty,' he whispered to them. 'We're among the best people now, an' I want folks to think well of you.'

'I guess we're as good as they be,' remarked Susan Ellen, looking at some innocent passers-by with dark suspicion, but Katy tried indeed to sit straight, and folded her hands prettily in her lap, and wished with all her heart to be pleasing for her father's sake. Just then an elderly woman saw the wagon and the sedate party it carried, and smiled so kindly that it seemed to Katy as if Topham Corners had welcomed and received them. She smiled back again as if this hospitable person were an old friend, and entirely forgot that the eyes of all Topham had been upon her.

THE HILTONS' HOLIDAY

'There, now we're coming to an elegant house that I want you to see; you'll never forget it,' said John Hilton. 'It's where Judge Masterson lives, the great lawyer; the handsomest house in the county, everybody says.'

'Do you know him, father?' asked Susan Ellen.

'I do,' answered John Hilton proudly. 'Him and my mother went to school together in their young days, and were always called the two best scholars of their time. The judge called to see her once; he stopped to our house to see her when I was a boy. An' then, some years ago – you've heard me tell how I was on the jury, an' when he heard my name spoken he looked at me sharp, and asked if I wa'n't the son of Catharine Winn, an' spoke most beautiful of your grandmother, an' how well he remembered their young days together.'

'I like to hear about that,' said Katy.

'She had it pretty hard, I'm afraid, up on the old farm. She was keepin' school in our district when father married her – that's the main reason I backed 'em down when they wanted to tear the old schoolhouse all to pieces,' confided John Hilton, turning eagerly. 'They all say she lived longer up here on the hill than she could anywhere, but she never had her health. I wa'n't but a boy when she died. Father an' me lived alone afterward till the time your mother come; 't was a good while, too; I wa'n't married so young as some. 'T was lonesome, I tell you; father was plumb discouraged losin' of his wife, an' her long sickness an' all set him back, an' we'd work all day on the land an' never say a word. I s'pose 't is bein' so lonesome early in life that makes me so pleased to have some nice girls growin' up round me now.'

There was a tone in her father's voice that drew Katy's heart toward him with new affection. She dimly understood, but Susan Ellen was less interested. They had often heard this story before, but to one child it was always new and to the other old. Susan Ellen was apt to think it tiresome to hear about her grandmother, who, being dead, was hardly worth talking about.

'There's Judge Masterson's place,' said their father in an every-day manner, as they turned a corner, and came into full view of the beautiful old white house standing behind its green trees and terraces and lawns. The children had never imagined anything so stately and fine, and even Susan Ellen exclaimed with pleasure. At that moment they saw an old gentleman, who carried himself with great dignity, coming slowly down the wide box-bordered path toward the gate.

'There he is now, there's the judge!' whispered John Hilton excitedly, reining his horse quickly to the green roadside. 'He's goin' down-town to his office; we can wait right here an' see him. I can't expect him to remember me; it's been a good many years. Now you are goin' to see the great Judge Masterson!'

There was a quiver of expectation in their hearts. The judge stopped at his gate, hesitating a moment before he lifted the latch, and glanced up the street at the country wagon with its two prim little girls on the back seat, and the eager man who drove. They seemed to be waiting for something; the old horse was nibbling at the fresh roadside grass. The judge was used to being looked at with interest, and responded now with a smile as he came out to the sidewalk, and unexpectedly

THE HILTONS' HOLIDAY

turned their way. Then he suddenly lifted his hat with grave politeness, and came directly toward them.

'Good morning, Mr. Hilton,' he said. 'I am very glad to see you, sir'; and Mr. Hilton, the little girls' own father, took off his hat with equal courtesy, and bent forward to shake hands.

Susan Ellen cowered and wished herself away, but little Katy sat straighter than ever, with joy in her father's pride and pleasure shining in her pale, flower-like little face.

'These are your daughters, I am sure,' said the old gentleman kindly, taking Susan Ellen's limp and reluctant hand; but when he looked at Katy, his face brightened. 'How she recalls your mother!' he said with great feeling. 'I am glad to see this dear child. You must come to see me with your father, my dear,' he added, still looking at her. 'Bring both the little girls, and let them run about the old garden; the cherries are just getting ripe,' said Judge Masterson hospitably. 'Perhaps you will have time to stop this afternoon as you go home?'

'I should call it a great pleasure if you would come and see us again some time. You may be driving our way, sir,' said John Hilton.

'Not very often in these days,' answered the old judge. 'I thank you for the kind invitation. I should like to see the fine view again from your hill westward. Can I serve you in any way while you are in town? Good-bye, my little friends!'

Then they parted, but not before Katy, the shy Katy, whose hand the judge still held unconsciously while he spoke, had reached forward as he said good-bye, and lifted her face to kiss him. She could not have told why, except that she felt drawn to something in the serious, worn face. For the first time in her life the child had felt the charm of manners; perhaps she owned a kinship between that which made him what he was, and the spark of nobleness and purity in her own simple soul. She turned again and again to look back at him as they drove away.

'Now you have seen one of the first gentlemen in the country,' said their father. 'It was worth comin' twice as far' – but he did not say any more, nor turn as usual to look in the children's faces.

In the chief business street of Topham a great many country wagons like the Hiltons' were fastened to the posts, and there seemed to our holiday-makers to be a great deal of noise and excitement.

'Now I've got to do my errands, and we can let the horse rest and feed,' said John Hilton. 'I'll slip his headstall right off, an' put on his halter. I'm goin' to buy him a real good treat o' oats. First we'll go an' buy me my straw hat; I feel as if this one looked a little past to wear in Topham. We'll buy the things we want, an' then we'll walk all along the street, so you can look in the windows an' see the han'some things, same 's your mother likes to. What was it mother told you about your shawls?'

'To take 'em off an' carry 'em over our arms,' piped Susan Ellen, without comment, but in the interest of alighting and finding themselves afoot upon the pavement the shawls were forgotten. The children stood at the doorway of a shop while their father went inside, and they tried to see what the Topham shapes of bonnets were like, as their mother had advised them; but everything was exciting and confusing, and they

THE HILTONS' HOLIDAY

could arrive at no decision. When Mr. Hilton came out with a hat in his hand to be seen in a better light, Katy whispered that she wished he would buy a shiny one like Judge Masterson's; but her father only smiled and shook his head, and said that they were plain folks, he and Katy. There were drygoods for sale in the same shop, and a young clerk who was measuring linen kindly pulled off some pretty labels with gilded edges and gay pictures, and gave them to the little girls, to their exceeding joy. He may have had small sisters at home, this friendly lad, for he took pains to find two pretty blue boxes besides, and was rewarded by their beaming gratitude.

It was a famous day; they even became used to seeing so many people pass. The village was full of its morning activity, and Susan Ellen gained a new respect for her father, and an increased sense of her own consequence, because even in Topham several persons knew him and called him familiarly by name. The meeting with an old man who had once been a neighbour seemed to give Mr. Hilton the greatest pleasure. The old man called to them from a house doorway as they were passing, and they all went in. The children seated themselves wearily on the wooden step, but their father shook his old friend eagerly by the hand, and declared that he was delighted to see him so well and enjoying the fine weather.

'Oh, yes,' said the old man, in a feeble, quavering voice, 'I'm astonishin' well for my age. I don't complain, John, I don't complain.'

They talked long together of people whom they had known in the past, and Katy, being a little tired, was glad to rest, and sat still with her hands folded, looking about the front yard. There were some kinds of flowers that she never had seen before.

'This is the one that looks like my mother,' her father said, and touched Katy's shoulder to remind her to stand up and let herself be seen. 'Judge Masterson saw the resemblance; we met him at his gate this morning.'

'Yes, she certain does look like your mother, John,' said the old man, looking pleasantly at Katy, who found that she liked him better than at first. 'She does, certain; the best of young folks is, they remind us of the old ones. 'T is nateral to cling to life, folks say, but for me, I git impatient at times. Most everybody's gone now, an' I want to be goin'. 'T is somethin' before me, an' I want to have it over with. I want to be there 'long o' the rest o' the folks. I expect to last quite a while though; I may see ye couple o' times more, John.'

John Hilton responded cheerfully, and the children were urged to pick some flowers. The old man awed them with his impatience to be gone. There was such a townful of people about him, and he seemed as lonely as if he were the last survivor of a former world. Until that moment they had felt as if everything were just beginning.

'Now I want to buy somethin' pretty for your mother,' said Mr. Hilton, as they went soberly away down the street, the children keeping fast hold of his hands. 'By now the old horse will have eat his dinner and had a good rest, so pretty soon we can jog along home. I'm goin' to take you round by the academy, and the old North Meeting-house where Dr. Barstow used to preach. Can't you think o' somethin' that your mother'd want?' he asked suddenly, confronted by a man's difficulty of choice.

THE HILTONS' HOLIDAY

'She was talkin' about wantin' a new pepper-box, one day; the top o' the old one won't stay on,' suggested Susan Ellen, with delightful readiness. 'Can't we have some candy, father?'

'Yes, ma'am,' said John Hilton, smiling and swinging her hand to and fro as they walked. 'I feel as if some would be good myself. What's all this?' They were passing a photographer's doorway with its enticing array of portraits. 'I do declare!' he exclaimed excitedly, 'I'm goin' to have our pictures taken; 't will please your mother more 'n a little.'

This was, perhaps, the greatest triumph of the day, except the delightful meeting with the judge; they sat in a row, with the father in the middle, and there was no doubt as to the excellence of the likeness. The best hats had to be taken off because they cast a shadow, but they were not missed, as their owners had feared. Both Susan Ellen and Katy looked their brightest and best; their eager young faces would forever shine there; the joy of the holiday was mirrored in the little picture. They did not know why their father was so pleased with it; they would not know until age had dowered them with the riches of association and remembrance.

Just at nightfall the Hiltons reached home again, tired out and happy. Katy had climbed over into the front seat beside her father, because that was always her place when they went to church on Sundays. It was a cool evening, there was a fresh sea wind that brought a light mist with it, and the sky was fast growing cloudy. Somehow the children looked different; it seemed to their mother as if they had grown older and taller since they went away in the morning, and as if they belonged to the town now as much as to the country. The greatness of their day's experience had left her far behind; the day had been silent and lonely without them, and she had had their supper ready, and been watching anxiously, ever since five o'clock. As for the children themselves they had little to say at first – they had eaten their luncheon early on the way to Topham. Susan Ellen was childishly cross, but Katy was pathetic and wan. They could hardly wait to show the picture, and their mother was as much pleased as everybody had expected.

'There, what did make you wear your shawls?' she exclaimed a moment afterward, reproachfully. 'You ain't been an' wore 'em all day long? I wanted folks to see how pretty your new dresses was, if I did make 'em. Well, well! I wish more'n ever now I'd gone an' seen to ye!'

'An' here's the pepper-box!' said Katy, in a pleased, unconscious tone.

'That really is what I call beautiful,' said Mrs. Hilton, after a long and doubtful look. 'Our other one was only tin. I never did look so high as a chiny one with flowers, but I can get us another any time for every day. That's a proper hat, as good as you could have got, John. Where's your new hoe?' she asked as he came toward her from the barn, smiling with satisfaction.

'I declare to Moses if I didn't forget all about it,' meekly acknowledged the leader of the great excursion. 'That an' my yellow turnip seed, too; they went clean out o' my head, there was so many other things to think of. But 't ain't no sort o' matter; I can get a hoe just as well to Ira Speed's.'

His wife could not help laughing. 'You an' the little girls have had a great time. They was full o' wonder to me about everything, and I expect they'll talk about it for a week. I

THE HILTONS' HOLIDAY

guess we was right about havin' 'em see somethin' more o' the world.'

'Yes,' answered John Hilton, with humility, 'yes, we did have a beautiful day. I didn't expect so much. They looked as nice as anybody, and appeared so modest an' pretty. The little girls will remember it perhaps by an' by. I guess they won't never forget this day they had 'long o' father.'

It was evening again, the frogs were piping in the lower meadows, and in the woods, higher up the great hill, a little owl began to hoot. The sea air, salt and heavy, was blowing in over the country at the end of the hot bright day. A lamp was lighted in the house, the happy children were talking together, and supper was waiting. The father and mother lingered for a moment outside and looked down over the shadowy fields; then they went in, without speaking. The great day was over, and they shut the door.

A WHITE HERON

★

I

THE woods were already filled with shadows one June evening, just before eight o'clock, though a bright sunset still glimmered faintly among the trunks of the trees. A little girl was driving home her cow, a plodding, dilatory, provoking creature in her behaviour, but a valued companion for all that. They were going away from the western light, and striking deep into the dark woods, but their feet were familiar with the path, and it was no matter whether their eyes could see it or not.

There was hardly a night the summer through when the old cow could be found waiting at the pasture bars; on the contrary, it was her greatest pleasure to hide herself away among the high huckleberry bushes, and though she wore a loud bell, she had made the discovery that if one stood perfectly still it would not ring. So Sylvia had to hunt for her until she found her, and call Co'! Co'! with never an answering moo, until her childish patience was quite spent. If the creature had not given good milk and plenty of it, the case would have seemed very different to her owners. Besides, Sylvia had all the time there was, and very little use to make of it. Sometimes in pleasant weather it was a consolation to look upon the cow's pranks as an intelligent attempt to play hide and seek, and as the child had no playmates she lent herself to this amusement with a good deal of zest. Though this chase had been so long that the wary animal herself had given an unusual signal of her whereabouts, Sylvia had only laughed when she came upon Mistress moolly at the swamp-side, and urged her affectionately homeward with a twig of birch leaves. The old cow was not inclined to wander farther; she even turned in the right direction for once as they left the pasture and stepped along the road at a good pace. She was quite ready to be milked now, and seldom stopped to browse. Sylvia wondered what her grandmother would say because they were so late. It was a great while since she had left home at half-past five o'clock, but everybody knew the difficulty of making this errand a short one. Mrs. Tilley had chased the horned torment too many summer evenings herself to blame anyone else for lingering, and was only thankful as she waited that she had Sylvia, nowadays, to give such valuable assistance. The good woman suspected that Sylvia loitered occasionally on her own account; there never was such a child for straying about out-of-doors since the world was made! Everybody said that it was a good change for a little maid who had tried to grow for eight years in a crowded manufacturing town, but, as for Sylvia herself, it seemed as if she never had been alive at all before she came to live at the farm. She thought often with wistful compassion of a wretched dry geranium that belonged to a town neighbour.

' "Afraid of folks," ' old Mrs. Tilley said to herself, with a smile, after she had made the unlikely choice of Sylvia from her daughter's houseful of children, and was returning to the farm. ' "Afraid of folks," they said! I guess she won't be troubled no great with 'em up to the old place!' When they reached the door of the lonely house and stopped to unlock it, and the cat came to purr loudly, and rub against them, a deserted pussy, indeed, but fat with young robins, Sylvia whispered that this was a beautiful place to live in, and she never should wish to go home.

The companions followed the shady woodroad, the cow taking slow steps, and the child very fast ones. The cow stopped long at the brook to drink, as if the pasture were not half a swamp, and Sylvia stood still and waited, letting her bare feet cool themselves in the shallow water, while the great twilight moths struck softly against her. She waded on through the brook as the cow moved away, and listened to the thrushes with a heart that beat fast with pleasure. There was a stirring in the great boughs overhead. They were full of little birds and beasts that seemed to be wide-awake, and going about their world, or else saying good-night to each other in sleepy twitters. Sylvia herself felt sleepy as she walked along. However, it was not much farther to the house, and the air was soft and sweet. She was not often in the woods so late as this, and it made her feel as if she were a part of the grey shadows and the moving leaves. She was just thinking how long it seemed since she first came to the farm a year ago, and wondering if everything went on in the noisy town just the same as when she was there; the thought of the great red-faced boy who used to chase and frighten her, made her hurry along the path to escape from the shadow of the trees.

Suddenly this little woods girl is horror-stricken to hear a clear whistle not very far away. Not a bird's whistle, which would have a sort of friendliness, but a boy's whistle, determined, and somewhat aggressive. Sylvia left the cow to whatever sad fate might await her, and stepped discreetly aside into the bushes, but she was just too late. The enemy had discovered her, and called out in a very cheerful and persuasive tone, 'Halloa, little girl, how far is it to the road?' and trembling Sylvia answered almost inaudibly, 'A good ways.'

She did not dare to look boldly at the tall young man who carried a gun over his shoulder, but she came out of her bush and again followed the cow, while he walked alongside.

'I have been hunting for some birds,' the stranger said, kindly, 'and I have lost my way, and need a friend very much. Don't be afraid,' he added, gallantly. 'Speak up and tell me what your name is, and whether you think I can spend the night at your house, and go out shooting early in the morning.'

Sylvia was more alarmed than before. Would not her grandmother consider her much to blame? But who could have foreseen such an accident as this? It did not appear to be her fault, and she hung her head as if the stem of it were broken, but managed to answer 'Sylvy' with much effort when her companion again asked her name.

Mrs. Tilley was standing in the doorway when the trio came into view. The cow gave a loud moo by way of explanation.

'Yes, you'd better speak up for yourself, you old trial! Where'd she tucked herself away this time, Sylvy?' Sylvia kept an awed silence; she knew by instinct that her grandmother did not comprehend the gravity of the situation. She must be mistaking the stranger for one of the farmer-lads of the region.

The young man stood his gun beside the door, and dropped a heavy game-bag beside it; then he bade Mrs. Tilley good evening, and repeated his wayfarer's story, and asked if he could have a night's lodging.

'Put me anywhere you like,' he said. 'I must be off early in the morning, before day; but I am very hungry indeed. You can give me some milk, at any rate, that's plain.'

'Dear sakes, yes,' responded the hostess, whose long-slumbering hospitality seemed to be easily awakened. 'You might fare better if you went out on the main road a mile or so to Winn's folks, but you're welcome to what we've got. I'll milk right off, and you make yourself at home. You can sleep on husks or feathers,' she proffered, graciously. 'I raised them all myself. There's good pasturing for geese just below here towards the ma'sh. Now step round and set a plate for the gentleman, Sylvy!' And Sylvia promptly stepped. She was glad to have something to do, and she was hungry herself.

It was a surprise to find so clean and comfortable a little dwelling in this New England wilderness. The young man had known the horrors of its primitive housekeeping, and the dreary squalor of that level of society which does not rebel at the companionship of hens. This was the best thrift of an old-fashioned farmstead, though on such a small scale that it seemed like a hermitage. He listened eagerly to the old woman's quaint talk, he watched Sylvia's pale face and shining grey eyes with ever-growing enthusiasm, and insisted that this was the best supper he had eaten for a month; then, afterward, the new-made friends sat down in the doorway together while the moon came up.

A WHITE HERON

Soon it would be berry-time, and Sylvia was a great help at picking. The cow was a good milker, though a plaguy thing to keep track of, the hostess gossiped frankly, adding, presently, that she had buried four children, so that Sylvia's mother, and a son (who might be dead) in California were all the children she had left. 'Dan, my boy, was a great hand to go gunning,' she explained, sadly. 'I never wanted for pa'tridges or grey squer'ls while he was to home. He's been a great wand'rer, I expect, and he's no hand to write letters. There, I don't blame him; I'd ha' seen the world myself if it had been so I could.

'Sylvia takes after him,' the grandmother continued, affectionately, after a minute's pause. 'There ain't a foot o' ground she don't know her way over, and the wild creatur's counts her one o' themselves. Squer'ls she'll tame to come an' feed right out o' her hands, and all sorts o' birds. Last winter she got the jay-birds to bangeing here, and I believe she'd a' scanted herself of her own meals to have plenty to throw out amongst 'em, if I hadn't kep' watch. Anything but crows, I tell her, I'm willin' to help support – though Dan he went an' tamed one o' them that did seem to have reason same as folks. It was round here a good spell after he went away. Dan an' his father they didn't hitch, but he never held up his head agin' after Dan had dared him an' gone off.'

The guest did not notice this hint of family sorrows in his eager interest in something else.

'So Sylvy knows all about birds, does she?' he exclaimed, as he looked round at the little girl who sat, very demure but increasingly sleepy, in the moonlight. 'I am making a collection of birds myself. I have been at it ever since I was a boy.'

(Mrs. Tilley smiled). 'There are two or three very rare ones I have been hunting for these five years. I mean to get them on my own ground if they can be found.'

'Do you cage 'em up!' asked Mrs. Tilley, doubtfully, in response to this enthusiastic announcement.

'Oh, no, they're stuffed and put in cases, dozens and dozens of them,' said the ornithologist, ' and I have shot or snared every one myself. I caught a glimpse of a white heron, three miles from here, on Saturday, and I have followed it in this direction. They have never been found in this district at all. The little white heron, it is,' and he turned again to look at Sylvia with the hope of discovering that the rare bird was one of her acquaintances.

But Sylvia was watching a hop-toad in the narrow footpath.

'You would know the heron if you saw it,' the stranger continued, eagerly. 'A queer tall white bird with soft feathers and long thin legs. And it would have a nest perhaps in the top of a high tree, made of sticks, something like a hawk's nest.'

Sylvia's heart gave a wild beat; she knew that strange white bird, and had once stolen softly near where it stood in some bright green swamp grass, away over at the other side of the woods. There was an open place where the sunshine always seemed strangely yellow and hot, where tall, nodding rushes grew, and her grandmother had warned her that she might sink in the soft black mud underneath and never be heard of more. Not far beyond were the salt marshes and beyond those was the sea, the sea which Sylvia wondered and dreamed about, but never had looked upon, though its great voice

A WHITE HERON

could often be heard above the noise of the woods on stormy nights.

'I can't think of anything I should like so much as to find that heron's nest,' the handsome stranger was saying. 'I would give ten dollars to anybody who could show it to me,' he added, desperately, 'and I mean to spend my whole vacation hunting for it, if need be. Perhaps it was only migrating, or had been chased out of its own region by some bird of prey.'

Mrs. Tilley gave amazed attention to all this, but Sylvia still watched the toad, not divining, as she might have done at some calmer time, that the creature wished to get to its hole under the doorstep, and was much injured by the unusual spectators at that hour of the evening. No amount of thought, that night, could decide how many wished-for treasures the ten dollars, so lightly spoken of, would buy.

The next day the young sportsman hovered about the woods, and Sylvia kept him company, having lost her first fear of the friendly lad, who proved to be most kind and sympathetic. He told her many things about the birds and what they knew, and where they lived and what they did with themselves. And he gave her a jack-knife, which she thought as great a treasure as if she were a desert-islander. All day long he did not once make her troubled or afraid except when he brought down some unsuspecting singing creature from its bough. Sylvia would have liked him vastly better without his gun; she could not understand why he killed the very birds he seemed to like so much. But as the day waned, Sylvia still watched the young man with loving admiration. She had never seen anybody so charming and delightful; the woman's heart, asleep in the child, was vaguely thrilled by a dream of love. Some premonition of that great power stirred and swayed these young foresters who traversed the solemn woodlands with soft-footed silent care. They stopped to listen to a bird's song; they pressed forward again eagerly, parting the branches, speaking to each other rarely and in whispers; the young man going first, and Sylvia following, fascinated, a few steps behind, with her grey eyes dark with excitement.

She grieved because the longed-for white heron was elusive, but she did not lead the guest, she only followed, and there was no such thing as speaking first. The sound of her own unquestioned voice would have terrified her — it was hard enough to answer yes or no when there was need of that. At last, evening began to fall, and they drove the cow home together, and Sylvia smiled with pleasure when they came to the place where she heard the whistle and was afraid, only the night before.

II

Half a mile from home, at the farther edge of the woods, where the land was highest, a great pine-tree stood, the last of its generation. Whether it was left for a boundary mark, or for what reason, no one could say; the woodchoppers who had felled its mates were dead and gone long ago, and a whole forest of sturdy trees, pines and oaks and maples, had grown again. But the stately head of this old pine towered above them all and made a landmark for sea and shore miles and miles away. Sylvia knew it well. She had always believed that whoever climbed to the top of it could see the ocean; and the little girl had often laid her hand on the great rough trunk and looked up wistfully at those dark boughs that the wind always stirred, no matter how hot and still the air might be below. Now she thought of the tree with a new excitement, for why, if one climbed it at break of day, could not one see all the world, and easily discover whence the white heron flew, and mark the place and find the hidden nest?

What a spirit of adventure, what wild ambition! What fancied triumph and delight and glory for the later morning when she could make known the secret! It was almost too real and too great for the childish heart to bear.

All night the door of the little house stood open, and the whippoorwills came and sang upon the very step. The young sportsman and his old hostess were sound asleep, but Sylvia's great design kept her broad awake and watching. She forgot to think of sleep. The short summer night seemed as long as the winter darkness, and at last, when the whippoorwills ceased, and she was afraid the morning would after all come too soon, she stole out of the house and followed the pasture path through the woods, hastening toward the open ground beyond, listening with a sense of comfort and companionship to the drowsy twitter of a half-awakened bird, whose perch she had jarred in passing. Alas, if the great wave of human interest which flooded for the first time this dull little life should sweep away the satisfactions of an existence heart to heart with nature and the dumb life of the forest!

There was the huge tree asleep yet in the paling moonlight, and small and hopeful Sylvia began with utmost bravery to mount the top of it, with tingling, eager blood coursing the channels of her whole frame, with her bare feet and fingers, that pinched and held like bird's claws to the monstrous ladder reaching up, up, almost to the sky itself. First she must mount the white oak tree that grew alongside, where she was almost lost among the dark branches and the green leaves heavy and wet with dew; a bird fluttered off its nest, and a red squirrel ran to and fro and scolded pettishly at the harmless house-breaker. Sylvia felt her way easily. She had often climbed there, and knew that higher still one of the oak's upper branches chafed against the pine trunk, just where its lower boughs were set close together. There, when she made the dangerous pass from one tree to the other, the great enterprise would really begin.

She crept out along the swaying oak limb at last, and took the daring step across into the old pine-tree. The way was harder than she thought; she must reach far and hold fast, the sharp, dry twigs caught and held her and scratched her like angry talons, the pitch made her thin little fingers clumsy and stiff as she went round and round the tree's great stem, higher and higher upward. The sparrows and robins in the wood below were beginning to wake and twitter to the dawn, yet it seemed much lighter there aloft in the pine tree, and the child knew that she must hurry if her project were to be of any use.

The tree seemed to lengthen itself out as she went up, and to reach farther and farther upward. It was like a great main mast to the voyaging earth: it must truly have been amazed that morning through all its ponderous frame as it felt this determined spark of human spirit creeping and climbing from higher branch to branch. Who knows how steadily the least

A WHITE HERON

twigs held themselves to advantage this light, weak creature on her way! The old pine must have loved his new dependant. More than all the hawks, and bats, and moths, and even the sweet-voiced thrushes, was the brave, beating heart of the solitary grey-eyed child. And the tree stood still and held away the winds that June morning while the dawn grew bright in the east.

Sylvia's face was like a pale star, if one had seen it from the ground, when the last thorny bough was passed, and she stood trembling and tired but wholly triumphant, high in the tree top. Yes, there was the sea with the dawning sun making a golden dazzle over it, and toward that glorious east flew two hawks with slow moving pinions. How low they looked in the air from that height when before one had only seen them far up, and dark against the blue sky. Their grey feathers were as soft as moths; they seemed only a little way from the tree, and Sylvia felt as if she too could go flying away among the clouds. Westward, the woodlands and farms reached miles and miles into the distance; here and there were church steeples and white villages; truly it was a vast and awesome world.

The birds sang louder and louder. At last the sun came up bewilderingly bright. Sylvia could see the white sails of ships out at sea, and the clouds that were purple and rose-coloured and yellow at first began to fade away. Where was the white heron's nest in the sea of green branches, and was this wonderful sight and pageant of the world the only reward for having climbed to such a giddy height? Now look down again, Sylvia, where the green marsh is set among the shining birches and dark hemlocks; there where you saw the white heron once you will see him again; look, look! a white spot of him like a single floating feather comes up from the dead hemlock and grows larger, and rises, and comes close at last, and goes by the landmark pine with steady sweep of wing and outstretched slender neck and crested head. And wait! wait! do not move a foot or a finger, little girl, do not send an arrow of light and consciousness from your two eager eyes, for the heron has perched on a pine bough not far beyond yours and cries back to his mate on the nest, and plumes his feathers for the new day!

The child gives a long sigh a minute later when a company of shouting cat-birds comes also to the tree, and vexed by their fluttering and lawlessness, the solemn heron goes away. She knows his secret now, the wild, light, slender bird that floats and wavers and goes back like an arrow presently to his home in the green world beneath. Then Sylvia, well satisfied, makes her perilous way down again, not daring to look far below the branch she stands on, ready to cry sometimes because her fingers ache and her lamed feet slip; wondering over and over again what the stranger would say to her, and what he would think when she told him how to find his way straight to the heron's nest.

'Sylvy, Sylvy!' called the busy old grandmother again and again, but nobody answered, and the small husk bed was empty, and Sylvia had disappeared.

The guest waked from a dream, and, remembering his day's pleasure, hurried to dress himself that it might sooner begin. He was sure from the way the shy little girl looked once or twice yesterday that she had at least seen the white heron,

A WHITE HERON

and now she must really be persuaded to tell. Here she comes now, paler than ever, and her worn old frock is torn and tattered, and smeared with pine pitch. The grandmother and the sportsman stand in the door together and question her, and the splendid moment has come to speak of the dead hemlock-tree by the green marsh.

But Sylvia does not speak after all, though the old grandmother fretfully rebukes her, and the young man's kind appealing eyes are looking straight in her own. He can make them rich with money; he has promised it, and they are poor now. He is so well worth making happy, and he waits to hear the story she can tell.

No, she must keep silence! What is it that suddenly forbids her and makes her dumb? Has she been nine years growing, and now, when the great world for the first time puts out a hand to her, must she thrust it aside for a bird's sake? The murmur of the pine's green branches is in her ears, she remembers how the white heron came flying through the golden air and how they watched the sea and the morning together, and Sylvia cannot speak; she cannot tell the heron's secret and give its life away.

Dear loyalty, that suffered a sharp pang as the guest went away disappointed later in the day, that could have served and followed him and loved him as a dog loves! Many a night Sylvia heard the echo of his whistle haunting the pasture path as she came home with the loitering cow. She forgot even her sorrow at the sharp report of his gun and the piteous sight of thrushes and sparrows dropping silent to the ground, their songs hushed and their pretty feathers stained and wet with blood. Were the birds better friends than their hunter might have been? Who can tell? Whatever treasures were lost to her, woodlands and summer-time, remember! Bring your gifts and graces and tell your secrets to this lonely country child!